I0749313

BRΩKEN

Excerpt from *Stars in My Pocket Like Grains of Sand* used by permission of the author, Samuel R. Delany.

Printed in the United States of America

Published by Silverthought Press
www.silverthought.com

ISBN: 0-9774110-1-X

BRΩKEN

A PLAGUE JOURNAL

PAUL EVAN HUGHES

ALSO BY
PAUL EVAN HUGHES:

FICTION:

enemy.
an end.

NON-FICTION:

Deconstruct
[dyingdays]

COLLABORATIONS:

to wound the autumnal city:
  a dyingdays.com 9-11 anthology
Alien Light:
  A Science Fiction Anthology
Silverthought: Ignition

FRAGMENTS:

for Pam Hall, Peter Hocking, Catherine Lord, and Ruth Wallen, four remarkable artists, for their guidance during my time at Goddard.

for Mark Brand, for his editorial assistance and swift kicks in the creative ass over the last decade or so.

for Samuel R. Delany, my mentor and inspiration, whether he knows it or not.

for Jacob, who still echoes.

and for Sarah, for our beautiful, fragile moments.

"You've blotted the rich form of desire from my life and left me only some vaguely eccentric behaviors that have grown up to integrate so much pleasure into the mundane world around me. What text could I write now? It's as though I cannot even *remember* what I once desired! All I can look for now, when I have the energy, is lost desire itself—and I look for it by clearly inadequate means. At best such an account as I might write would read like the life of anyone else, with, now and again, a bizarre and interruptive incident, largely mysterious and completely demystified—at least that's what it has become without the day-to-day, moment-to-moment web of wanting that you have unstrung from about my universe. Without it, all falls apart, Japril. In a single gesture you've turned me into the most ordinary of human creatures and at once left me an obsessive, pleasureless eccentric, trapped in a set of habits which no longer have reason because they no longer lead to reward. And if I had enough self-confidence, in the midst of this bland continual chaos into which you've shunted me, for hate, I should hate you. But I don't have it."

Samuel R. Delany
Stars in My Pocket Like Grains of Sand

ALPHA

ALPHA

A

and all broken tomorrows: bracketing those dead to us, delineating the forms and histories of our desires, in a breath, in tears, in the pattern two opposing collections of striation compose in the catalytic reaction of palm to palm, all physics are bent, and all probabilities, all convenient presuppositions and extrapolations of futures not yet lived are erased: all we have is now, this moment, this beautiful, fragile moment, and

He inhaled.

"Storm's coming in."

"You sure this is him?"

She nodded. Across the gulf, lightning licked at waterspouts. She brushed the fine salt spray from her cheeks.

"Specifics?"

"Pattern confirmed. Subject is Fourteen-Seven When intact. Age twenty-three... twenty-three years and thirteen hours. REM signature confirmed; this is the author."

"What's a kid from the sticks of New York doing alone on the Gulf Coast on his birthday?"

"The library's empty." The mathematician shrugged. "Watching the lightning. Getting high. Running away?"

West nodded. "He wanted to die down here, away from everyone he knew. Tonight was the night."

"Shit, he's got another fifty years before—"

"That's why we're here."

"It's all there, everything we need?"

"It's there."

Benton sighed. "Hard to believe this kid caused it all."

"Wasn't really his fault."

"What if we—"

"Hope, I'm disappointed." West took a handful of sand, let the grains sift through his fingers. They danced with the wind. "You of all people should know that killing him wouldn't stop this."

"I'm just a mathematician."

He scoffed. "Our best quantum X theorist."

"Just a maths egg."

He wiped his hands of the beach. "You ready?"

"Guess so."

"Unlock the When."

Benton tapped the subdermal in her throat. A halo sparked to life around her head. "Agents West and Benton, Fourteen-Seven When, request immediate unlock on my mark. Play."

nav fix on your position. jog to play in three, two—

And I knew somehow that on that night in Lincoln, Nebraska, Abigail wasn't sleeping well. Thoughts of tomorrow's flight to Vermont, the uncertainty of a future spent mostly between airports and stages, behind cameras, and I knew that a baby was born, and his parents would name him David for his father, Smith for his mother's side. The family lived three blocks east of Abigail, one block west of the recording studio where Lullaby recorded the album I couldn't get out of my head.

All I saw was silver: in the lightning, in the waterspouts, in the sand. The stillness between stars.

"Paul?"

❧

He jumped.

West studied the tension of muscles, hardening of jawline, narrowing of brow. Eyes lost somewhere between green and gray and mud went to one, went to other, went to one. Even in shadow, he saw the boy's nose was sunburned.

"Eri—?"

"No." She bent, extended her hand. Shake. "Benton. Hope. And you're Paul?"

"Yeah." Something crawled behind his eyes. Heartbeat and suspicion. Names of people and places and scents and tastes; this was... This was. "Have we met?"

"No..." Benton looked to West.

"What do you want?" He stood; he brushed sand from cargo shorts filled with bottlecaps and cigarettes, golden discount cards to the strip's most popular clubs. "I don't have any money, and I'm not into—"

"We're not here to hurt you. We're just—"

"Spring break?"

"No." West regarded the thousands amidst light and sound behind them. There was such stillness in the impending storm. "We're here for you."

The author stepped back. "I don't know you."

"You do, though."

"I've never seen you be—"

"You have."

Black coat flapping in the breeze over black uniform, burn fresh on temple. Gray eyes.

He smiled. "Great. So you've read the book, right? You're a big fan. You tracked me down and want my autograph, right? Listen, this is flattering, but—"

Benton grabbed his arm. He looked into colorless blue eyes. "You know that's not true. You know who we are."

"I—"

"You see her in me. You're right; she's a part of me, but you knew the character wouldn't be purely her. I'm a combination of many. The name Hope because she loved it, the name Benton because of that band. You feel it behind your eyes. You—"

He shrugged her off. "Don't touch me."

West pulled the pack of Marlboros from Paul's chest pocket, withdrew one. Lit.

"They were right." Exhale. "Every possible world that ever could have existed will someday exist in perfect emulation in machines. Every possible you that ever could have existed will."

"Will you—"

"You're carrying a virus. A contagion. You can feel it. You know it's there. That's why you write. You have the silver. You write about things from pasts and presents and futures that you shouldn't be able to see."

Paul was silent.

Benton squeezed his hand. "There are holes all over this When. You're making it all fall apart. You're ending so many worlds with each breath, and you have no idea. We're here to take you out of this. We need you."

"You aren't real."

"We are now."

He took out a cigarette. West smiled.

"Let's go out to the pier."

❧

I'd gone to the edge of the world and thrown myself against all that I knew: safety and solidity and the past. Life became a fluid somewhere out there in the thousands of miles between the stagnation of home and the brilliant, beautiful uncertainty of the edge. Life became metaphor: I walked wearily to the ocean after the long and dangerous station wagon journey across the country, just standing there in the sunshine and the gulf breeze, feeling the cleansing grit of sand beneath me, working its way into every pocket of my clothing, every hair-covered limb, underneath contacts and between toes and fingers and scouring the gold sheen from my Zippo. The sand worked its way into me, making me feel at once totally alien to that place and an integral part of the landscape. The sand would eventually blister my feet, itch my scalp, grit every last exposed bit of flesh with its silicon scour, but not before I'd simply stood there for a while to appreciate its exotic warmth.

Many tens of thousands of my generation had gone to that city of sand and sunrise. Few of them shared the reason that I had for being there... We all went to escape from life for a while. We all went to be the bad people that we were told not to be the other fifty-one weeks of the year: we drank and smoked and smoked and fucked and otherwise debauched on the beach at the edge of the world. We gathered in groups of thousands and flailed the primordial dance of existence to overplayed rap songs and paid too much for beer in plastic cups and smoked cowboy killers and bummed cowboy killers from a stranger with long hair and dark eyes that looked at and through you with his intricate, recording gaze.

i contain multitudes...

By the hundreds, by the thousands, I watched them. I detached. I separated myself from the organism that was humanity. Hovering over the crowd, poised against a wooden railing that had seen the sun set into the emerald coast too many times to count, carved a palimpsest with the initials of the past spring breakers who thought themselves cool enough to brand their love forever on the treated wooden logs of the upstairs bar of Harpoon Harry's before moving on to the Fountainbleau or the Reef or the Chateau for a night of refrigerator beer cans and horny sorority girls free for the week from the confines of relationships and morality. I peered over the edge down into the beast of raw abandon, people by the thousands engaged in grinding, undulating, dripping sexual frenzy, arms in the air supporting beer in plastic cups and beads ripe for the swapping of bare breasts or muff shots, sometimes even supporting smoked-to-the-filter cowboy killers bummed from the dark stranger watching from above, ashes poised eerily outward, defying gravity to the beat of the music.

I could have made an army of them.

Jolted from that realization, a weakness, a thin nosebleed and a smile. I smiled once. I bled more than once.

I watched from above. That frenzy. Detached. Not a part of it. My generation. Not a part of it. At all. I was the cigarette man. I had the Cobra long-sleeved t-shirt. I made people smile. People told me to "Smile! It's Spring Break!" I watched from above. And felt alone in a crowd of thousands. It was not for me... none of it. It never was for me. I was a voyeur. I thought too much. About. Things. There. In the midst of thousands. I was. Lost.

But I could use them. Stir them.

an army seven million strong by the time i

Walking. Along Front Beach Road. Sand grinding between pinkie and second toes on left foot. Grinding away flesh. Walking along the road because it was good for us. Walking faster than traffic, slow enough to be witness to any and all displays of flesh that we could find. Beads for tits, tits for beads. Instant cameras and Daddy's hi-8s by the dozens. An experiment in humanity: *i am not a part of this.* There was cleansing and rebirth in that experience. Finding the correct outlet was the key to the success of the rebirth. Finding that place to be in the midst of that chaos that would channel the fury into creativity...

waves.

Sitting before that inescapable wall of water... Burning tobacco and burning flesh and thoughts of She and thoughts of the blank void that was the future burning away the Paul that I once was. A limit experience in the liminal zone: fire and water, humanity and the great impossibility of the edge of the world. Sitting on the sometimes-wet sand, grit in my eyes, staring blankly off into the world that we can never have, inasmuch as we think that we've conquered it with small wooden and metal constructs with which we can skim along and just under its surface. Place cigarette in mouth, extract golden Zippo from right pocket, flip open lighter, flick flick flick until the stubborn flame finally licks the delicious tip of the Marlboro 100. Smoldering. Deadly. Inhale, exhale. Pause. Inhale, exhale. Pause. Wind howling from the gulf, internal wind painting my respiratory tract blacker with my divine purpose of living up to the ouija board's predictions.

Flood of thought, sunrise, sunset... Sitting in that place of beauty and edge and impossibility. That was the place that I had so yearned for... That was the place that embodies everything that I'd felt since the loss of. Of. Dark skies in the daytime: impending storm, impending downfall, impending torrent. Sleeves pulled up around tanned but not burned arms, left still exhibiting the eleven lines that had so defined the last five years of my life, eleven lines of scar tissue now barely discernible from the surrounding scarred tissue, except for the fact that the lines were a lighter shade of tanned. Barefoot, toes buried in the sand, absorbing warmth and grounding me in that world, as the fingertips of Sakyamuni called the earth to witness not his divinity but his enlightenment. Hand outstretched, fingertips touching the earth as the armies of Devadatta raged around him, hand outstretched to call the earth, all of existence, to be witness to his enlightenment. Toes dug into the sand as seagulls raged around me, wind blew through seabreeze-knotted hair, not brushed since November, sky above growing darker in defiance of any human definition of Spring Break.

i contain multitudes.

Moments of lucidity: the screams of the interior fell silent as the rage of the exterior filled me. Struggle for peace; struggle for silence. I'd gone to the edge of the world to do what every good metaphorical struggling author does: find himself. I sat before the kingdom and the power and the glory; I looked into the face of the closest thing I'd seen to god. I sat until the doubt and the rage and the mourning were replaced. I sat until I was filled up again. Beauty. Sitting before that amorphous canvas and watching the power of existence paint itself in waterspouts illuminated from behind by divine lightning. There was such a peace in submission to that divinity... Take me, destroy me, tear me apart so that I won't have to return to the places I fear. Standing out on the pier, hundreds of feet out into the surf, wishing for the overhead lamps to extinguish into black... Waves crashing into the pier, swaying the massive construct, waves illuminated orange and pink by the garish strip of humanity stippling the beach with light. All of mankind behind me, alone in that journey out into nothingness... Perfection in that black. Perfection in the relentless cycle of waves crashing against the pier. Crash into me, through me. Destroy me in your wake.

I needed that. I needed to approach the edge of the world, to abandon everything behind me, to leave everything that mattered in the sand and walk out into the surf. On that last night, I spent a moment of solitude alone on the beach. Harpoon Harry's raging behind me, thousands of generation enjoying the meat market that was the drunken bliss distilled in Panama City. I walked out into the ocean, took a final drag from my cigarette, launched it out with a flick of my fingers into the great black gulf until it hit the water and extinguished. How appropriate that gesture: the extinction of the spark. For years, I'd struggled with the knowledge that I'd once had a spark, and had lost it somewhere out there. What a symbolic move: killing that spark with the world screaming behind me, the noise of tens of thousands being slowly supplanted by the rage of the waves and the flood of voices that roared from within. I walked out into the waves without bothering to roll up the legs of my pants, without bothering to care about the couples swapping their own waves of fluid on the beach behind me, thinking only of that limit experience. Merging with the unknown, feeling it caress my skin, enveloping all that I'd given to it. Sound became nothing but heartbeat and voice and voice and

I thought. Of her. Out there.

The future was unwritten, but I was almost there. Accelerating into turns, plummeting into the future with each instant. Somewhere out there... I felt it, the falling, the gravity of our situation. I felt the desire, the need, the utter insignificance of

Guitar strings, nylon, strummed savagely, then gently, then the pure, resigned voice of yesterdays... Beauty in that submission. Minutes left before my ascension. Moments left, and

Almost there. I'm almost there.

West tossed his guttering cigarette into the gulf. "You're a smart kid. You can handle it."

The author's hands gripped the guardrail. Palms pressed: texture of the names carved beneath. Fingers clawed down, nails on treated pine. Smell of brine. The wind brought with it fragments of the hurricane. A crack and lightning flared behind the veils of approaching rain, fell to black, uneasy, uncertain in that night. Music intruded from behind.

"It's true?"

Benton sat between the railing and the overflowing garbage bin: popcorn boxes, beer cans, empty suntan lotion bottles, half-eaten barbecue, smokes, rubbers, detritus and evidence that people were here to play, to drink, to fuck, to burn. The shadow of the overhead pier lamp fell over her face. Arms draped around her knees, she focused on something in the gulf, something approaching with vicious silence and wind. "It's true." Voice barely audible, Paul didn't know if she was answering or meditating. He felt what she saw behind blue eyes: the physics of immortality, the intersection of ineffable paths, the tangents, the blessings. *He is knowing* but he knew he wasn't.

"How's the book going?"

"It's going."

"Yeah." West studied the weathered planks below. "It would've been okay for a while longer."

"What do you mean?"

"Something's going to happen in just under six months. There'll be a crossover. Something's going to happen in this When that shouldn't."

"And you're here to tell me that it's my fault, and I have to help you fix it?"

"No." The rain started. West pulled his collar up. "It can't be stopped now. It's going to happen regardless of your help."

Paul noted that the scarred man's eyes tracked the running lights of a plane knifing takeoff through the rain above. "How?"

"Tell me about silver." Paul turned to Benton, still on the ground, still in stark shadow. An instant, an instant and those blues were something else, a tugging, and gone.

"'Au' on the periodic table—"

"'Ag.'"

"Art major."

"Your silver. Tell me."

"Invasive biological contaminant, airborne, replaces flesh with—"

"No." She got up. "Go back further. When did you first think of it?"

He frowned. "*Enemy*? I don't know; it's been a long time since I really thought about—"

"That's the danger of revision." She shook her head. "You lose track of the beginnings. It all merges into one."

"I don't—"

"The sixth revision was the first time you wrote about it. You shifted focus from the mystical nature of Shadow drives to a hard-edged quantum physical explanation for the technology. Original versions of the book barely contained the word 'silver.' Where did your obsession come from?"

"It just..." He considered. "I don't know."

West wiped rain from his brow, fingers lingering momentarily over his temple code burn. "We do."

And as the sun rose, he knew that he had to leave with them. Hope sat at his side, her head on his shoulder. He smoked his last cigarette. The storm had wet the beach; they were apparently alone on that strip. Clubs dead behind, early-morning traffic just beginning: an army of chambermaids and custodians. West stood down the beach, staring into the western remnants of night.

"I remember you."

She looked into hazel. "I'm not her."

"Maybe not here." Inhale, pause, exhale. "But somewhere."

Coffee, black, served in a chipped cup. There was sugar on the table, a dangerous little container of cream that he'd never trusted. He drank his coffee black.

"Why this city?"

Sip, cup to tabletop. He didn't answer.

"You were never specific in your locations. People wondered where Maire's complex was. The only clue was the fact that the orbital gun rose from a body of water. Was it Seattle?"

"No." He answered too quickly.

West nodded, looked away. Paul wondered what semantic thread he'd just uploaded to the Judith Mind-Essence.

Late afternoon crowd. Outside: rain. Nirvana on the jukebox. President Jennings on the link.

"It was always this same coffee house. Why?"

Paul shrugged.

"When did you first write it?"

He considered. "The first book. One of the last versions, the final scene. I wanted to give some form of closure to the novel, not just let the characters cut off without some acknowledgement of a positive future."

"Ninety-eight? Ninety-nine?"

"Let's say ninety-eight."

A middle-aged man had come in since they'd arrived. He sat at the counter, spoke to the proprietress. She gave him a pack of smokes. Marlboro 100s.

"You know anyone here?"

Paul surveyed the crowd. "Simon. Maggie." He stole a cursory glance of the woman behind the counter. "She looks familiar, but I can't quite—"

"We pulled you out of Fourteen-Seven before—Well, it's amazing what the mind allows you to forget."

She rang up the bill for one of her customers. His girlfriend walked to stand next to him. There was a silver ring on one hand. The coffeehouse owner smiled, revealing one gunshot dimple.

you know... you do.

Paul blinked away the recognition before it could take hold in that stillness between the heart and memory.

"Who else will I meet before our business is done?"

West sipped. He took his coffee with one sugar. "Not all of the characters survived. Some were just too far away to rescue. Would have been impractical to rescue some of the others. We're still tracking the major players. They'll produce a more viable calculus."

"When do we go back to Judith Command?" Something about the owner... She'd laughed at something her cigarette customer had said. Something.

West marked Paul's gaze, uploaded new matrices into the Judith ME. "I think we're done for the day."

"Right." He sloshed coffee around the cup. "What's your favorite book?"

West's hand moved instinctively to his codeburn. "The one you haven't written yet."

❧

of Samayel, of Katre, of countless others: Berlin, Frost, the Judiths, the Wests, the ocean of gods who were Michaels and Windhams, Hunter and Joseph. I could tell you of so many.

I could tell you of their plans. Of purposes.

I could tell you of the place they built in the stillness between times, that catalogue of the remnants, how it stretched away into universes filled with typing monkeys.

when i close my eyes, who do i see there?

Walking down the passages that looked like metal, a charge to the air of static and nothing. Heart beating in my throat. *and i can't even compose a single fucking coherent sentence anymore.* I'd been taken from a beach and immersed in this: *self-referential, indulgent bullshit. No discernible plot, no outstanding characters, no sympathetic developments.* I asked myself if I could begin to explain that which I could never begin to comprehend.

They'd been busy since I'd first written them into existence.

And I realize now that what I'd seen in those sleepless hours and daylight moments paused over a cup of coffee, a cigarette, lightning in the gulf was a pale fragment of what I was supposed to have seen. Maybe I wasn't supposed to have seen it at all; maybe it would have best been left hidden behind the clouds, hovering behind veils of shadow and doubt, in that place where hopes and dreams

becoming so much more than this

I'd developed the bad habit of masking any semblance of a plot in fancy metaphors.

I exhaled when I first saw Judith Command, and I don't know if I've ever again inhaled. How could I have written it so? It shocks and amazes, the fundamental mistakes a sleeping mind can translate into truth. A feeling of falling, the distracting and disturbing euphoria that accompanies a mind's incapability to name or place or begin to understand.

West walked me down the metallish corridors, introduced me to a fraction of the war machine of Command, the harvested systems powering its core, the fields and valleys of gods, the endless possibilities, each a complete specimen of a particular Judith. I saw the walls lined with host bodies, the breeders whose only purpose was to bear variants of the only god we had left. I watched the moment of cycle completion: bodies raised from nutrient baths, abdomens flayed by light, the wailing cargo removed by gentle silver strands, scanned, plunged immediately into their own variant chambers, their wails choked off by the thick biological slurry as the breeder process began again.

Promising variants were taken from the chamber and grown to adulthood in personalized heavens.

Is that too much? I could tell you of the host debris, the gaping caverns of fetid birth chambers, the bodies swept forcefully from the breeder rooms into waste tunnels, trails of blood and amniotic fluid still slurping from the wounds of Purpose, intestines reaching like fingers toward sex-less daughters. Judith was a beautiful woman, but multiplied by forevers, split apart with cutting beams, the infant cargo removed, her bodies became ugly beyond explanation, not the classic demure beauty that the original God host had been but a bastardization of female form, a violation of reproduction and natural life cycles.

It was disgusting, and I questioned which Purpose was truly the evil.

West understood. He didn't expect me to trust any of it. He knew that I'd been shown a different forever.

"It's just the way things have to be done here. It's the only way of restoring the broken

❧

tomorrow we can go to the park. Sit on grass. Maybe go to the zoo?"

"Or the jazz festival?"

The man at the counter grinned. "Of course."

West stood as Paul got up to pay the bill. "Do it like I told you, son." As Paul approached the counter, he heard snippets of conversation: but we just, so you see, I don't know maybe we can, but if Hesse had meant to, and that's why in the first book, music's just, cookies are delish, and at the counter: "This is where the fish lives."

The owner smiled up at him: one dimple. The smile faltered, returned, a blink, a vague sense of

The man at the counter turned. One white streak in his salt-and-cinnamon hair. Eyes narrow, a blink, a sense of

"Keep the change." Paul left a handful of silver dollars on the counter and began to walk away.

"Wait." The owner reached out her hand: silver band on her ring finger, pattern. "Do I—"

Man: "You're—"

West watched.

Paul cleared his throat, regarded the man. Stepped in, pulled him close, whispered. "Erase."

Pause. Play.

The man gone, Paul sat down in his place at the counter, hands shaking. The owner, maybe seventy, maybe fifty, let her hand fall. Her ring was gone.

He stumbled over words, eventually succeeded in voicing. "I hope—I know you can't understand."

Eyes watered. Dimple retreated. "You're—"

His hand hovered over hers.

"A bench outside a dorm. A box of cigars. A white t-shirt, paint-spattered hands, holes in the knees of my jeans, plastic-tipped cigars. Snow. It was cold. That's all you'll remember. Nothing more."

"Paul? Paul *Hughes*? How—"

"It never happened. We never happened. I died on a beach before we met again. No ghetto apartment, no cigarettes in bed, no pears, no ice cream. No broken hearts, no broken tomorrows. You lived and loved. Without me."

In a pocket, two light blue marbles disappeared.

Paul pulled back his left sleeve and saw a line of scar fade.

"I'm sorry." He reached out, placed rough hand against the dimpled cheek.

"Paul?"

He nodded, smiled with a sadness beyond stillness, beyond that yesterday.

"I'm sorry." A whisper, an approach, lips speak into a soft warm curl of ear. "Erase."

She faded.

West studied the floor.

"Get me out of here." The author choked back something, swallowed those concepts and closed his eyes. "Program stop."

❧

Time heals nothing by itself.

Survival depends on forgetting. Excision. Formatting. Re-formatting.

an exhalation, a lip upturned, the infinitesimal field of blonde, crow's feet from a life too

Pattern slams back into form. Hiss and release, a chamber door opens. Billowing steam. (Where does it

The author cracked the release system of his helmet, which opened in a dozen places and peeled away to reveal a face studded by whiskers and scar. He wondered why helmets in science fiction novels were almost always big globes of glass. Vulnerable. The helmet he'd designed for this novel used direct sensory submersion behind an armored collapsible blade paneling system. Safer. No glass. In the armor, he breathed slurried nitrox gel, if you could consider it breathing at all.

West, Benton. Displays. He slumped into a vacuum chair beside the girl.

"It was a good run."

He looked up. "Guess so." Ran fingers through hair. "Scissors?" And they were.

"The triumphant warrior begins another transformative process?" She grinned, but her teeth didn't show.

That sound the scissors make on sweatened hair, the tickle just before depattern of the severed strands. Scentless flashes of

"The helmet needs work."

"Could've saved time by thinking it away." West walked to another display. "Drama queen."

The scissors paused in Paul's hand. "I know."

Benton brushed some pre-snap curls from his shoulder. "Containment's at ninety-eight over. Just a few more."

He grabbed her hand and removed it from his shoulder. "You're hyperkinetic."

"And you don't like to be touched. Sorry. I forgot."

Short squeeze of hand-to-hand. "No sorries."

Healing by primary intention: leaving the wound open to the elements, visible to all. Scab, scar. Public replacement of flesh, of memory and heart, filling in the places between and

Scissors disappeared. Hair stood on end, clumps, moist, a tangle of muddied fire burned up to nothing in particular.

"Hugh Grant? Michael Madsen?"

"Not quite. Terrible combination of neither." He felt his cardiac shield twinge.

"Come on, kids. Stop your grab-assin'." Light traced a new code burn on his temple. "The boss wants a progress report."

❧

feeling screams, burning ends in that night, and it was beautiful. the touch of self, the touch of alters, galaxies of altars, and trees, trees singing and flying, echoes before dawn, a moon, a gasp, the chill that midnight makes when inhaled, the loss of exhalation, the yearning to breathe that scent again, ever again, to be there ever again

the way things break, the way tomorrows break, the way we struggle to correct yesterdays

and in one she frowned as a nacelle tore from the craft, crew pulled to death between the planet and the star, and in one she fought robots made from wood and organic paste, wiring spun from the silk of system-sized spiders, and in one she had a twin, and in one she watched a planet cut cleanly in half by a light from the stars, and in one she found no enemy left, and in one she sipped a bitter liquid that would keep her awake for hours, and in one she slumped, exhausted from breathing, as a door opened and

❧

Judith sighed.

They'd finally located that rock in the center of the silver infestation. Centuries of searching, centuries without form or substance or duration, they'd searched; they'd found. West had been in the original rescue fleet, tattered remnants gathered from the first Enemy war and the temporal refugees of the Forever Dust, the human residue of all broken Whens. Data cycle errors, reflexive overruns, cyclic redundancy checks, cache corruptions: humanity.

The trouble with his stories is that they happen concurrently... People who were killed in the third chapter walk in and ask for coffee and a cigarette in the fifth. He can't keep it straight; it's not worth it to the reader to attempt to make sense of something so inherently flawed, something so innately incomprehensible.

"Thanks for the vote of confidence, Jud."

"Come in." The warm smile barely contained the acid tongue beneath. "You two fucking yet?"

"Oh god." Hope sat on the edge of the bench next to the author.

"That's what they used to call me. Where are we?"

"Ninety-eight over. Last run was almost a complete success."

"Rad." Hands went to face, fingertips traced temples as her smile fell off. "You have to get better at this, Paul."

"It's not like I even know what the fuck I'm supposed to have lived in these Whens. You have the advantage of knowing everything already."

"If I could erase it myself, I would."

"I wish you'd find a way and let me get out of here."

"It's not up to me anymore." Judith stood from her chaise, walked over to the window that showed the latest crop. "It's up to one of me down there."

West cleared his throat. "Combat runs have been marginally successful in Fourteen-Three, Seventy-Nine-Nine, Two-Hundred—"

"Stop." Something behind a god's eyes, something crawling and caustic. "They're waiting for something before striking back. Secure our positions along the When—Ha!—*Time*stream and fortify the forward bases."

"You're getting good at this." West bit a nail.

"That's why they pay me the big bucks. Next time, you can have god inside of you and hand out the orders."

Benton activated the sheet of glass she'd carried into the room. "Theory reports that we have a 60/40 lock on Linear.

A/O position lock expected within three runs." Figures danced from the display across her chin, cheeks, half-glints in colorless eyes. "Static's quiet, though. They could be ghosting our sensor fleets."

"No..." Judith shook her head. "This time they want us to find them."

"Could be a trap."

"They don't have anywhere to run. This isn't the first war. We're in charge now."

"Right."

Judith turned to Paul. "Something smart to say, sugar-tits?"

Layers of frown clouded with uncertainty. "I wouldn't have made it so simple."

"You thought too much. Made a very messy existence for us to clean up."

"Yeah, sorry about that." The author's eyes narrowed. "Most books don't become real."

the war was beautiful

"Was it?"

"Just slipped out."

Judith walked to Paul's side, demure smile on her face. She goosed him. He jumped.

"As long as we're in your brain, Paulywog, try not to let things 'slip out,' alrighty?" She walked to Hope, took the glass from her hand. "60/40? We can do better. Get back in. Take some help. Take... Hope? You up for a field trip?"

"I've never—"

"It'll be good for you. Apply some of those fancy theories." She turned to Paul. "Get out of here."

"Yes, dear."

⁂

amidst rivers Lethe and Styx
an enigma wrapped in lies
healing by primary intention

an enigma wrapped in truths
we are forgotten as easily as

❧

"Paul, you need to—"

"Adam?"

West turned. "Hmm?"

"Can we have a moment?" Paul nodded toward Benton.

Eyes slit. "Sure." West walked down the corridor. "But make it fast."

Benton sagged against the wall. "What is it?"

"We're at ninety-eight over. Sixty/forty lock. You know you don't have to come in with us."

Starlight in eyelight. "Are you saying you don't need me?"

"It's just—"

"Afraid of what you'll find in there?"

"No." He sighed. "But if we—"

"Paul." Hand to shoulder. "I've seen it all before. You don't scare me."

"You should be scared."

"I shouldn't."

"You will be."

"I won't."

"Fighting with you is useless."

"You wrote me." Lips upturned.

"And you," lips to cheek, "have no idea."

❧

Screaming.

Agony of broken bone within the face. He snuffled back blood, choked on copper, spat. Eyes slicked shut with

He ground earth from his vision, blinked. Sitting up from the mud and shit and snow, he pried his arms from the impact mark, rolled to free his legs. His helmet was gone.

He heard the stutter and stammer of his cardiac shield attempting to lock on to

West at his side, face gouged by

"This isn't good."

"Hope?"

She crawled through the trench towards her partners. "Lock's splintered."

"Yeah."

Stutter.

"Shit. Let me see that."

Chest heaving, breath a whisper, the author rolled to his back. Benton checked the readings on his shield. "Okay, it's stabilizing."

"Where are we?" West held his riflescope to a silver eye.

"Over/under target, that's for sure."

"Okay." He patted Paul's cheek. "Can you move?"

"Yeah. Just a little headache."

"Nose's broken. Maybe your cheekbone. You'll be fine."

"I'm placing a beacon in the Stream. Should be able to lock in a few."

"Good. Let's head toward the ridge."

❧

Lights flickered in the valley around the lake.

Their landing in this time had been particularly rough. West now saw the probable cause of the temporal disruptions in the worldline.

There were scores of black vessels surrounding the lake. One had crashed into an island at its center. From the sky, the stiletto shapes of Judas warships strafed the ground with lances of white laser. Smoke and fire, screams and static snaps. A shattered upload generator struggled to connect to the Enemy mind-essence under a barrage of weapons fire. Judas and Enemy fought hand-to-hand by the thousands. Humans fading into the shift, humans downloading from the mind-essence, a sweep of snow and cutting wind. The lake was frozen. Ice splintered with shadow.

A squadron of Judas Mujahadin passed over the huddled Judith, dropping dozens of pattern-charges into the midst of the Enemy horde. One vessel slowed, a fan of zeros and ones sprinkling West, Benton, Paul. Landing struts descended, and retro-forces kicked up spatters of mud.

It landed.

∽

I remember the throb of nose and right cheek, splintering into eye socket above and rattling teeth below. I don't remember writing Judas or Enemy into anything else. It concerned me. More blood. I spit again. Breathing was getting easier, marginally, as my blood slowed and thickened. The cardiac shield was quiet.

I guess I'd never really seen a spaceship. I knew it wasn't just that, but the tickle behind my eyes grew into suspicion and fear. A lucky shot from the valley below slammed into the starboard nacelle of the Muj and dissipated harmlessly into phase shielding. Returning fire from the craft ignited two of the disabled Enemy ships. Shards from the blast tore into and through the field of combatants.

I'd seen it all before... but I'd never *seen* it before.

A hull ramp descended from the Muj's belly. Armed Judas soldiers ran down the plank, surrounded us. At least the weapons were pointing out, not in. That was a good sign. And one Judas—

"Commander West?"

The frown and flicker of confusion was unmistakable, but he proceeded to hide it well beneath his mask of coagulating blood and diced cheekbones.

"Yeah, I'm West."

Silver eyes swept forth, back under furrowed brows, sculpted with laser precision, fixed on Adam's again. "Sir?"

"Listen..." The firefight below and above intensified. "I'm not *your* West. Where are we?"

Realization. "Shit, sorry. Let's get back to the ship."

They ran.

❧

That disconcerting joggle in the stomach as inertial dampening systems compensate in an alien atmosphere, butterflies: monarchs? and he felt the suck of the vacuum chair as they rose into a sky shot through with beams of light and plumes of black.

Beside him, Benton wiped beads of nervous sweat from her upper lip. One eye was developing an unpleasant bruise from their rough entry into the wrong When. She caught him looking and smiled quietly, looked toward the front of the cabin where the battle chamber elevator was falling to the floor. The Muj captain got off.

"Okay, let's figure this out. I just checked with our batteries; nav's taken us to strato, so we're out of the battle for the moment." She palmed the release mechanism on her armor, and silver blades retracted across torso, limbs, settled in seams. "You're not Commander West."

He pried himself from his seat, reached to shake her hand. "Not yours. We seem to've landed wrong."

She shook. "It happens. Captain Mindel Frost, Judas Mujahadin Kate, out of Fort John Wayne."

His eyes lit up. "Mindel Frost? You know Breine Frost?"

"My father."

"He served with me in the first Jaguar war."

"I know." She shrugged. "Same here, too."

"Is he—"

"Pattern erased two years ago standard."

"Sorry to hear that."

"So what's your business in this When?"

"Well..." West looked over at Paul. "It's complicated."

Frost turned to the author. "You are..?"

"Paul."

"Right."

"We're here to fix some things, but it might not be exactly here. Can we take a little trip north?"

"Where to?"

"Search Judith ME for coordinates for Lascaux."

"Judith Em Ee?"

Fuck. Paul gave himself a mental slap to the forehead. "Can you find where France will be?"

"Yeah."

"Good. Let's go."

❧

the most painful of our memories jarred loose from the recesses and wrinkles of gray-pink flesh by that most poignant of our senses: scent, and I knew watching her wasn't good for me. Smelling her was worse.

Scent and taste intrinsically linked: mouth-melting mints, fireplace logs, the claw-footed table, the brown ceramic cup into which he'd spit chewing tobacco juice and saliva, the taste of tongues and lips, teeth closed to bar entrance into mouths, adolescent, yearning, to be rid of the heat and roofing nails, the tear of white t-shirt and back, scars now, wounds then (and this is how we heal by primary) intentions uncertain: cigarette smoke and vodka? The pressure of three on a green flannel comforter, giggles, sisters, shaking hands move to breasts, necks, cheeks, and taste and scent collide in their spectrum, lost in themselves, the self a wondering observer from the periphery of my own world, taste and scent collide in the thrash of limbs, descent of clothing to tiled floor, callused fingers within softest folds, the shudder and gasp, the disconcerting slap of flat sweetness, sweat, the tang of exertion and desire, and desire across all senses, all pasts brought forward into tomorrows constructed solely of impossible memory and the loss of

"What's in Lascaux?"

My attention snapped from Frost, now poised over viewscreens of the battle at Jaguar. Hope Benton beside me: her scent accompanied an entirely different spectrum flood of memory into the conscious. She was adjusting her armored left arm; a snap of her wrist and silver plates *schhhicked* forward.

"Snow. Wind."

"You know what I mean."

I knew what she meant. The Judas weren't supposed to be here, weren't supposed to be anywhere. Now we were aboard Judas Kate watching Mindel Frost assess the progress of her fleet's attack against an Enemy insurgence force. Judas? Judith? Where could I have gone wrong? We'd been within two percentage points of A/O stability.

"Maire's here."

I saw her eyes flick to Frost and West at the screen. The Muj hit some slight turbulence. The scene required thunder. She leaned in. Whisper.

"That'd explain a lot."

It didn't require a response.

"Should we tell them?"

And a commotion from the screen: Frost's hands moved over controls. "You should see this!"

Walls faded from non-reflective alloy to the snowflake-stippled battlefield around Jaguar. The vacuum chairs upon which Hope and I sat seemed intensely out-of-place from our vantage point in the sky above the battle, a parasite image drawn from the eyes of another Judas.

Frost's hands clasped, unclasped. Eyes were drawn, slight smile. "Wait for it."

Hundreds, thousands of Judas soldiers fled from the valley; Enemy stood motionless, flickering. Flocks of Judas focused fire on the upload generator sunk into the lake. Great black shards splashed to the surface, ice cracking from a glacier into frigid Arctic waters. Three focused phase bursts at the spire's base and it shattered, a wave of purple and silver leveling the Enemy vessels and downloads across the valley floor. The Judas flocks arced to the sky to escape that explosion of stolen souls.

To be above it, to be within that wave of chaos and screams, was the closest I'd found to stillness.

Frost waved a hand and the image merged back to black walls, cold walls.

"We win."

❧

within
and within
shattered images: a star, an inhalation, silver and blood
the poetry of us
loss is
ruse, a
delta
converge, assess, act
alpha. omega.
hidden from and Delta
purpose will be
forgiveness; please forgive
a gnashing of teeth, a rending of flesh
stutter
c:\format c
It begins.

❧

"You've won the battle, but not the war."

"Nice. Cliché."

"Thanks. I'm an author."

Faint look of disdain from Frost. "We're approaching Lascaux. Want to tell me why we're here?"

Paul walked to the screen, still guttering with images from Jaguar: smoke, flame, stars. "Show me the Stream."

Frost paused, looking skeptically into eyes torn between green and mud. Fingers slid over depressions and the image changed: the linear temporal path from Alpha to Omega, branches of charted Whens and alternities spidering out in the pipecleaner cartography of the collected knowledge of eons.

"Illuminate known Enemy progress in this fragment."

Fingers: a pale blue-green field washed a majority of the time/space in the direction of Alpha from Omega. With few exceptions, blank areas on the Stream's spine, the Enemy had already uploaded a majority of this universe.

"See those?"

"What?"

He pointed. "Magnify this."

The area he indicated filled the screen; there was a noticeable fluctuation in upload success during that time.

"Bring it to two-dimensional." The image flattened. It could have been a depiction of a recorded waveform. Just below his finger, there was a severe decrease in uploaded pattern. "There it is."

"What am I looking at?"

"Delta Point."

❧

maybe it was the interlocking of those life strands that made the loss of both so poignant, so unbelievably painful.

I'd considered writing it into *Enemy*, but it was one of those ideas that just wakes me from hesitant sleep, accompanies me through a cigarette, two, three, and the hours of trying to return to dreams, only to have left in the morning (afternoon) light. Judith had told me of the next book I'd supposedly written; there was no mention of it there, either.

i met her again after two years at the first performance of his i'd seen in two years. the last time i saw him was with her. a month separated their physical and metaphorical deaths.

Writing histories into existence, writing men and women into life...

the most difficult part has been convincing myself that i'm not the focal point of these destinies, that i have no right to ascribe my ownership of these histories. i've been selfish and vain to assume that i linked anything together.

Alpha and Omega.. and Delta. How could I have forgotten that strand?

i'm not the focal point of history, but a simple man swept along within it. i don't deserve to be the intersection of life paths; i'm just paul. just paul.

Maire. The name tasted like blood.

i am ugly in every way.

i am bitter and selfish.

i could take pills, but they'll never help.

i am incapable of love.

i'm sorry. i'm so sorry.

❧

"Don't—Just stay back."

West grabbed Benton's elbow to stop her forward motion. She looked into his old gray eyes with cold precision.

She activated the panel above her right forearm. Blade shielding retracted from her hand and she—

"Stay shielded!" Paul shouted back from the impact crater. "I don't know if it's still active."

Blades slid back into place.

Frost surveyed the frozen plane. "What are we dealing with here?"

"Silver." West's grumbled answer.

❧

contained multitudes.

and I felt like weeping, knew that I couldn't, forgot about it for a while.

what have i done?

Knowing that each time I put pen to paper, each time callused fingertips traced lightly over plastic lettered keys, a world began, a world died, knowing that each time I thought too much, that each time I woke from a nightmare, a daymare, knowing, just knowing that it was real, it was blood and bone, the gasp of terror or lust, the cry of pain or release of

I knelt next to the mark her body had made in the earth. In the Earth.

Imagine a bipedal alien, cold eyes and flowing hair, jettisoned from a galaxy whose death she'd guaranteed, thrust into the veil of black between galaxies, caught in the wake of a vessel: a glorified photographer, an artificial lover, a traitor with two broken hearts. Imagine the impact of a body, a body and the snow, ice, the wind between then and now, and silver.

I knelt by the human-shaped crater, dragged armored claws over the compressed snow. Ice. I carved faint paths across its surface.

I could see the silver crawling. Merging, diverging, coalescing. Still very much alive, still very much a threat. She'd been here recently.

The husk of Task's vessel had stopped smoking. A path of footprints and blood stretched to it, around, to the caves beyond.

I stood. Melting silver dripped from my claws, puddled and danced across

❧

"Frost?" Paul returned from the crater, holding his right hand before him. "You shielded?"

"Shielded? I—"

"Have phase armor on?"

"No, but—"

"Shift up. Just a little. Have something to show you."

She flickered into the shift. Lazy light spilled over Benton and West.

"What is that?" She reached out to touch Paul's silvered hand.

"Don't." The light from the shift bent toward his hand, shivered.

"But what—"

"Silver."

Paul reached to finger the release mechanism at his neck.

"Don't—!"

The helmet hissed and released, retracted into his clavicle armor. The silver leapt. He exhaled, closed his eyes.

Benton gasped as the silver blackened, fell to the packed snow in lazy swirls of ash.

Paul cleared his throat. "Adam, what's your wife's name?"

West blinked. "What?"

"What's her name?"

Eyes narrowed and jaw clenched. "Abigail."

"Right. Frost, what's your West's wife's name?"

She looked from West to Paul, confused. "Patra."

"Any children?"

"Two daughters. Twins."

"West?"

"One son."

"And therein lies the problem." Pasts and futures intertwined in the knot of an impossible present. "How'd Abby die?"

West blinked. "In childbirth."

"Right." Paul flicked the last of the silver from his claws. "Judith and Judas, Patra and Abigail, West and West. Frost, have you ever met her before?" His outstretched hand indicated Benton.

"I don't think so."

"You wouldn't have. She doesn't exist here. West does, though..."

"What's this mean?"

"Maire's breaking through. She's achieving Delta point completion."

Paul's cardiac shield began to beep. Benton rushed to his side, looked over the monitor. "They're locking on to our signal."

"Save these coordinates."

"Done."

"We'll be back, Frost. As soon as we can. We'll bring reinforcements."

"But what if—"

"Just wait for

and all was static, shimmer, shift as the three soldiers of the Judith faded from the plain of snow and silver.

Frost, alone now, palmed her communications panel. "Get me Commander West."

A formation of Judas Muj fighters screamed through the sky of perpetual winter.

࿐

"Great timing, Jud. What happened with our insertion?"

"Call it a short circuit. We don't know yet." An army of Judith technicians plugged, unplugged, analyzed, removed armor, placed nitrox masks over gasping mouths.

Paul felt the ache of reality begin to pound once again in the place behind his eyes. "There's been a few developments. Do you have our output coordinates?"

"They're locked. Rest for a while. I'll debrief you after you're reloaded."

"Sounds like kink."

"You wish."

Paul smiled, sighed as he leaned back into the reload chamber. Technicians removed his armor. They slammed the chamber door shut above him. Through its clear metal cap, Paul observed Benton's already-reloading figure in the oven next to his. Cutting lights moved in to flay her. His eyes crawled from peaceful, sleeping eyelids to gentle philtrum to supra-sternal notch, the placement of her nipples, the indentation of navel and the soft southern path to the pudendal cleft. Flesh flew away in the thinnest strips as the spinning whiteness recycled her body. Skin, fat, muscle, bone were removed and then rebuilt with untainted code from the Judith ocean. Hairless. It grew. Muscles toned. A wash of freckles, a mole, a scar. Breath of life and her eyes opened. She caught his gaze and threw it not ungently back.

He closed his eyes and felt his layers of offense and defense stripped from him by harsh, beautiful, sensual light.

"Feel better?"

"Like a summer's eve." He toweled tousled hair. "You're looking better."

Judith leaned against the chamber entrance, arms folded. She looked over the flesh constructs: the aged West, the hairy author, the ripe smoothness of Benton, brutal cardiac shield scar painfully visible above and between hanging breasts. She self-consciously suited up under the feminine gaze.

he has good taste

Paul reached out. *so does she. now stop ogling her.*

fair enough. "What'd you see?"

schlick of armor closing over his arms, legs, chest. Cardiac lock. "Your favorite one-hearted psycho is bleeding through into the Whenstream."

"Fuck." Judith slumped. "You're the author. What's this mean?"

"It means

two distinct universes colliding, splintering both along that fault to history-sized fragments: rupturing, rending, riving, splitting, cleaving. It meant that two distinct universes that I'd written into existence were merging into one.

dissolution

then strike in my name. Strike for all of those whose lives were shattered. For the trillions dead and broken. For those who still bear scars of flesh and thought. Strike because I don't want my children to die for the Purpose. Strike because there is evil, and it is not me. Strike because history will remember the loss if you don't.

fading

I've begun a war of desire. A war of technology.

All fears realized, all hopes questioned, all boundaries erased, all secrets of form and space brought forward into hesitant light.

None of us will survive this

❧

intact, but it's not a good chance. If she's in the Stream already, chances are she's started all over again."

"And you're convinced this Jag When is the crossover point?"

"It's Delta. Silver is off the scale, and Enemy pattern exhibits a sharp decline. It's where she broke through."

"No good... No good." Judith activated the display. A glowing representation of the Timestream flickered to life. "Okay, we can divert forces from—"

"It won't be enough."

"The Fleet's—"

"She'll equip the Enemy with silver. If she's focusing on Delta Point, I wouldn't be surprised if she has forces en route to the trees right now."

"Shit, never thought it'd come to this." West tapped nervous fingertips on the display surface. "Place any bets, Miss Maths?"

Benton thought for a moment. "Negative to at least five decimals."

"That's reassuring."

"Enough." Paul's fingers went to his temple: throbbing with the silver ache. "We gather forces, we travel back, we take out the Zero-Four probe before silver infestation."

"Easier said." Judith smirked. "But you can do it. Get out of here."

"See you tomorrow, Jud." Paul rose with West and Benton. "Whenever tomorrow might be."

"Watch your ass." As the chamber door sizzled shut, something crawled between her hearts, took residence there, and began to gnaw. She shuddered.

They left.

OF LOSS, OF RUIN

OF LOSS, OF RUIN

Four hearts: one, and frequent exhalation, shudder, the scrape of exquisitely-manicured nails over flesh, over metal, over flesh and:

She realized through closing her eyes, opening to watch the ceiling spin, the gritting of teeth, fingers through hair, that the absence of stubble was a refreshing and welcome change, and that she could feel the inverse imprint of dimples on her inner thighs as Maire smiled, looked up, went back to work, the drape of raven locks, curled with effort, hours, sweat, hiding most of their collective sin:

The inhuman tongue shaped, re-shaped, the central division splitting, flicking, rearranging and reconceptualizing the meaning of pleasure, of desire, as the interior vocal cords housed within resonated reflexively, whispering without thought through muscle, through the tips of the snake's voice, one ruddy finger caressing, one circling, both speaking into wetness and soft, soft magenta: *do we* and with a frantic shifting of position to the other tongue, to other, darker recesses, bound not with teeth, but with lips, kissing, dragging, inhaling the essence of *have an agreement?*

Maire arose from thighs, wiped moisture from her mouth. She smiled over a tongue closing upon itself, sealing with mucus both her own and another's. Shattered voices repaired as one: *Do we, sweet-ness?* The tugging of a voice formed beyond the vibration of flesh, somewhere within the electricity, the halo.

The response was slow, not as a result of thought or consideration or reticence, but simply because Kath couldn't calm her hearts enough to form words. Hands now idled from intertwining with hair danced lost across her bare thighs, abdomen, breasts, settled over her cardiac plate. La-la-duh-dub. La-la-duh-dub. Slowing, the edge of orgasm, the recession of the interior oceans of loss, of desire for a moment, an hour, a day with this dark partner, replaced with the richness of pleasure.

"Of course... Of course."

"Good." Her smile seemed misplaced, given the decision, the alliance. "Blinds off."

The panels walling the entire chamber shifted from murky gray to reveal a projection of the planet surface far above them. Realized in four dimensions, the outside was a disconcerting veil of sensuality: the bitter wind, the brittle scrape of the lumber schools drowsing through waves of chlorostatic mist far above the surface, the heady intrusion of pine pitch into membranes just now waking from aromas hidden in uncovering, in opening, in sex.

Maire rolled on to her back and snuggled against Kath's side. It started from above: the singing of the trees, lilting, howling, branches miles long quivering through the mists, sparks floating down, a lazy display of fireworks that sputtered out long before planet impact. The song...

"This is where it begins." Maire looked into her eyes, lids narrowing, lips bracing with resolve. "This is how we win the war."

Kath looked into a night sky brazen with perpetual sunset from the system's binary stars, the great black forms of the sentient trees blocking out swathes of meager star-points, their own shower of silver falling to ground, never reaching, never reaching:

Silver.

❧

It was terror and it was beauty and it was all.

Michael made the final decision and launched the Zero-Four probe from a Gauss pipeline that stretched miles within the planet to the void between stars, between times: one hundred grams of alloys and plastics and the echoes of biology. The primary propulsion rockets separated and the solar sail deployed in a flash of gossamer golden filaments. The sail spread out to grasp the stars, and a fusion concussion fed the ever-increasing velocity of the precious spacecraft. At several million astronomical units and several hundred thousand years, the unit achieved nine-tenths light speed. The journey of infinity had begun.

Nanotechnological ramscoops collected the materials required to procreate, and in the night between the galaxies, the tiny vessel created an exact copy of itself. The two remnants of a civilization now eons dead separated, and for an instant, the first machine felt an emotion. It dismissed the feeling and began to replicate another child. The second vessel set off on an alternate trajectory, the translucent solar sail sweeping eerily before it, mute golden wings in the void of silence and nothing, forever departing from its immaculate and sole parent.

The process continued for billions of years. In time, out of time, the original machine died, but its infinite spawn carried the message forever onward. The universe became populated with the machines. The expansion of existence eventually forced the universal heat death. Organic life became an impossibility, and the technological lifeforms flourished. The machines continued onward, waiting for the time that their precious cargo could live again.

When the universe fell back together, having achieved maximum expansion, the machines fell silent. When they encountered a solar system, sometimes they could reconstitute organic life from the biological patterns recorded so long ago on a planet in a system long dust. All that they could do then was wait for that life to grow anew.

In those days between the death of everything and the rebirth of less than humanity, the Zero-Four probe hurtled into the dark and spawned. Its progeny spread outward and consumed everything in their path. Before Omega, it judged that all that it had created was good and redeemable, and it sent the newborns back into the blackness to save those unfortunate enough to have remained behind.

They would live forever in the ocean of silver fire. Omega would be the salvation and the nirvana and the extinction and the

❧

wind bit at her still-flushed cheeks. She pulled her hood forward, forcing her hair into a flailing mane. She pulled errant wisps from her sticking lips. She'd left the scientist Kath drifting into sleep between silken sheets. A part of her still longed to be there.

Concussion from above of static thrust, cycling engines tracing the planet surface with gentle force, currents of dust and needles. The transport was magnificent, drawfed only by a migrating school above, the scavenging parasite herds trailing silently behind.

Clawed feet, jointed legs hinged from the transport's belly. It more crawled to the surface than landed. As ramps descended, as sides split and smaller vessels thrust into the mist, as ground vehicles began rolling from the transport as a burst eggsac releases spiderlets, Maire was proud of the army she had gathered.

Her mind reaching, her tongue flicking behind parted teeth, no longer filed to barbarian standards, she tasted the communications blinking across the plain, the battle language, the grunts and hisses of action, of anger. Fear: hidden below bravado, hidden not deep enough.

A tracked vehicle approached the compound. Maire frowned, not at the approach, but at what she had begun to taste on the edge of the passenger's thoughts, a strange, bitter, hazel confusion.

Treads came to a rest. The passenger jumped from the top hatch.

"Maire—"

"What've you found?"

"We don't know. Just—"

A tugging and she saw, heard, smelled: a ridiculous beeping, two sets of tones with silence interrupting: blip blip blip, beep beep beep, blip blip blip, silence.

She frowned.

❧

From dreams, the warmth of the bed, the coolness and fragility of panic, she thought of the freedom that Black Space promised. She thought of Berlin, now so far from her on the planet of machines and nears. She had been unfaithful. She struggled to find calm, but the potency of memory intruded with yesterdays of stubble, stretching, and good pain.

She sat up in bed, drew the sheets around her still-nude form. She wasn't cold, but she was.

To be so far from One...

To what end had she agreed? How could she ever tell Berlin of the plan that had been set into motion? He was due to return on the next outward tide with the harvesting fleet for the chlorostatic flora.

Black was on fire, had been for decades. The animals, the machines... Maire had told her of a childhood, living but not *truly* living. Underground with the fires above (literal and figurative), the horrible memories of feasting on the rotten flesh of her fallen parents, of her friends. The time when the plains of wheat had died in the chemical scourge and white light had shot the emergency aid shipments from the sky.

There were legends that they'd once made the machines, but Kath didn't believe them.

Berlin's mutterings in his sleep... The final battles before the nears, before the artificial lifeforms had made it all the way to Planet One. Hers was a species enslaved by automaton baubles.

He'd whispered of a tower of black falling from the sky, crushing the planet surface, a line of white through the sky, and then words fell victim to slumber's confusion and grief's overflow. Tears choked him and he turned over, coughing, pulled the covers closer over his shoulders. She'd reached out to touch him but hadn't.

Pieces of a grand puzzle slid into place with liquid and silver precision.

She wasn't cold, but she was.

❧

Closing her eyes as the waldoes gripped the treadcar, swung it up through the chaos of troops, fighters, other land vehicles, coming and going, loading and unloading, up through sparks and static and jets of super-heated gelatin, she thought back to the calm of war, that moment before impact and combat, that moment when all becomes honed senses: the waft of the protein sludge sloshing in the biobombs, the tickle of phased silica shielding, that scream the weapons arms of land vehicles made, lacking lubrication, as pallet after pallet of twelve or fifteen medium-range slash-and-blow missiles slam into place, the muffled tinkling of contents: enough compressed shrapnel slurried with acid to disperse five square miles of unshielded ground soldiers, the stink, the stink of decay and exhaust, blood, sticking to sand, sticking to bones burst through flesh.

She opened her eyes.

The car bounced to a landing platform, quick-sealing deck fudge locking it into place. Maire jumped down from the vehicle, her stomach lurching into place under the pressure of ship gravity. Her first few steps were impressing, sucking, as the fudge completed its curing process.

She stood in place as an internal transport tube lowered over her body and flew her to operations. Her hearts pounded through thousands of feet of lowlight tubing.

Gentle landing.

"Where is it?"

Maire stepped forward into the ship's core. Helmeted technicians worked at a ring of consoles, their manacled limbs projecting and determining the courses of vessels in wait above the atmosphere, hordes of ground troops spreading across the surface, things as simple as the waste reclamation system and limiting the level of toxic oxygen in the living spaces on-vessel. Dozens of distinct projection bubbles clouded dozens of consoles.

One bubble unclouded.

"We found it in the Seychelles Drift."

Nude limbs undraped from its squat, shaking interface gauntlets loose to the floor. It stood, stretched, skin pale gray, the juncture of legs revealing nothing other than the signature evacuation slot of the unsexed neuter. Maire's thoughts drifted briefly to the disgust and anger that even three decades of star travel couldn't erase entirely from her mind, made even more potent by her lust for Kath, the evidence of their union still on her lips.

"Maire?"

"Hmm?" but that voice, that *voice*. She hated the middle species.

"Seychelles Drift. Remind you of anything?"

A cave, and teeth, and eyes. And silver. And a voice: reaching, reaching.

"Just show it to me."

ꩰ

The lock cycled open in the chamber forty levels above the operations deck, in a secluded area housed between drives and weapons, just under the coolant pond. She felt the heat of engines, of lights, of something else, something just besind the eyes, just besind now.

Hiss and release of atmosphere shielding. Rivulets of steam and sparks.

"That's it?"

The neuter walked in before her, fingers tracing over wall-mounted displays. "I'll boost the outer barrier and run the interior down to visual. You have to see this."

In the center of the circular room, tracing lasers faded, swept, intensified. Waves of phase shielding rippled out, slowing as force gradation shifted within the containment perimeter. The item hanging at the room's center flickered into Maire's vision.

"Readings?"

"Nothing atypical. It's absorbed a lot of radiation, but that's to be expected if it'd been in the Drift for a while."

"What's it made of?"

"Mostly gold, titanium.. But there are some elements we haven't yet identified."

"Metals?"

"Yes."

"Anything else?"

"Trace biologics on the interior. We can't sequence them."

"How's that possible?"

"Alien genetic patterns. Our printers haven't been able to build from them yet."

It was a ball of yellow and gray metal, an imperfect ball, flattened gently like the exterior reproductive shells of the flying reptiles that frequented the coastlines of ocean planets. It could fit in the palm of her hand. Maire leaned in closer. "What are those ports?"

"Propulsion, I'd imagine, although it appeared to have been free-floating for quite some time. Wait..." Its fingers activated something on the control mounted on the wall. "I'm lowering the solar range to half."

Maire watched as the light in the room dimmed to half-standard. The alien ball whirred to life, a panel slicking open on one flattened end, two tiny masts deploying, the silken sweep of a golden solar sail filling the space between.

"It's a vessel."

"Might be."

"Has it opened before?"

"Not when I've been in here."

"Scan it again. Maybe we can pick up something from the inside now."

Maire watched as the neuter's grotesquely long fingers traced over the control panel. A scan arm swung down from the ceiling, dug into the phase shield around the tiny golden vessel. The ball didn't react to the scan; its sail still stretched out, reaching for purchase on the meager supply of photons the half-solar bombardment could offer. Its scan complete, the arm withdrew.

"Okay, I'm getting—Well, that's different."

"What?"

"Scan analysis usually takes a few seconds to complete, but the system's locked up."

"The system hasn't had an outage in—"

"It's back."

The neuter activated room display, and the scan results began to stream across a virtual plane beside the vessel. Document after document, cross-referencing, linking, red-coded secret documents flashing and opening, photographs, four-dimensional re-presentations of centuries of accumulated scientific knowledge, all tore across the field of vision too fast for Maire to comprehend, such was the glut of the information ocean results on the scan query.

"It's accessing the entire library of temporal sciences."

"More than that..."

"Time sciences, threat science, metallurgics, genetic databases, megascale engineering, quantum—"

The image froze.

"—physics. What are we looking at?"

The neuter didn't have an answer.

A representation of time and space: bent physics, a blinking dot linked through forty-thousand years of drift in the Seychelles, a line denoting forward travel through time traveling exponentially outward, the edge of another galaxy, another time, another blinking dot.

"Okay. Tell me if I'm reading this right."

"Sure."

"Either the libraries are fucked, or it's telling us that this vessel has been sitting in the Drift since the machines appeared, and before that it traveled forward in time from a place on the other side of Black Space?"

"Um... Sounds about right."

"How's that possible?"

"It isn't. It's bent physics, time travel, deep space travel wrapped in one. This thing is ancient, but it's from the future. Not even our future."

"That explains the genetic patterns."

"We're looking at the machines' creator. It has to be. There was nothing else in Seychelles that long ago."

"If it's true, this rewrites everything. We'll finally know where the machines came from. We'll finally be able to—"

Movement.

The solar sail retracted.

"Neuter?"

"Yeah?"

"What did threat science say about this thing?"

"No known weapons present. No toxins, minimal radiation, no—"

The phase shielding bubble around the vessel gave a last static burst and shattered to the floor, splashing across the expanse in a small wave. Maire's boots and the neuter's bare feet stood submerged in an inch of crystal sludge.

"Don't move."

Can one forget war? A succession of brittle images: a knife cutting through the flesh of a sister, calf muscle, open fire, black streaks in the sky and the scent of burning plastic. Can one forget war? Those humans, non-humans, eyeless, faceless, hordes falling, following, flying, the way she hid in the rubble, grew in the rubble, became an adult under the bloody rule of those who were not flesh, were not calf muscle, but who more resembled open fire, black streaks in the sky, the scent of burning plastic.

Maire screamed as the vessel opened, as the field of silver tore through her body, as the neuter beside her was stripped from the room, skin flayed, muscles and bone ground to dust against the wall, as she felt the same process begin within her, as silver, as silver, and then nothing.

The vessel closed.

❧

Frozen in place, she hung next to the neuter inside the nothing. Dream, fog, without reason or movement. Her chest couldn't move; she couldn't inhale, but her lung bladder didn't burn.

And where did the light come from?

All she could see, if it really was seeing and not a nameless sense, that ineffable crawl behind eyes and between times, was the neuter, its arms held before its face, mouth agape in horror of an end, frozen. Waves of

And she considered how horribly they'd always treated the slave class, the third sex (gender? or the precipitous lack thereof?). They weren't even given clothing to hide that place between their legs where phallus or cleft appeared in the rest of the species. Realization: here in this dark, Maire was without clothing, uncovered, vulnerable, the only movement of her form her raven hair, swimming about in the nothing as if there were wind, a current, a prehensile ability to abandon her paralyzed form. It was cold, but she couldn't feel it. Gooseflesh. Her nipples were erect on either side of the retracted cardiac shield cage, usually open to permit the free-flow of nitrogen into the inhale areas on the underside of her external ribbing, but now closed tightly around her hearts, making her chest a ridged plain crevassed by cleavage.

She thought the nameless neuter was trying to look at her, but its eyes remained clouded, fixed elsewhere.

Hundred of thousands of years of star travel and all her species had to show for it was a third division of the race, sexless, and enslavement at the silver hands of faceless machines from worlds buried deep in the Drift. The neuters weren't treated as a part of the species. They were a workforce valuable only for their ability to withstand long flights without sterility and the occasional act of kink between non-breed partners in more-progressive joining communes.

She'd never fucked a neuter. The idea disgusted her.

But to treat them as a subspecies, to treat them as the machines treated the dominant groups of the race, to marginalize and persecute them for being breed-null... She wished she could have changed it.

With a wave of light, a tracing projection, the neuter was released from its motionless state for an instant filled with screaming, thrashing agony, and then it was gone. Maire was left alone in the nothing.

A tickle, an itching, a biting instant of pain between her eyes, and

❧

the acrid sting of toxic oxygen, but she wasn't choking yet, wasn't feeling nauseous or dizzy. She reached for her cardiac plate to test the temperature of her inhale slits, but gasped and looked down: there was no plate. Her chest was smooth, unbroken by even the ridges of retracted secondary ribs.

More than just the atmosphere was wrong.

Rain outside, its tattoo on the rooftop of the building. People sitting at tables, drinking from white cups, steaming, and the scent of smoke: a person sitting at the counter inhaled a smoker, exhaled.

"Who are you?"

She started at the voice, from a young man sitting across the table from her. A sip of black liquid, napkin to the corner of lips. She reeled from the flood of new senses, alien experiences all around her, the physical changes that her body itself had gone through.

"I—" And she heard, felt the difference of her voice. She attempted to modulate the sound with her ancillary vocal cords, but she had none.

"Hmm?" He looked at her with kind, gray eyes. "Cat got your tongue? Who are you?"

"Maire." She sat up in her chair, eyes wide, surveying the people around her. "Who are you?"

He chuckled. "The name's Michael Balfour. I bet you're wondering where you are."

She nodded.

He took another sip, swallowed. Napkin. "I'll let you in on a little secret. See all these people?"

At tables, in twos and threes: a young couple, hands held, the woman's now displaying a silver ring on one, a black glove on the other, another at a table of books and laughter, red curls and sighs, the two at the counter talking so closely they could have been one, muddy brown and blonde intersecting in gray streaks, a white dot, a single dimple. A spattering of others, reading, watching the moving images projected on the wall, sipping, sipping.

"This is heaven."

The word meant nothing to her.

"Heaven. Dig?"

She shrugged her shoulders, and Michael wondered exactly how a species could have no concept of heaven but could still exhibit the same mannerism denoting confusion as his once had.

"We've been watching you for a long time, Maire. Coffee?"

She looked down at the steaming cup he held between mocha fingers, the nails bitten in true Delany fashion to the quick. Her new fingers were tipped by the same translucent (chitin? protein?) shields, each with a setting moon crescent at its base. "No. Thanks."

He sipped. "Took us a while to make contact. We've been waiting out there, dabbling here and there. You're an interesting species."

Cup to tabletop. She was trying not to breathe too much, breathe too quickly. Her chest hitched under her blouse as she attempted to spread her gills plate, but it was no longer there.

"I myself only arrived in-system about forty-thousand solar cycles ago. I wanted to check to see what my kids had made. I must say, you're among the most interesting pattern variants yet."

"You're a god?"

Michael smiled. "Not quite." His smile opened to a grin. "I know what you've done to your gods before, and I wouldn't want that to happen to me. Just consider me a neighbor. A cousin, sort of."

"What are you? What is this place?"

Hands folded on the table. "You have no concept of virtual worlds; I've done my homework. Guess I'd better start by telling you of a

❧

sky blackened by war and disease and centuries of gaiacide. The only lights studded the rim of the launch tunnel, and even they were murky in the dead air of the dying world.

"Almost time, Michael."

"Yes."

"There's still time to change your mind, you know."

He shook his head across his pause. "I can't go."

The earth shuddered beneath them almost imperceptibly. Men in clean suits ran to the vehicles and sped away from the edge of the launch tunnel, forty miles away. Michael took the binoculars from his eyes and wiped away the stale sweat that had collected on his eyebrows and in the hollows of his eyes.

"Starting final countdown sequence. Any more to board?"

Expectant eyes regarded him with almost pity. He shook his head.

"Shut down the upload link. Irrigate the lines and initiate primary engine test sequence."

The earth began to resonate with the power of the massive engines that lay hundreds of miles beneath the surface. There could be no turning back now.

"Test shows positive across the board. Waiting for coordinate lock."

The binoculars went back to his eyes. The edge of the launch tunnel looked deceptively calm, bereft of the hundreds of clean-suited workers that had toiled over every inch of its interior for decades.

"Coordinate lock achieved. Planetary position is a go. Launch window open. Launch on your order, sir."

Michael nodded his understanding. All hope for the continuation of the human species lay in the precious golden machine bundled safely within the launch vehicle.

Millions of emulated humans living emulated lives in emulated worlds where the emulated sun still shined and the emulated water was still pure. Someday they would come home. They were the ark. When the planet had finally healed, they could come home and live again.

"Engage Gauss cycle in launch tower."

"Gauss engaged."

"Engage primary thrusters."

"Primary thrusters engaged."

With this machine, all hope lay.

"Launch."

"Launching vehicle."

The binoculars revealed a tunnel entrance that flickered with the Gauss cycle. Michael held on to the bunker wall with one hand to steady himself; the ground beneath them shook noticeably and fiercely. Never before had a vessel of such size or power been launched from the planet surface.

Where is it?

"Gauss cycle at max. Vehicle launched."

Michael took the binoculars from his eyes and replaced them with blackened blast goggles. The vehicle emerged from the launch tunnel with a stark white ferocity that painfully illuminated the bunker interior and flash-reddened Michael's face immediately. The sound and heat and light were unbearable even from forty miles out, but then it was gone, and the vehicle was out of the atmosphere.

"Launch successful. Vehicle has broken orbit."

Goodbye, my child. Goodbye, my children.

"All right. Good." Michael regarded his launch crew. "Start the disassembly process. Everything has to be taken apart before we abandon the city. There's sure to be a resistance attack now that they know we've

❧

launched, and that's where the story really begins."

He regarded his empty cup, motioned for the server. She smiled, one bullet-hole dimple, and went behind the counter for another pot.

"We're here to bring you home."

"Where's 'home?'"

His fingers tapped one through four on the plastic tabletop. "I wasn't even supposed to be on the probe. I guess one of my over-eager or over-compassionate technicians must have ghosted my pattern while I wasn't watching. They always had far more respect for me than I had for myself. Difficult to believe in yourself when you're nothing more than a fourth-gen clone."

The dimpled server returned with coffee. On her way back to the counter, her hand went to her partner's back, lingered as she whispered something to him. Maire saw: the scar on her fingertip, the prominent bridge of her nose, the way her lips brushed his ear, brushing and whispering, perhaps the scent of smoke, perhaps the taste of him.

Maire absently rubbed the place where her hearts should have been.

"I know of your ambitions, Maire."

She frowned.

"I built a machine that would save a world. And this is what it made, a thousand variants of my species scattered about our universe, a million variants spread across a million timelines, forevers expanding and contracting, and here, only here, have I found anything remotely resembling me. You know how hard it is to talk to crystals? To bioneural sludge? To control that evolution, to hope beyond hope that somewhere, somehow, things have lined up to create a semblance of familiarity? I'll tell you the greatest secret of life: we're all alone out here. No little green men, no hives or alien queens, no beings of pure energy. All we have is us."

She didn't know what to say, so she didn't say anything at all.

"Those silver machines that you hate so much? I made them."

Eyes drew to slits.

"Something happened after the heat death. Maybe it was that dark matter, the holes in the universe we'd not been able to explain. My machine bred, its children bred, and somewhere along the line, something went tragically wrong. They don't yet know we're here," his hand extended to indicate the air, the interior of the coffee shop, its patrons, "and I intend to keep it that way. They have to be stopped before they reclaim it all."

Laughter from the counter. Michael turned in time to see a playful bite on the cheek, man to woman, tip to tip of nose, bite from woman to man: he had known love once, albeit unreflected. He closed his eyes and saw Richter's spectrums of gray there.

"Why am I here?"

He looked at and through her question as it hung in the acrid air between them. "I need you to do something for me."

"What?"

"I need you to kill a god."

❧

and she slammed to the floor from her stance, the lifeless body of the neuter falling beside her in a heap of unclothed flesh, a sickly crack as its fragile skull gave to the floor, the slap of meat on metal as legs bounced once and fell still.

Her first breath was fire. Her second was fire. She remembered

i contain multitudes

everything.

Hand to heart(s?) and she knew it had been real.

Her third breath was easier as she adjusted to two lungs, one heart.

She fastened the closure on her chest, concealing her lack of cardiac shield to anyone she might encounter in this vessel. She stood, dizzy, but stopped to bend and gently close the open eyes of the dead neuter.

She left the chamber without looking back at the Zero-Four probe.

i contain multitudes

❧

Kath stirred in the bed from hesitant dreaming, the games of flesh remembered, the reward all around her in that bed, the tang marking sheets and lips with memory.

A brush of and then

She heard hushed movement in the adjoining room and knew Maire had returned.

With schlick and hiss, the door opened to the bedroom and she entered, still believing Kath asleep, moving to the wall panel where clothes were stored. She removed a rucksack and began shoving clothes in. From under a pile of stockings, she took out a shiver gun, checked the vibration chamber, placed it in her sack.

A pattern of light in near-dark: Kath knew the outline of the weapon by the spaces between shadows.

"Maire?"

Her hands stopped over underthings, fingers curling to fist. "I didn't know you were awake." She didn't turn around.

Something was wrong. Kath couldn't place it, tried to, failed, considered, almost gave up. Insight and

"What's wrong with your voice?"

Fingers dragged against the wall, and the room gently illuminated. Maire placed her bag on the floor and sat on the edge of the bed. Her eyes avoided the touch of Kath's. Reaching, reaching still

"Maire?"

She looked and Kath knew it wasn't right, would never be right again, could never possibly be right again. The eyes were swimming between black and gray, each blink swirling tendrils of color into non-color. Blink and

"I have to go." That voice, the horrible flatness of its tone, the single pitch, and grating, wheezing breath... "I'm going."

"But—What happened? Maire, what happened to you?"

She was silent.

"Please, just tell me. I can—" and she reached for Maire's shoulder.

"Don't *touch* me." The shoulder shrugged away in time to her growl. She stood from the bed and lifted her sack from the floor.

Tears verged. Kath's breath came in halts and stops, the choke of sob, the confusion of the not-knowing. "Whatever happened, let me help you."

"I have to go away. Now. I don't know for how long."

"Will I—"

"You'll see me again when it's time."

"Time for what?"

The illusions our eyes play in night, without light or reason: an instant of static, a halo of silver, and Maire's form returned to normal. *Don't touch me*

"When it's time to strike."

She turned and walked out the door, leaving Kath to an empty room, echo, and fear.

❧

"You're quiet."

The observation platform hovered miles above the surface, the "grass" of thousand-foot trees, the embryonic stage of the lumbers. Kath had once seen a hatchery where a surrogate mother had nudged those infant flora into the sky with great cracks of vestigial root structures and the dusting of centuries-old branches to the forest floor. Those first hesitant leaps into the sky, that keening song, the wind made by the mature herd swimming above them... It had been beauty, steeped in the scent of pine pitch.

"Hmm?" Her gaze met his.

Berlin grinned. "Exactly."

"I'm sorry." Her fingers threaded through his, now wrapped tightly around the safety ring of the platform. She'd forgotten how disconcerting an observation flight was for those usually confined to galactic or surface travel. It was a different kind of falling. "Just thinking too much."

"About what?" His fingers squeezed. That scar, those infinitesimal hairs, the ridge of callus denoting the bellies of knuckles.

Her answer hid in the tilting down of her eyes, the thin exhalation of carbon triox evidenced in the cool of the upper lower atmosphere. He smiled at the redness of her ears and the flush of her cheeks.

"What? ((Cat)) got your tongue?"

She frowned, awash in a memory not hers and a word not possible. Maire and smoke and bitter, bitter

"What did you say?"

"Kath, what's wrong? You've barely spoken to me since I arrived in-system."

"It's just..." The thought was lost somewhere between wind and the long fall down.

"If it's about the lumbers, I've told you. They won't feel any pain. We need to do this. It'll all be over in—"

"It's not that. It's not just that. I mean..."

She unlocked fingers and wrapped her arms around him. He pulled, squeezed, noting her height, the tickle of her hair in the scattering wind, and the scent of

In the distance, he saw the first harvest vessels begin to chase a small school of the enormous trees. Flash and snare, the screaming of wood, the foul defensive odor of burning and something intensely sweeter than sugar could ever be.

She jumped in his grasp at the screams, and he pulled her closer.

The harvest continued.

❧

Just a taste at first, a few hundred lumbers. They took the screaming specimens into orbit, held them in dissection freighters, took them apart and looked inside for that shimmer, that echo.

They found it in the tricarboxylic acid cycle, mitochondria resonating with an energy, a metal, a something they couldn't explain. They took more samples.

The machines were confused. Concerned.

A breakthrough: isolation of a limited flux passage, buried deep within the pattern, teased forward and brought to the rippling surface. Vacuole inversion. They could ride on poisons. Liquid space travel became not a dream but a soon-to-be-realization.

Planet One sent orders.

❧

Weeks, months and

the air burned with cold above the lumber plains on the night that she'd been so convincing. Winter had arrived in the hemisphere. The embryo forests stood snow covered in their first hibernation, sleeping through the frigid night until a spring that wouldn't arrive. The platform didn't offer much protection against the wind.

It wasn't dancing, and it wasn't singing, but the flora hovered in formation below them, basking in the phosphorescent hydrostatic mist of the mid-atmosphere. The canyons echoed with their midnight song.

Berlin wrapped his arms around Kath, hands clasped in front in a bundle of their intertwined fingers. Squeeze. Sniffle and one hand went to her face as demure form shook with sob and fear. In moonslight, twin tracks on windburned cheeks: just two tears, but they were two too many.

"They'll all be harvested."

"Analysis was conclusive. We can isolate the flux ability."

"Then why—"

"Because they can. And they don't want anyone else to figure it out."

"So that's it? They take a few lumbers for sampling, isolate the tech, and kill the rest?"

"That's the way we work."

"No." She turned around in his arms. Gray eyes swallowed by black pupils. "That's the way *they* work."

"I can't—"

"You can't. But we can."

She slipped from his grasp, walked to the other side of the floater, leaned precariously over the edge. The vehicle swayed in the wake of a forest passing above them. Berlin walked to join her.

"We?"

Kath hesitated, cleared her throat. "You don't have to know about this."

"Do you think I'd—"

"No." She squeezed his hand, let go. "But they'd kill you if they knew about it."

"Tell me."

"I've met someone."

Berlin stood in a silence only that phrase can assemble.

Kath remembered her indiscretion, stumbled through clarification. "There's a woman who can help."

"Help what?"

"She comes from the outer. Came in months ago on a transport. Just something about her..."

"Who?"

"She knows what to do. To make it right."

"Kath—"

"She's not like us."

"If you're talking about—"

"She wants to help. Not just this planet. She can make it right again."

"Make *what* right?"

Kath's hands balled to fists at her side. "The last war.. Nothing's been the same since. Planets in slavery, One ruled by machines and nears. Gods dropped into the slumber. Nothing's right anymore."

"We had to fight that war."

"But we didn't have to become this." Her fingertips traced the insignia on her chest, moved to her temple, where the metallish uplink writhed under her skin. "We didn't have to give up our—

"It was for the best."

"*Whose* best?"

"Our best. It had to be done."

"We're killing the system! The stars can't support us anymore. The energy load alone between the two—"

"That's why we need the lumbers. Deep galactic survey missions, colonization hives—"

"We have all that we need right here. We've just forgotten how to live within our means."

"We can't turn back now. We're pushing the saturation mark as—"

"We don't *have* to be pushing the saturation mark."

Berlin felt the throb of the comm uplink, but kept it static. "You can't be talking about—"

"Planet One alone uses eighty percent of the system resources."

He said nothing.

"A lot of bad people on Planet One."

"Not all."

"They started the war."

"The war's over."

"It's not over. Not yet."

He'd never heard her talk like this: such determination. Passion. He never suspected that she felt so strongly about the civil war that had split the binary system a decade before.

"If we take out One, we solve everything. Decentralize the machines' power. Make room for real people again."

She reached out. His response was uncertain, but he did hold her hand.

"And you know someone who can do this?"

"A woman from the outer, where the planets still burn. She says she can kill the machines."

"And her name?"

"Maire

~

shook from the release of the shiver, stilled. The headless form in front of her fell to the floor in a splash of destabilized proteins.

The gun an extension of her arm, she turned, slowly enough to stir a ripple of widening eyes and furrowing brows in the circle of people before her weapon.

"I'll ask again. Who can give me a ride into the Drift?"

A jagged chuckle from behind was the only response to her inquiry. Its distance from perceived origin to her ears spoke of safety, but the whisper behind her eyes still warned her to be wary of a drawn weapon. Weapon and head first, body trailing not far behind, she met the source of laughter with a sharp inhalation and her firing finger poised on her shiver gun's trigger.

"You're already in the Drift, woman. Come on, sit down." His hands waved off the concern of onlookers. Business returned to that particular brand of normal that only the edge of Black thrived upon.

He wasn't short, but short enough, and he wasn't fat, but fat enough. He leaned forward in his chair and poured another steaming cup of fermented protein gruel for himself. Tilting it toward Maire, he wordlessly offered and she wordlessly refused with the wrinkling of her nose bridge and the downturn of her lips.

"You're looking for something, this far out. What is it?"

His enormous brow sloped down into a hooked nose. Underneath, two black eyes blinked away drunkenness and crawled over her body, darting imagined tonguetips over erectile tissues. A badly repaired cleft palette barely drew attention away from the ledge of his underbite. His voice reflected more than simple physical impairments.

"Speak to me, woman. I've saved your life by inviting you to my table. You stink of sex, of women. Blood and fear, rage. You're desperate for something out here, looking for something, and I'm the man who can lead you home."

There were no machines on this vessel, at least none of the thinking machines from the last war that now held the inner planets of the system in a death grip. Her thoughts flashed to Kath and the trees, Michael and the

"You're a mercenary?"

"A trivial term at best." He sipped from his meaty cup. "An appropriate term at worst."

"I need a ship, and a team of—"

"Slow down, woman." Black beads surveyed the mess interior. "You can't just come to my home, kill a member of my crew and expect service immediately. First I have to get to know you."

Her gaze was the empty that encompasses all of fury.

"I'm going to ask you a bunch of questions, and I want them answered immediately."

"And if I—"

"If you refuse, I'll have my troops space you into Seychelles. Not a nice way to die."

Eyes dimmed.

"What's your name?"

She placed her shiver on the tabletop and thumbed the echo chamber release.

"Maire."

"Where you from?"

"Seychelles Edge, two-seventy under."

"A local girl!" He grinned through teeth that were somewhat there, mostly broken. "But you've been gone a while, haven't you?"

"Long enough."

"Fantastic." Another sip, his eyes still gouging into hers, and now a playful flash. "So that's where your taste for flesh came from. Your entire family? Friends? Did you have to eat your children, or did you escape before—"

Her bared teeth and a barely-audible hiss cut him off.

"Poor girl. You stink of inner worlds. Why'd you come back?"

"Business."

"Yes, business. You need a ship, and troops. And you're heading deep into the Drift, looking for something. Sounds like standard fees are in order." He pulled a data panel from a pocket at his side, placed it on the table. His fingertip traced over schematics. "We can work together."

"This isn't your usual fuck-and-run. I'll need the best vessel you have, your strongest troops, your—"

"Tall order from a stranger."

Her eyes scanned the ceiling, fell back to meet his. "I can see you fought in the wars." She tapped her temple, indicating the regiment brand not gracefully gracing his own. "And this vessel," she waved around them, more indicating the raucous crowd drinking goofy gravy, smoking the copper from old wires, and savagely fucking in the darkened corners of the mess than the superstructure of the gutted ship itself, "is an Inner Worlds destroyer from the machine conflicts."

"Your point?"

"You hate the machines. I've not seen a single thinker since I arrived, save that glorified abacus with which you're about to take my order."

His frown, a constant until now, explored deeper definitions of itself.

"There's something out there in the Drift right now. I need to go get it."

"And why's this 'something' so important to you?"

"It'll be important to you, too."

"And why's that?"

"Because when I have it, we'll use it to kill all the machines forever."

He smiled.

*

Back arched, she swung down through the cockpit tube, her grasp on the ladder releasing when she felt the not-unpleasant suck of the vacuum chair on her buttocks and thighs. She adjusted her robe to allow a better grip.

"You don't have to wear that here, you know."

Cork had paused long enough from his startup routine of toggling switches and locking interface ports to his wrists and eyes to crawl his vision over her drab-draped form. His tongues absently explored the corners of his mouth.

"I get cold."

"Right."

She wondered how the mercenary had managed to squeeze through the access tube into his nest. Rolls of hairy flesh poured over his pilot chair, pulsating to the suction. His breasts dwarfed her own. Above, his cardiac shield heaved for breath. She checked and double-checked the enclosure on her garment.

"Comfy?"

"I guess."

"Okay. I'll lock you into waste systems—"

"No." She couldn't take the risk of slaving into the ship if the urethral, vaginal, and anal links were fully aware biosensors. Cork would find out in an instant that she wasn't exactly normal anymore. "I can hold it."

His eyes narrowed. “Suit yourself.” His hand waved over the dashpanel. He grunted as his body loosed to the ship’s probing and gave a satisfied exhalation. “You can clean up the mess yourself if we hit rough water. And shitting on my boat costs double.”

The bulbous drives forward and above the cockpit began the resonance cycle. Maire felt the vessel shudder and jerk against the docking grips.

Tickle.

She studied the panel, the levels, the systems. “What’s your mix?”

“Dark, seventy over.”

“How’s she run?”

“She gets by.” Cork patted the viewshield affectionately.

“Try boosting the dark level to seventy-two five. It’ll compensate for outside interference from resident dark streaks as we get farther out.”

Frown. “Ever sailed the Seychelles, woman?”

“Just trust me.”

“Fine.” He bumped up the level of dark matter in the shred drive to 72.5%. The vessel immediately calmed, the drives above them shivering steadily instead of randomly. “Well, shit. You’re just full of surprises, aren’t you?”

“I try.”

∽

The shred peeled away from the belly of Cork’s destroyer and fell into the black endless of Seychelles, the jungles of empty, the machinery of night. Maire felt the ratcheting of the mercenary sleepers as the pods fell into place in the chain of the vehicle. Snaking through the debris of ancient and [recent] wars, the shred spermed around the hulks of abandoned warships, metal worlds whose interiors had been torn into the suck and cold. Occasional freeze-dried soldiers sparked and ceased before the forward energy sweeper.

"How long've they been asleep?"

Cork's fingers traced over the biologics readings. "Brand new batch. Twenty, thirty years."

"Good."

"What's it matter?"

She shrugged. "I prefer fresh meat."

His eyes performed unmentionables. "I bet you do."

The passage through the vessel graveyard was uneventful. Maire froze images as Cork's ship increased speed: the shell of a destroyer, a planetship scuttled and taken apart for spares, smaller shreds transporting reclamation teams through the complex of spinning metal and hollowed asteroids.

Cork yawned.

He caught Maire's glimpse and tossed it back.

"You're different."

"Hmm?"

"Exactly." He wagged his tongue from his mouth, the tips circling and rubbing together. "Your voice is different. Flat."

"Yeah."

"It's alright. I'm different, too." He wiped saliva from the badly repaired cleft on his lip. "But you... There's something wrong with you."

Maire smiled. He disgusted her.

∽

around and never through those nonspace tendrils, the black matter that stippled, and swung, and reached

All time went flat.

She'd gasped for a while as the cockpit bubble flooded with nitrox gelatin. Cork's breathing was steady; he'd been sucking the shielding for decades, and inhaling that bittersweet fluidish was a comforting return to the non-womb of space.

"Let me know where to point this thing." The voice was choked, slurred. His tonguetips flicked over slicked lips, teeth. Sludgy echoes. Flat time.

"Give me flight control."

"Listen, no one flies this shred but me, and I'm—"

"Give me flight control."

Eyes narrow, relent. Cork thumbed the panel release and slid the sticks across to Maire's side of the bubble, where they locked into place. Her considerably smaller hands gripped the shafts.

"You know how to run one of these?"

"Should've asked that before you slid these over." Smirk.

He watched as she expertly adjusted the shred axes. She boosted the dark mix to 75%. "You'd better know what you're doing with that mix."

She gunned the engines. "I was a pilot. Don't worry."

They flew.

৩

She locked coordinates and eventually lilted off to sleep in the sway and slosh of the mineral slime's warm caress. Cork took the opportunity to extrapolate the path she'd set into the vessel's slave. She was taking him deep into the Drift's crotch, that hook of realspace bordered with dark matter so thick that entry was a suicide and exit was just as deadly.

He scratched an itch buried beneath suck.

Maire shifted in her seat. Her face rolled toward Cork, her mouth open, struggling to inhale the bubble sludge.

Gotcha.

He leaned closer. There *was* something different with her; her tongue was deformed. He absently fingered the scar of his cleft palette. He'd seen other deformities who'd been born in the wake of the trinary collapse, but never anything like that...

Her robe had come unsecured in the bubble's tide.

He considered.

He acted.

Reaching out, his hand navigated around her shoulder, below and through the loosed interfaces above her eyes. He tugged on the front slit, gently enough to mimic the natural pull of the sludge. The robe flapped open.

Her chest was smooth, marked only by the small canyon of her cleavage between two breasts and a scattering of moles. No cardiac shield. No—

Her eyes opened.

She struck out at him, a savage blow to the throat with a backswing that shattered the bridge of his nose. The bubble blackened with the blown ballast of his blood.

For an instant, just an instant, Cork could have sworn that Maire's eyes were silver.

She pulled her robe shut. "How dare—?"

Klaxons roared to life.

Maire spun to the flight control sticks. In her sleep and Cork's distraction, the shred had pirouetted dangerously close to a tendril of dark matter. She flailed the sticks and the vessel spun away from the reaching black, over a ridge in the texture of space, down through a valley and

the ships, if they were ships, lay in wait.

Maire gasped.

They scattered, converged, enveloped. Michael had told her what to expect, but what she saw was beyond expectation or reasonable comprehension.

A wave of light swept the bubble. The vessel shuddered.

All around them, the ships swam through space, the tendrils of dark matter licking and following. It was a dance of horror and beauty, the magnificent school of black spiders thrusting through light and something deeper, something ancient and

a tug and

❧

Maire sat alone on the floor, vomiting shield gel into and out of the spot of light in which she wretched. Cork was gone; the shred was gone. Beyond the circle of light, all was the absence of light, but she sensed something there, someone there, someones there. Another fit of coughing wracked her as bubbles of gelatin worked their way out of her lungs.

It was cold.

a heap of shattered images and

zero

flicker

zero one

flicker

one zero one

resolution

you are

fear and

you are ((?))

Maire stood, covered her now-nude breasts with goose-pimpled forearms.

you are ((?))

"I—I've been sent." She struggled to remember what Michael had told her. "I've been sent by your creator."

silence and

you are of loss, of ruin

"I am."

purpose. completion. forevers.

One heart: one, and frequent exhalation, shudder, the scrape of exquisitely-manicured nails over flesh, over metal, over flesh and

"I am Omega."

SYSTEMS OF DESIRE

SYSTEMS OF DESIRE

"Do you believe in werewolves?"

Samayel shrugged as best he could beneath her, his nacelles rising and falling in lubricated silence.

"I do."

She clambered to the edge of his central hub, looked down upon the captured star. The heat was a pleasant slap compared to the months of timestream cold in which they'd been. She rolled to her back and let her nest of hair dangle over the side.

Looking up, away from the stark light of the sun below, she saw a scatter of wounded forms returning home, Judith vessels with phase scoring, here and there a vessel being dragged along by one nacelle. They couldn't afford to leave the wrecks behind anymore. She glanced the tickle of tight-beam signals Sam sent to his returning soldiers.

It made her sad, so she turned over and looked down again.

"Fort Myers, good ol' Fort Myers. I'm gonna miss this place."

The orbital ring had been split into halves, into quarters, into countless fragments of metallish, but remarkably, the containment layer that held the miles of breathable atmosphere in place above the star was still in place. Alina loved the smell of *air*, the heat of *sun*, the exposed warmth of

Sam's hull beneath her. How many Judith captains could say that they'd ridden their mounts on the outside?

A flock of three Judiths passed close enough to generate *wind.* Alina giggled as they tipped their nacelles in salute.

"What's gonna happen to the Fort, Sam?"

retrieval crews will salvage what they can from the shell. they'll collapse the star and conceal the evidence.

"It's a shame. I really liked it here."

The atmosphere parted as a Judith destroyer entered the shell, towed by at least a dozen smaller fighters. Alina stood, shielding the light from below with her still-gauntleted hands as she tried to get a better look. "Who's that?"

i'm not getting any signal from it... but the markings say it's from Fort Johns.

"Flagship Jasper. He's—Uhh.. It's coming in a little fast, isn't it?"

The destroyer picked up speed as it plummeted into the atmosphere. The Judith tows fell behind as its billions of tons of metallish fell faster and faster toward the sun below. Caught by a flailing particle cable, one Judith rolled dangerously close to the destroyer's hull, slammed against its side and erupted with fire and splinters of black. Other Judith began to disengage their cables as the destroyer fell out of control.

Alina smelled the smoke as it surged past Sam: something between plastic and flesh, something between bitter and sweet. The sound it made: screaming.

The helpless destroyer erupted miles below against the containment layer, great arms of black and fire blotting out the brightness of the star.

"There goes another one."

yeah.

Alina felt dizzy, not from the disconcerting vertigo of standing on a vessel without protection miles above the shield layer, but a deeper sickness wrought from two-point-five decades of servitude and horror.

"I think I'll come back inside now, Sam."

ⵓ

She loved Samayel, but she hated her command. She hated the war. She hated that even in a world of war, even when those last scattered remnants of her species were trying to make a stand, people could still be cruel. Boys could still be cruel. They could still work up the balls to call her "Banana Tits." She hated those boys. She hated her breasts. She wanted them to be fuller. She hated her face: how it drooped, how her eyes looked perpetually sad and her high, high cheekbones, that in another time and place would be deliciously inviting for biting and nibbling, just made her feel so intensely ugly. Round face. Banana tits. No ass. She had a funny nose, and her body, even in stripped-down emulation, was still stippled with patterns of freckles and moles. She thought maybe if she improved her posture, just stood a little straighter, smiled a little more, maybe then she'd be beautiful.

She hated that space and time had made her sterile, removing the monthly threat of droplets of blood gumming up the systems of the ship, but hair still grew in the places where she wished it wouldn't. Not that it really mattered. Everyone caught in this war seemed too tired to fuck. She wanted love. She wanted to *make* love. She wanted someone to love her. She wanted someone to remember her or care if she didn't come back from a combat run or think of her as he drifted off to sleep, or at least what true sleep this war would allow between the killing frenzies and the running.

Sam loved her. She knew that because she knew everything he knew, but it just wasn't the same being loved in that way. Besides, Samayel was a machine forged from metal and plastic and stars, and his soul, older than hers by at least four decades (he refused to tell her his real age), was forever and hopelessly queer.

She sighed a lot.

❧

To one, it was a Paris cafe, filled with American expatriates of the fin de siecle. To one, it was a Laredo saloon, the rough-and-tumble crowd clustered around an overworked barhand. To one, it was an East Village dive where Bob Dylan had once been slated to perform as the opening act for a science fiction author. To Alina, it wasn't much of anything. A few tables, a few smokers, a few glasses. She caught Sam's beckoning smile and sat down beside him.

"Have a drink, little lady." Hank tipped his glass to her. A smoldering Marlboro hung from his lips, the ashes considering the jump to the table. "It'll help."

"Not tonight, sugar."

"I don't know if you've heard," Sam's deep eyes swept the non-space construct, "but we lost Fort Myers today. Cleanup and collapse crews are en route."

"Tragic." Whistler hissed through his teeth. "Tragic, tragic. Sorry, my dears. It seems each day the Delta's redrawn." In his version of the projected construct, an attentive garcon placed another bottle of absinthe on the table. Whistler poured green over the sugar cube. "And each day, we lose more ground."

"Shit, Jim. You know that ain't true. Why, just last week we—"

"Which week?"

"Last week."

"Which last week?"

Hank reddened. "You know what I mean. They're doing their best to fix it all."

"Bullshit." Alina bummed a smoke from Sam's pack, used Hank's scarred Zippo to light it. "That kid doesn't know what the fuck he's doing."

Sam pushed his ashtray closer to his captain. "Sure that's not the jealousy talking, Al?"

She blew smoke into and through his chocolate face, frosted with bushy vanilla beard. "You of all people should know there's nothing to be jealous about."

"And you, of all people," he stole the cigarette back, inhaled, "should know there is." He tousled her hair, which was already and perpetually tousled. "Benton needs some competition. It's good for her. Keeps her maths pure."

"It's not her." Alina blushed, a furious bloom of red across nibbleable cheeks and nose, neck and down through the periphery of her banana zone.

"Somebody's got a crush!" Hank swigged back the last of his beer. "Ain't it wonderful, Jimmy?"

Whistler's eyes rolled under the swirl of his mane. "Charming. You dirty old men should leave the poor child alone. Intellectual badgering and Old West hullabaloo. You're an episteme all your own, Messieurs."

"Ally needs some competition. It's good for her. Keeps her strats pure." Hank grinned.

"Oh, fuck off. I'm out." Alina snapped from the construct, leaving the three Judith emulations at the table.

"Aww. Something I said?"

Sam patted Hank on the back. "Not our fault. Just young love."

"Has she ever even met the author?" Whistler dipped his sugar cube.

"Not really. A few words in passing here and here. But there isn't a young woman this side of Omega who doesn't have a hard-on for him." Sam's eyes indicated a group that had just arrived within the construct. "And not an inconsiderable percentage of the young men, too. Oh, to be young and foolish again. To feel—anything."

At the entrance point along one of the far walls, three figures faded in. They shrugged off their blade armor and found an empty table. Metal retracted to reveal the old soldier, the author, the maths egg.

"To the young and foolish," Sam raised his glass. "May they contain multitudes."

❧

"I still don't get it."

"What?"

"This." She indicated the room. To Benton, the walls and tables were bare metal. Before her on the table, a simple flask of nutrient slurry steamed.

"Use your imagination. It's a nice way to spend our recharge time. People need people. As long as we have the resources, we'll keep this place running." There was a Killian's Red and a charred steak in front of Paul.

"I don't need people." Benton plugged the slurry flask into her arm. "It's a waste of bandwidth."

"Spoken like a true child of the Judith." West took a fishstick from his plate, bit into it, wondered why he'd chosen fishsticks of all things; Judith knew there wasn't a squirt of tartar sauce available for centuries around them. "If you'd known a world, a real world, you'd appreciate this place."

"I appreciate it. There's nothing trying to kill us here." She adjusted the pack on her arm. "Most days, at least."

Paul caught Sam's wave from across the room. "I'll be back." As he stood, his hand traced across Benton's shoulder.

West waited for a safe distance before he asked. "So?"

Benton leaned in. "A/O reports sixty-five/thirty-five. We've lost ground, and—"

"No, no." West cleared his throat; his eyes locked hers. "What's going on? With you two?"

Benton sat back in her chair. "How many times do I have to tell you? There is no 'you two.'"

"Not the word on the street, kiddo."

"What's the word on the street, then?"

West shrugged. "Apparently Judith brought the author in from his When to fix all this shit, and now she sends him out on missions with that old man West and the delicious young Hope Benton. Word is that I'm a mere chaperone."

"Bullshit, and you know it." Benton scoffed. "One more reason for me to hate this construct. Gossip."

West bit into a fishstick. Flecks of what could have been fish glinted in his grin.

❧

"Good run today?" Sam offered a smoke. I accepted and sat down with the characters at a table that looked suspiciously like it had come from the old U Inn. I blinked and noticed the booths in the back, the chubby drunk sorority girls. Music from a wedding reception seeped through from the back room. Heard myself on the jukebox. Smoke, shadow, echoes: illusions, all.

"It was okay. How're you guys doing?"

Sam did his best Burl Ives impression, but his grin faltered. "Lost Fort Myers. Al's pretty upset."

"Fuck." I'm better with words in my head. "How about you two?"

"Still lookin', son." Hank scooped a slug of Red Man into his mouth. "Ain't much out there, but we're still lookin'."

"What my dear cattleman is trying to say," Whistler smoothed his lapels, "is that we've run out of promising leads, and we've not yet found anyone of significant tactical value."

"There have to be more characters out there somewhere. You were."

"So we were, but we're not, shall I say, entirely *truthful*?"

I knew where Whistler was pushing the conversation. "Sometimes it's hard to be truthful about people you never really met."

"Perhaps you should have focused on biographical research. I would *never* have worn this ridiculous cape."

Hank guffawed. "Sure makes you pretty, though, Jim."

Whistler hissed at the cowboy.

Sam just shook his head. "Any leads on Delta yet? Anything new you can tell us?"

"It's there." And it was, a great stabbing tickle behind my eyes, a tugging toward and a pushing from and the words escape: it was. "Just haven't excised it yet."

"Word is we've slipped to Alpha seventy-over."

"Sixty-five." I hated how fast the Judith mind essence relayed everything to everyone, and how fast that relay distorted truth. "That's the word. Watch my mouth and call me the horse."

"Rough insertion today?"

Dirty old man. I drank, swirled the beer around my mouth, over bruised gums and a loose molar. "Could say that."

"Meet anyone interesting?" He considered. "Again? Any words of wisdom from the Great Within?"

Thinking back to the shattered images I'd catalogued that "day": "People shit when they die."

Sam chuckled.

I pulled on the cigarette, exhaled through my nose. I vaguely remembered when that had used to hurt. "Just another day. Erased a few more post-silver characters."

Hank spit tobacco juice into his empty bottle. "Seem to be getting better at that, buckaroo."

It didn't matter that he sounded artificial. He *was* artificial. His television show had never really existed. The dialogue did concern me, though. I knew I could do better.

"We've almost got a lock on the bear. Should be able to grab him in the next insertion."

"You bringing him in?"

"Might as well. He's a fragment we can use to get a better lock."

Whistler sighed. "'Fighting wars outside of time and space,' with a cowboy, a painter, and a teddy bear. Whatever would the Hugo committee think?"

"Doesn't matter. No one's gonna read this when I'm done."

"I know I wouldn't." Sam's face broke from stern steel to friendly laughter.

"Ah, well." Whistler pushed away from the table. "Ready to get back to work, my captain?"

Hank spit, gouged the spent tobacco from his lip. "You betcha."

"On the morrow, gentlemen." Whistler smoothed back his hair, twirled his white streak into the air. "One question, dear boy... Why does Hank get to be the Captain and I his mount?"

I shrugged. "Never really thought about it."

"He just hates my spurs. Let's go, Jim." Hank tapped his subdermal and became static and nothing.

"Next time," Whistler pointed his cane at me, "I'm the Captain." He snapped and faded.

"Those two make a cute couple." Sam thought another beer to the table.

"You think?"

We laughed.

"Just like you and..." His eyes indicated Hope, who was lost in conversation with West at their table, her glass displaying the day's kill stats.

I'd heard it all before. "Sam, there is no 'me and...' Regardless of what you hear. This place is such a soap opera sometimes."

"You sure about that?"

"Jesus, I'm sure, okay? She's in love with her integers."

"And you're in love with impossibilities."

"I've killed almost everyone I've ever loved."

"And you'll have to kill the rest before this is done." Sam had a way of cutting not only to the chase, but to the end credits.

"Pretty much."

I studied the table, my bottle. I knew he was staring at and through me.

"You should meet my Captain." Some smiles, the most conspiratorial, evidence in eyes.

"Oh yeah? Why?" although I already suspected. I'd written her to cursory life, but my characters always had a way of growing into themselves, adapting, becoming people without any input from me.

"I shouldn't tell you this," his eyes swept the construct, "but Al has a little crush."

Suspicion confirmed. Only in a universe I'd made would that happen. "Well... Huh. Send her my regards. Tell her to keep up the good work. The Author appreciates all she's done. Purpose be and all that jive."

"You conceited prick." Another sip through the grin. "'The Author,' huh? I'll be sure to tell her." He winked.

West called to me from the other table.

"Better go, Sam. I'll see you tomorrow."

"Good luck with your insertions."

"Good luck with your own." I patted his back as I stood. "Bring Alina with you tomorrow."

"Ha! Will do, buckaroo." Sam snapped to fade through the echoes of his best Hank impression.

❧

"How're the boys?"

"Getting by." Paul sat down, the now-cold steak on the table before him. He thought it away.

"Nice Jedi powers, Obi-Wan."

"Nice fishsticks, Batman."

Benton looked from West to Paul to West, rolled her eyes. Her gaze fell flatly back to the numbers on her glass.

"Working through recess, Hope?"

"No rest for the quantum theorists."

"Any leads?"

"If we pick up the bear, it should push us to Alpha fifty-five-to-sixty-over. Seems that toy was a big part of our target's pattern."

"God, I hated that fucking cartoon." West grumbled over his ketchup and maybefish. "And those toys were just creepy."

"I never had toys." Benton didn't look up from her calculations.

West studied his plate.

"You can play with Honeybear once we get him. Fair enough?"

"Great." She snapped the glass shut and it faded from the construct. "I've mapped the insertion for tomorrow. You boys get some sleep at some point. We want a good run."

"Yes, dear.": unison.

Benton shattered from the construct.

"Enough exposition for today." West wiped his mouth. "I'm turning in. Night."

"Goodnight, Adam."

After he'd faded, Paul sat at the table until the bar construct was empty and he was alone. Well into the non-night of his consciousness, he mulled over the select regrets, fears, and dreams that had created the person he had become, and when the false sun had risen over the false horizon, he decided to sleep.

❧

There's a moment when panic becomes sensual: you can taste the copper of your blood, the tang of adrenaline and sweat, and the deeper wash of terror. Suddenly I felt that the innovative new helmets I'd designed for insertions were entirely too suffocating.

My breath came hard and ragged as I began to choke on the blood filling my left lung. I felt the suit envelop the shard of phase flak and begin to repair me.

I struggled to my feet. Another wave of splinters from the wrecked vessels coming apart in the atmosphere above us struck the city.

"Take cover! Jesus fuck, take cover!" My words sounded like a blood clot feels.

I glanced right to see West throw himself over Benton as the shards fell. His armor was fluctuating phase; one shard hit his leg but harmlessly faded from being. He grabbed Benton and hefted her to safety under a shattered concrete support tilted precariously against the nearest building. I crawled into a doorway across the debris-littered street.

"They're not here!" Benton shouted over the roar of the battle above. She had her glass out, and I saw numbers flickering through the display. "Something's wrong with our position!"

"Stay here." I heard West speak to Benton over his subdermal. He ran from the protection of the overhang across the street to my side. "You okay?"

"Just some flak in the lung. Suit's fixing me."

"Okay... Okay. Hope! Can you make it over here?"

She did.

Her eyes and hands swept my armor. "Is it bad? Oh god... Are you—"

"I'll be fine." I sat up against the wall under the grind of my still-shattered ribs. "What's your glass say?"

"Half-empty. Position's off. The attack's happening, but our target isn't at the Maire complex. Neither's his mother or the toy."

"Any readings at all on them?"

Another blast of flak hit the street. Benton flinched. "Too much shit in the sky. Can't get a lock."

"Okay." West rose from his crouch. "Maybe they're still at home. We have to go check."

"He's wounded. We could log out and try a closer insertion."

"I'm fine." I grunted through the words and stood with West's assistance. "We can't risk slipping even more."

"Fine. Where do they live?"

I paused. "You have the stats."

"You wrote the book. The stats are fucked, anyway."

"Okay." The hole in my chest sealed. The grating of bones was almost gone. "Let me remember."

By the time they reached Helen Windham's humble apartment, Paul's wounds had healed and he was walking without West's assistance. The veils of phase flak falling from the sky became more and more sporadic as the battle ended. The quiet in the city was broken only by the collapse of the massive cannon to the west as it broke apart and fell into the ocean.

West kicked down the door to the apartment.

It was dark. The curtains were still drawn. They activated their halo lights and began to search the home. There wasn't much to search.

They found the figures in the living room, two husks of silver dust prone on the floor, the larger mostly concealing the child below.

"Don't touch them." Paul sighed. This was an unfortunate development. "Got any signal on the glass, Hope?"

She opened her panel. "Yeah." She hesitated. "Running at Alpha ninety—"

"Shit." West shook his head through blades. "Must have just missed 'em."

"What about Honeybear?"

Her face brightened. "He's here. He has to be! The reading's off the scale."

"Okay, where's the kid's room?"

"No..." Paul walked to the far side of the living room. "I remember where he is." He reached under the couch and pulled out a ragged brown bear. "At least that didn't change."

Benton ran her sensors over the toy. "It's a close enough signal match. Should bring us back down to Alpha sixty-over."

"What about those two?" West stood over the dead shells of silver that had recently been Helen and Hunter Windham. "Does this seriously fuck up our line on Delta?"

"It shouldn't. I can bring in Helen from one of the Seattles, and Hunter... We can try to bring Hunter and Lilith both in at once."

"That's gonna be tricky."

"That might be mathematically impossible."

"We'll do it." Paul tossed the bear to Benton. "Trust me."

---

retrieval and concealment crews are finished with the salvage and load placement.

"I guess we're leaving now?"

time to hit the road.

"Alright." Alina stood up on Samayel's hull. She'd miss the warmth from below. She'd miss the light, and the wind, and the real air. "Real" air. "Sam? How far down to the shield layer?"

three hundred miles or so.

"That's enough." She ran toward Samayel's edge. "Catch me at fifty!"

al, don't—

But she did.

The rush of vertigo, the wind and heat around her body, caressing in ways no lover could, enveloping, becoming. She spun to see Sam dropping away above her, his nacelles flickering to life as he dove after her. She swam.

The heat grew.

It was freedom; it was everything.

She laughed through the tears of that limit experience.

Falling, falling through light and heat. Falling through silence. She felt the stillness, but knew she was falling. How the senses are deceived into stasis; how the senses lie through the truth of the heart.

It seemed hours before Sam matched her descent and she landed gently on his back. He coasted along the shield layer, swept upward on an exit vector.

girl, you're crazy.

"I know." She couldn't force her grin from her face.

By the time Sam had reached the atmosphere barrier, Alina was snuggled into her command chamber, sleeping peacefully the sleep of those who had fallen into a sun.

They left Fort Myers forever.

⁂

"Mmm *hmm.*" Judith looked at the bear with skepticism. "That's it? A toy?"

"Not just any toy, Jud. Honeybear Brown."

She picked him up and turned him over. "And this toy is important to our mission how?"

"He's a character in both timelines. A potential Delta crossover in and of himself."

"Paul," her metallish eyes betraying her disbelief, "it's a fucking *toy.*"

"Not to Hunter." He took the bear from Judith's grip. Static and shift and

The bear moved. Jud jumped.

"Honeybeeeeear, Honeybear Brown!" The toy's eyes lit up. "I'm the nicest little bear in the whole darned town!" He looked around the room. "Where's Windy?"

Jud looked like she was about to answer Honeybear, but she shook her head. "Paul, that thing's god damned scary. I should know. I'm god."

"You're neat!" Honeybear smiled at Jud.

Paul stifled a chuckle.

"Take that talking bear and get back to work, author. Next run, you'd better bring me back a human being. No stuffed camels or ostriches, you freak."

"Gotcha, sweetness."

He picked up Honeybear and faded with a smirk.

⁂

She'd heard that their counterparts on the Judas side of the Delta bleed piloted vessels powered and protected by black holes, and the captains linked with their ships through mechanical gauntlets and webs of silver (not exactly *her* silver, but a silver nonetheless). She'd heard that they had fought a war against an army of consciousnesses emulated with machines from the future. She'd heard that they were cannibals. She liked cannibal movies; she still believed in werewolves.

Sam draped her with *her* silver, the veil webbing and penetrating her skin, concentrating over her cardiac shield plate. Locked securely into the firing chamber, she shared all that was her existence with all that was Samayel.

She wondered how different she was from the Alina on the other side, if there even was an Alina on the other side.

"What's on the plate for today?"

smash and grab mission. we're meeting up with remnants of the fort john wayne fleet.

"Frosty's fleet?"

captain frost, yes.

"Wait.. This is a frag or a bleed?"

bleed.

"Oh."

well, lock and load, kid. we're hitting the stream.

❧

"Jim?"

shut up.

"Jimbo?"

shut UP.

"Come on, pardner. You gotta talk to me sometime."

no i don't.

"You just did." Hank grinned from his command chamber. "Anyhow, what's it look like out there?"

whiter than jo's inner thigh.

"That white, huh? That must be pretty white. You know, one time I was at a saloon in—"

for the love of all things holy, shut UP.

Crawl, crackle.

"You feel that?"

certainly did. initiating full sensor sweep.

"Looks like we ain't alone out here, buddy."

They fell through time.

❧

tomorrow and tomorrow and

just make a thread that says "no" and

"Hey, dude."

I won't lie. His voice caught me off-guard. No one had ever been with me before, not there, not in the little bubble I'd carved for myself, just for myself, deep within the registry of the Judith ME.

"What's goin' on?"

I'd thought people into existence before, but they'd only been characters. Whistler and Hank. Benton and West. Jacob's voice slammed into and through me, echoed through the sphere of nothing within which I floated, and all became my parents' living room: the old green carpet snaked with guitar cords, the bite of woodsmoke, brownies for us in the kitchen. I knew this without vision; I was too tired and broken to open my eyes.

Lithe fingers climbed over nylon strings, coaxed forgotten songs from a long-dead soul.

"I don't know anymore." I knew that choke in my voice.

He stopped playing.

They'd told me, of course. I'd asked to be inserted into the fourteen-seven variant, just two years into the future from which West and Benton had removed me. Hope had come with me, had stood with me behind the mourners at the burial. Wraiths. She'd held my hand between its frequent trips to my mouth, choking back sobs that no one but she could hear in that when.

When my future self placed a guitar pick on the coffin and touched it, he looked up for a moment, and in those eyes, I saw everything that I knew I must end. What tragic cycle, what series of events could inspire such madness in those once-forever eyes? The then-gaunt frame sweating under a gray suit suddenly entirely too big, the sun-burned nose a red foil to those pools of teared ash, hands and wrists shaking, scarred with

He was the madness I must end.

Other friends would have asked if I wanted to talk about it. He knew better. He started playing the guitar again and

bonfire, scorching the leaves of the ice storm-tilted tree that was now entirely too close to the pit and the wind was entirely too cold for the early-summer night I knew it was from the taut skin on my nose and arms and neck, the slivers of chaff now roiling beneath the surface of my forearms, placed there not tenderly by hundreds of bales of hay stacked mindlessly into the mow.

His song never changed, never faltered. He hummed along sometimes.

"I miss you."

A string snapped. His hand went to his neck, found the speck of blood and wiped it away, red from flesh too lifeless, too gray. I thought color back into him.

"Miss you, too, dude." He pulled the broken string from the guitar and threw it into the fire. He kept playing; he could do that.

There were so many things I wanted to ask: the hows and whys of his hanging, those last moments. What happened after the electricity had flickered away? But I knew that there were no answers in this place. No one within the Judith or Judas programs had any idea what happened when we died. I guess I'd written it that way for a reason. I didn't really want to know.

"We'll have to get together the next time you're home. I should be around."

The broken string crimped and danced as it burned.

"Yeah." From that side of the fire, he couldn't see eyebrows furrow, lips twitch, two lines of tear slip down stubbled cheeks. "I should be home again soon."

"It's easier when nowhere feels like home."

Jagged exhalation. I struggled to maintain.

"Well, the bed is looking pretty good right now." He placed the guitar back in its battle-scarred case: stickers, newspaper clippings, scatter of plectrums. Snapped the snaps, stood up, brushing ash and bark from his knee-holed jeans.

"Damn, I want some eggnog." He smiled that sly, shy smile. "Goodnight." He started to walk down the driveway.

"Jake?"

"Yeah?"

"What do I—How do I—What am I supposed to do?"

He frowned. "Huh?"

I forced a smile. "Want me to drive you home?"

"Oh. Nah. I'll walk. Stars are out."

"Be careful."

"Yeah."

He walked down the driveway and the image faded to nothing: bubble.

I sat there for a long time.

midsagittal plane breached
it's spread into
ready lesioning probe on my
physiologic confirmation of the target location
initial pass in three
two

but if i take a few days between sleeping, my dreams have answers in them, and

a pain so great and sudden that he dropped his cup of coffee to the table.

"Paul?" Hope's voice: confusion and concern.

He felt tissues give way as blood surged from his nose. He coughed in reflex, a fine mist of red spattering his hand as he clamped off the flow with a napkin entirely too flimsy to contain it all.

"Jesus, boy." West pulled more napkins from the dispenser at the table's center. "You okay?"

He waved away the extra napkins. His eyebrows furrowed, and the blood was gone as he thought it away. "Don't know where that came from."

Benton's eyes met West's.

"You need to sleep. You can't stay awake like this."

"I don't need sleep."

"That wasn't normal, kid. Nosebleeds don't just happen like that. Maybe you have high blood—"

"Cardiac shield's not beeping, is it?"

"Well, maybe—"

"I'm fine. Just have a headache."

"You need sleep." Benton touched his hand.

"I'll be fine." His words were cold and final. He pulled his hand from beneath Hope's.

She'd noticed the shaking.

"Seems empty here tonight."

"Lots of ships are out. Myers meeting up with John Wayne, Spear and Riley for a Fuck-Run-and-Go."

Benton shook her head. "You boys and your cute little names."

"Behind your back," Paul took a sip of coppered coffee, "we call you 'Sugartush.'"

"Now I *know* you're sleep-deprived."

Paul and West looked at each other and grinned.

"Hi!" Honeybear jumped onto the table.

West flinched. "God, I hate this bear. Don't sneak up on me like that!"

"I'm sorry, Mr. West! How are you today?"

"Shut up."

"Okay!" The bear sat down between Benton and West, glassy-eyed smile directed at Paul.

"I guess we have to take him out on a run sometime?"

"Yeah... Should be able to get a pretty good lock on Windham with him."

"Great."

"Oh, he's not so bad." Benton patted the bear's scruffy head.

West grumbled.

"Big run tomorrow. You two should get some sleep." Paul picked up his cup to take another sip of coffee, but Benton took the cup from him. It snapped from the construct.

"You, too. No more coffee."

"Yes, dear."

"We close enough yet?"

fleet on scope.

"Bring Mindel up on gel."

calling.

Alina slumped against her interfaces and leaned into the warm slurp of the neuroflux gelatin. She blew a few bubbles from her mouth, which danced outward to her command chamber's metallish crust.

Eddies wrapped, swirled into a form a little taller, a little more angular than Al's. Static snap and the form sculpted a translucent smile, swam forward to embrace her. Sam adjusted the gelatin consistency accordingly to make the contact convincing enough.

"Frosty!" The two young women, one molded in flesh, one carved in jello, giggled and covered each other's cheeks in slimy kisses. "It's been forevers."

"Too long, babe. How's it hanging?"

"Oh, you know. Mediocre, but it gets the job done."

"Ready for a little midnight special?"

"Fuck and run, you know it. How's your fleet holding up?"

"Just fine until they pulled us out of the Jag. Sent us to patch up hotzones closer to A-Point. Lost our fort sometime last—Well... A while ago."

"Time flies in the mind of—"

"Minolta. Oh! You're going to hate me for not telling you sooner, but I met him."

"Met who?"

The gelatin form's eyes pinched to mischief. *"The Author."*

The bridge slime Alina inhaled took on a bitter cool. "Really?"

"Jud's little retrieval team misfired into our Jag When. Kate and I got to personally deliver him to the suspected Delta bleed at Lascaux."

"You bitch!" Her stage frown became a smirk. "What's he like? I mean, in real life?"

"Didn't say a lot. Didn't smile, either. His hands—"

sorry to interrupt, darlings, but we're closing on-target.

"Okay, Sam. Meet me after the dance in the construct?"

"Sure thing, Al. Let's lube up."

"Bang their bottoms out, hon." Wink.

"Later!" Mindel Frost's gelatin form drizzled back into the bridge tide.

Alina sighed and sank back into her gauntlets. "You get that?"

it's all recorded. Judith ME confirms Delta bleed on Fort John Wayne patterns.

"Bring them to visual."

All around her, the dusk of Sam's bridge faded to the intense white of the Timestream. A scattering of Judith vessels flocked according to home forts.

"Secondary confirmation?"

neurological extrapolation confirms Delta bleed. tainted code. she's silver.

"Sweep for crawlies?"

negative on enemy pattern.

"Okay, open channel to my kids."

done.

"Judith Ft. Myers fleet," her fingertips raced over the projected timescape, "close on these targets and engage on my mark."

Her finger hesitated over Mindel Frost's vessel, Judith Kate.

"Open fire."

❧

tracing these constellations of flesh, greater silences than stars provide

"You, too. No more coffee." Benton pushed back from the table. She was about to stand up when she saw Samayel and his captain approaching.

"Yes, dear." Paul's eyes were locked on hers. He hadn't seen Sam & Co. yet.

"Al, don't—"

The young woman walked right up to Paul's side and struck him across the face before Sam could grasp her flailing arms, hands pulled to fists. West jumped up and took one of the fists harmlessly to his barrel chest. He growled as her forced her arms behind her back, slammed her to the tabletop.

"Shit. Fuck. I'm sorry, Paul. She's—"

"The fuck's your problem?" West bore down on her, incapacitating her against the metallish table.

Paul said nothing. He wiped a line of blood from his crumpled nose, upper lip split by that inherited chisel of teeth. With a thought, it was gone. Silver burned behind muddied eyes.

"I don't care who you are." Alina struggled beneath West's heft. "If you send me on another mission like that, I'll fucking kill you." Her bared teeth looked entirely too sharp.

"Wanna help me out here?" Paul searched Hope's eyes.

She activated her glass, waited. "They went on a bleed containment run today. Took out the Fort John Wayne fleet remnants."

Paul sighed.

"She was my best friend!" Alina blinked back tears.

"Captain Mindel Frost." Benton snapped the glass shut. "Delta-infected, 99% certainty."

"We met her... When this all—"

"Get off me." Alina shrugged from underneath West. He lifted her with one hand to her feet.

"You gonna control yourself?"

She didn't answer as she fixed the tie in her hair.

"Have a seat. You three let me handle this." Sam, West and Benton faded from the construct, now empty except for Alina and Paul.

She sat. Two distinct lines of tear wet her too-big cheeks. She wiped them away.

"I'm sorry. Really." He reached out to take her hand, reconsidered and withdrew. "I know it wasn't easy."

She scoffed. "It was easy. All I had to do was reach out and think."

"I know the feeling." He thought a scotch into his hand, drank most in one draw.

"Listen—" She studied the tabletop where she'd been splayed and writhing a minute before. "I shouldn't have hit you."

"It's okay. I can't feel anything anymore."

"I don't believe that."

"I do." He placed his now-empty glass on the table and extended his hand. "Let's try again. I'm Paul."

"Alina."

"Sam's told me all about you."

"Ditto."

Awkward silence.

Paul's glass filled itself again. Sip, swallow, clink.

"I'm sorry about Frost."

"Yeah."

"You know you didn't really kill her."

"I know she's out there somewhere, outside of this."

"A ghost."

"Shaking chains in the attic, droning amps in the basement."

Something twinged behind Paul's eyes.

"It's all going to be okay. Trust me."

"I can't." She took his glass and drained it. "I don't know you."

"Then know me."

Flush of red. "I'd better go get sliced. More fun tomorrow." She stood.

"Keep up the good work."

"I'll try."

❧

i want to know your midnights
to bear witness to your
yawns, twists and turns
your valleys and
your breath, neither better
nor worse than mine.
i want to be your stars
and sunrises, first kisses
of ever and of morning.
i want to see your
first smile and hear
sleeping mumbles and sighs.
i want to see your waking face
in the stillness of our quiet dawn.
i want to be your

❧

Cowboy lately?" He shrugged off the drape of sleep as he got out of the slicing chamber, the blades retracting, still wet with the flesh fragments of his previous day's body.

Benton not-shyly toweled pattern scum from her pubis. "Haven't heard anything from Jud. Adam?"

"Nah. Last I knew, they were heading outer. Trying to draw a bead on young Windham."

Paul blew pattern from his nose, wiped it from his ears. He felt the final touches solidify: scars, wrinkles, hair. He caught Benton's stare.

"What?"

"New scar." She approached, touched the right side of his face. "Blade impact."

"Yeah, well—" He wiped his face dry. "Your tits are bigger today."

She scowled. "Glad you noticed."

"It's true." West chuckled. "What have *you* been dreaming?"

She ignored him, snapped her glass open. Figures illuminated face and chest. "We'll be out on runs for a few days. Recharge in the forts. A few little hotspots to seal up before we hit half-and-half."

West shielded with a ssschiick and sheen. He flexed the blades of his right arm and slammed a needle cartridge into his right shiver pistol, repeated the process with his left, flipped both back into their forearm holsters. "Let's fucking do it right this time. I'm getting old, kids."

Benton shielded and locked her glass into place on her chestplate. "We'll be good to go. Coordinates are golden."

"Silver." Paul pulled his faceplate down, locked it into place. His cardiac shield hissed and frosted blue as it blinked an affirmative. "Coordinates are silver."

They went

❧

back into the wind and it amazed me, all of it, the incomprehensible enormity of the system within which I now operated, the Judith Mind Essence. They'd taken some of the best parts of each book and combined them into the hive mind generated by the countless Judiths held in metastasis in the construct.

A twinge: too much. Right eye watered, from pain or from the sunlight reflected from white stretching away in every direction.

"That ridge. We'll find the cave there."

The hulk of Task's vessel still smoldered on the ice plain of Lascaux. I smelled, tasted his blood in ice crystals, in the bite of the wind, the singe of melting metallish.

We trudged, West and I crunching down through the surface skin of melted and re-frozen snow, Benton walking along beside us, sweeping the field with her instruments and colorless eyes.

"I got a reading. Faint."

"Human?"

She shook her head. "Two hearts. Berlin or Task?"

"Don't know." And I didn't.

"We takin' 'em, or bleed?" West unslung his shivers.

"This one's pure Judith patty. We'll take him."

৵

They walked from wind into the dark of the cave, flooded it with schools of halo dust, lighting their way over ridge and around protrusion and under overhang.

"Reading's close." Hope's voice was barely a whisper.

She need not have consulted her glass to conclude the proximity of their target; the two lines of tacking blood in the snow draped on the cave floor were barely freezing, two imperfect plow rows through drifts, the scrape of shattered femurs across ice.

It was an ugly place to die.

The tunnel widened, bubbled, tapered off into a series of smaller shafts into the rock. Laying propped against the ledge, the dying man who was Task gasped his agony through bloodied mouth. His glass eyes swung to view his three visitors in a way that suggested he was already dead.

In the plastic interface glove of his left hand, he still held a twitching, sparking something. It appeared to be the index or ring finger of his dead lover, the near Elle.

His right hand was crushed into a smear of bone and strips of flesh.

His legs were held on by what muscles hadn't torn completely through in the crash of his vessel.

As Benton crouched beside him, surveying his damage, another twinge needled through and besind and before Paul's eyes.

"Who..? Who—"

"Don't try to talk." Benton injected him with numby mist from the kit at her side.

West remembered a young doctor from Michigan who'd designed something like that once. Sweeping, flailing, tides of memory and something else, deeper and darker and alien.

"Task," Paul took a knee. "Where are they?"

Blinking confusion and fear. Red teeth, crusting and browning.

"Berlin and Maire. Where are they?"

Task clutched the finger tighter. "Elle..?"

"It's dead. You know that. You saw it die. We need to know where the others are. What happened after the crash?"

Eyebrows furrow, a gasp, exhalation and drift into meds-induced coma.

"He's out."

"Dead?" Paul reached to check Task's pulse.

"Metastasis for now. He'll die if we stay here much longer. He'll cross over with us, minimal damage."

"Looks like we're heading home early."

Paul stood. "You prep him for exit. West, let's check out the rest of the cave for signs of

❧

silver erupted everywhere, that piercing brand of light that exists beyond our concept of vision.

The force of the blast was enough to knock Hope from her feet. She not-gently hit the stone and snow floor, her head snapping back in a sickly and palpable crack of shielding.

I saw Task's limbs flutter in ways that human arms and legs shouldn't. Now passed out, he couldn't have realized that what had remained of his left leg had just sheared off.

The blast knocked me back against the cave wall, but I kept my footing. I immediately thought my shielding to its highest phase.

The mountain that was West bore the explosion the best of us all. He had his weapons drawn and was returning fire before I even realized what was happening.

Blocking the light with an outstretched hand, I looked into the white that the tunnel entrance had become to finally see somethings that had crawled behind my eyes for centuries.

I hadn't imagined them that way.

Beyond simple words or concepts, the Enemy spidered along the cave walls, tens, dozens, fifteens of them, a flickering, sub-screaming mass of writhing silverblack silverthought.

Each of West's shiver blasts, accompanied along its trajectory with a stream of profanity that only he could seem to muster with such aplomb during combat situations, struck home on its intended Enemy target. The intruding Judas timeline patterns shattered and were re-absorbed into the Enemy mind-essence.

More came.

Bent physics fucked my mind for an instant before realization, but I tore myself from the big picture and focused on smelling the roses instead: I lifted Hope from her crumple on the ground and snapped the emergency exit pin on my chestplate. I did the same to Hope's. I reached down to grab hold of Task's arm.

"West! We're out!"

A few more kills, a dozen more new arrivals, the cave ceiling cracking and collapsing into dust and chunks. He walked backward, dodging silver tendrils, almost to us—

He tripped.

The uneven ground met his bottom and back with a rough slap, but still he fired, the shiver blasts echoing and rupturing rogue code from the ME. He slid back, kicking with his feet, trying to get as close to us as he could before the jog jerked us back into nowhere.

He'd almost reached us when a shot went wide, an Enemy got too close, a silver tendril snaked and severed his right arm from the elbow down.

The shiver fired once upon impact with the ground, taking out the Enemy's legs. It snapped to grid.

West dropped his other shiver and tore the emergency exit release from his chest. When he was within reach, I helped him into what was supposed to be our exit bubble.

It wasn't there.

I knew something was wrong. There was no tickle, no copper anticipation of jog or exit, no visible shimmer.

I was covered in other people's blood.

The Enemy patterns stopped their advance. Silver snakes paused.

A fuzz of static, a shared mind, orders from beyond. I could seetastehear them speak as one: that horrible One, the Enemy mind-essence, that which had kept me awake for years as I'd attempted to unravel its intricacies, its secrets and horrors.

It spoke.

❧

The voice was ancient. The magenta bib overalls looked brand-new.

Click.

She walked lazily around the still Enemy patterns, each leg she passed a veritable tree trunk in comparison to her five-year-old form. As she passed each pattern, the silver-black rippled, reached, retreated from her purity.

Maire wasn't smiling.

“Ah, Author. You think too much.” She sat on the floor before the four where their exit bubble should have been. Her raven curls bounced and settled. “Let’s talk.”

The Enemy didn’t move.

Paul ignored the child for a moment, checked Benton’s vitals from her plate. She was stable. West held his cauterized stump with his good arm. “I’m fine,” to the silent question in Paul’s gaze.

“I’ve been watching you, Paulywog.” Her voice was playful, singsong. “Nice job with the bear. I never would have guessed that he was under the couch.”

“Thanks. It was a shining moment in literature.”

“So what should we do now? I could have my shiny dead soldiers back there kill all of you right now. That’d be the easiest solution.”

“I die, you die.”

“Unfortunate, that. You shouldn’t have written me so well.”

“You weren’t meant to be a main character.”

“Good thing I was, though. Brought credibility to an otherwise-sappy space soap.”

“I should’ve deleted you.”

“You never did like kids.” Her finger dragged through the slush of mixed blood on the floor. She stuck the tip in her mouth and smiled. Dimples. “How’s Judith?”

“You won’t find her.”

“I will.” She sculpted the child’s face into a scowl. “We will.” An adult gesture, that: the slight tilt backward of her head, indicating the Enemy patterns.

“A simple keystroke. You would never have happened.”

“Too late. I’m coming. I’m here. We’re here, and we’ll find her.” Maire’s eyes sparked silver.

Paul’s eyes sparked nothing in the mud of his gaze.

“This concept of ‘Delta Point’ as you so lovingly call it.. It’s—”

The space where her hearts had once been erupted with white

❧

and I saw the Enemy patterns shatter one by one. All was fire and scream and shiver as

❧

Alina shifted her weapon from where the girl had been and started taking out the Black. The cave crawled. Her troops surged forward, confident with the courage that new-Awake gives them. The Black patterns destabilized, crumbled, sunk into the rock of the ground, but the Judith forces didn't let them get far; Alina tight-beamed orders up to Samayel, and he doused the hotzone with phased tethers, securing their codes in that When.

Alina charged through the still-dissembling patterns, throwing a few fuck-you shots into a few black skulls as they melted. She saw the author and his glorified bodyguard West scramble to their feet as they realized what was going on, that they were being rescued.

Alina's kids cleaned up the cave in no time.

Benton wasn't moving. Next to her, Task lay dying. West tried to hold his blood in.

"Alina!"

It was the first time Paul had said her name. She felt something.

"Judith ME picked up your exit request before the Enemy blocked the signal. They sent us in. Sam's waiting above to take you back."

"Good. We have serious wounded. Task's critical, Benton—"

"Paul?"

He turned to meet West's gaze.

"She's—Hope's—"

"No" and he fell to the floor, pulled off the girl's helmet, placed his hand over her chestplate. He frantically tried to revive her, activating the shield suit's recharge system, and when that didn't work, he leaned over her and fisted his weight down into her chest. He stopped to check her breath, her pulse.

West gently placed his remaining hand on Paul's shoulder. It fell, rose to the rhythm of the attempt to start her heart.

"Stop it, Paul."

He kept going.

"Paul—"

The author threw West back and almost succeeded in tumbling the man over. West reached forward and one-armed Paul off of Benton.

"She's dead."

These systems of desire and ritual, silver lies and betrayal: what love could breathe in a world of such uncertainty and echo, what morning whisper or crawling dawn could ever replace that scent, that taste, that perfect moment in which we look into eyes not our own and realize that they are?

Paul again shrugged off West's hand, walked past Alina and her troops as he studied the ground in front of him. As he passed Alina, he looked up, and in those eyes, she knew the fragments of him.

Alina thought she felt something in that moment.

WIND{S}WEPT

WIND{S}WEPT

Flatline.

affliction had been isolated and the source identified, it was far too late for the forward combat crews, who had been exposed to fatal levels of the alien metal as they

Do you know of blood? Of wind? Of loss, of ruin?

to the waft of black, bitter coffee and she followed them into the empty streets, finally moon-lit, finally casting aside the day's embrace of mist and fog, the earlier downpour retreating into the

sound of their footsteps, his ancient black boots, her new black boots, a drift of laughter and conversation. She had hesitated before the cafe, finally allowing the door to swing shut to the bell's call. The jingle brought the proprietress's thin gaze from an emptying pack of Marlboros to the door. The jangle brought her customer's thin gaze to his wife's. Eyes locked as the bell settled; they would make love that

ঌ

night that Hope was killed, West found Paul sitting alone in the construct. This time it wasn't decorated with his typical college bar layout. It was gray and empty. Mostly empty. West thought most of the gray came from him. He thought in, saw Paul, and thought out. West knew the author needed time alone.

West talked to Jud, and she sent him back to a semblance of home. She'd handle the repairs.

Abbie was in bed already, the lights out. West had been downstairs reading a parenting magazine half-heartedly between paying bills and watching the game. She'd bought the magazine and many more like it and put them in a stack on the coffee table. West was younger, skinnier, his hands still callused. Before the war. Before she'd...

So he read the magazines, not that his wife put any faith in them. She knew they'd work it all out eventually. They wouldn't learn how to love a child by reading articles on the right diapers to buy and proper vaccination schedules.

West crawled into bed next to her, and her weight shifted as his lowered. A whispered, slept inquisition to which she knew the answer: *Adam?* She moved into a spoon against him. As he gave her a goodnight kiss on the cheek, he smelled toothpaste and Noxzema and her shampoo, the expensive stuff she felt guilty buying on a farmer's paycheck, but the stuff that he loved her to have and needed her to have.

It was a quiet night in Nebraska, away from his missing arm, Hope's dead body, Paul's emotionless face in that gray, empty room.

He didn't want to go

ঌ

back downtown after they'd watched moonrise by the water.

She was always just behind them, always close enough to taste them, once reaching out for Maggie's halo of curls, her hand stopping just short of target. Not yet. She didn't yet trust herself enough to not savage their

❧

bodies all around her, an imperfect circle on imperfect sand.

Hunter's body slumped to the ground, the shattered skull splashing gray and crimson on impact, the shiver gun cratering sand at his side.

It was in the perfect silence that she screamed, her wail growing younger faster as the silver spread through the sky, the stars, all

❧

the energy they'd expended on the development of weaponized silver would be for naught if the test failed. Already, there were reports from the many fronts across shattered space that the lumbers were adapting, evolving, fighting back against the harvest fleets.

Ever cut your grass one day, and the next, you notice a foot-tall dandelion towering above the green, white fluffy seeds spreading in the phantom wind? The lumbers were just as hardy, just as determined to resist harvest.

You don't know what freedom is until you've seen a system-sized school of trees, branches bare and brittle from the nothing of space, defensive spines bigger than continents firing from ridged, cavernous bark, tearing apart slithers with petrified wood.

The keening, the screaming: their calls weren't answered in that void.

Their song was one of

❧

morning West left the dream of Abigail's arms and retreated to the horror that was the final book.

Paul was already in Jud's chamber. When West greeted him, his hand waved him to silence as his head cocked toward the obscured cove of Jud's sleeper. The lights were at work carving her apart, flaying layer after layer down to her silver core where god lived. West never got used to seeing that. Blood, guts, and a pretty little marble. The lights wrapped her in a new Jud body and sealed her up. She stretched, the incision lines still sealing on her face and chest.

"The answer's 'No.'"

"We need to get back out there." Paul's voice wasn't.

"You need some time."

"I don't—"

"You need some time." She wrapped herself into a robe and reclined. "It's too soon."

He spun, mouth curling to a snarl. "There's no fucking time left. We need to get out there, full-force, and—"

"Paul." She held out her hand. "Take this."

West knew what it was already: Hope's marble, now lifeless and useless. Paul snatched it from her grasp and stormed from the room. When the chamber door had cycled shut, Jud patted a place next to her on the dais and motioned for West to join her.

"He'll be okay." West didn't believe it, but he said it because it was the only thing he could think of.

"Yeah." She leaned her head against his shoulder. "I liked Hope."

"There's no way...?" He let the question fall.

"Not this time. Maire fucked the code. She's lost to us."

He didn't want to think about the implications of *to us*.

"Who'll be our third?"

"Fourth, with the bear."

"I hate that bear. Who's fourth?"

"Ever meet Banana Tits?"

❧

This is where I take them when they've died:

Jacob was wrong. It's not easier when nowhere feels like home. It's easier when no *one* feels like home.

It was a close cousin to the first book's Chicago crater, I suppose, a great gouge in the surface of the planet, the cliffs of the edge entirely too sharp on the periphery, the upload generator tilting precariously miles away at the impact's center. The sky was empty.

I walked past the older graves, their shadows inking the glassed dust with darkness deeper than that feeble sunlight should have birthed. Simple stones, simple names. Each contained multitudes.

I buried her marble next to another.

I wanted to say something when I was done, as if vocalizing the loss would validate her importance to my life, to my sanity. I couldn't find the right words. The words I did find were inappropriate and filled with a venomous mix of truth and emotion that I could no longer afford.

I remembered that first night: the beach, the shadows, the voice. Another life. The grating of sand across skin. Too many kisses on the cheek. All of that, all of that, now ruined by the corrupt code of a child, a monster.

I stood and walked away from my cemetery, certain that I'd visit it again before long.

❧

There are no mechanics to a shiver gun.

The basic physics are those of particle acceleration and molecular resonance. The gun itself is nothing more than a shaped form of phase-ready metallish, available in any sculpt one could desire. In the history of her, she'd eventually see shivers like six-shooters, the traditional claw form of the inner worlds, the stylized driftwood grip and sliver barrel of the outer worlds, blocky extended cubes and tubular bells, rifles, billion-barreled shatter arrangements mounted on destroyers.

No matter the size or shape or taste, the shiver gun she remembered most was the pistol with which she'd been repeatedly raped after her capture and interrogation following the initial invasion of her homeworld. The Inner forces enjoyed such torture. They viewed her lifekind as barbarians; the condition in which they found her blockaded planet certainly helped that assumption. Continental fires, cannibalized cities, necromancy and sacrifice and an innate resistance to the machines.

She refused to talk. They enjoyed the aftermath.

A swift and brutal beating to tender her up, to get the juices flowing: blood from her broken nose, her split lip, her torn ears, tears, snot and spittle and vomit. A particularly brutal impact to her chest had split the bottom of her left breast open. They'd stopped the bleedout on that one even as they bit off her right nipple and carved and branded their marks on the soft gooseflesh of her belly, her descent to sex, her thighs. A broken finger, an extracted tooth, a clump of raven hair torn from her scalp and waved as a prize above: she still wouldn't talk.

A thumb in her eye: an audible pop, but they kept her alive. She was beautiful.

The first at her sex was the commanding officer. The only lubrication between her legs was her own blood, the torn labia and excised clitoris providing her a semblance of new virginity, and the splash of seed he left behind, his pathetic penis quickly deflating and retreating below codpiece armor to the congratulations and admiration of his subordinates. The other officers took their turns, filling her, ripping, inverting and bypassing walls of flesh, cervix, uterus, bruising and abrading the softness, the holy tender profaned.

She screamed until she couldn't catch her breath, blacked out, woke to new horrors. She'd bit into and through her bottom lip, which hung wordless and kissless in two pieces painting her chin and cheeks.

Still alive.

The stood in a circle around her, jerking their members to attention, ready for ensuing rounds, waiting for orders, waiting for questions and answers they knew she'd never give, as if they could fuck the truth from her, bring her to confessional orgasm, ply the coordinates and movements and statistics from her body with their pricks, slick with her truths, blood spattering the floor in revelations.

Her ears covered with rough hands, armored hands, the fury in his eyes capturing what attention she couldn't hold dear and safe behind tear-wet eyelids, she couldn't hear their barks and grunts, couldn't realize her next coupling until the soldier shot, grinned, crawled out of and off and she saw him then, a former lover, a former underling in her resistance, standing with his hands bound behind him, matching bloods and tears masking his face, sobs because he saw what they'd done to her, what he was about to do to her.

He fell under the rifle stock. Unable to stop his collapse, his hands bound, he slammed onto her front, their collision producing a unison exclamation of pain. Soldiers adjusted his position, tore his pants down and from his legs. His tears dropped to her face, cleansing unremarkable tracks across tacking blood.

I'm sorry. I'm so sorry.

The soldiers laughed at him: flaccid penis and tears and the mutual sobbing he shared with her. She looked up to see the commander drinking from a flask, his foreign orders sending a scurry of soldiers to her lover's sides and rear, a flurry of hands coaxing and encouraging, violating him as they'd violated her, forcing him to a half-erection with their manipulation of his shaft, his testicles, his prostate. His was a different form of resistance.

All through the rape of him, he remained still above her, his two eyes locked on her one, their inhalations and exhalations matched, the paths between their gazes and breaths a hesitant solace. He grimaced through the pain and when they judged him hard enough, one enterprising soldier guided him into her.

Through blood and the seed of a dozen others, she'd produced enough of her own wetness for him. Only for him.

The position wasn't impossible, but difficult because of the bindings holding his hands at his back. They were chest-to-chest, and he whispered to her, knowing he was crushing her, knowing his weight took her breath, which he tried to replace with hitching whispers: *i love you, i love you, please forgive me, i love you* and she ground beneath him, pain spiking from the groove where her clit had been, where her vagina had been grated and gouged, where the blistering brands split across her navel and inner thighs.

He hated himself for building to orgasm. Her eye comforted, knew.

When he shuddered and released, she barely felt his cum splash within her. A last look and she definitely felt his weight release; they pulled him up by his hair and shot him in the back of the head with a shiver gun, the resonated needle of metallish emerging just below his left eye, covering her with chunks of his brain and skull and the cartilage of his nose, a rain of blackened blood.

His dead weight slammed back against her, and in his death his body opened, his penis shrinking with awful speed even as it pumped urine and remnants of his semen into her gaped hole, mixing with her blood and slick, his shit and sweat running against her thighs and buttocks, puddling in that puddle that surrounded her broken body.

The soldiers laughed and cheered as they dragged his corpse from her and began their rage again, being sure to keep her alive, just keep her alive.

Maire screamed out to no god in particular.

❧

Some months, some times.

Jud tapped her fingers on the table.

"He's the only god here, you know."

"Well, fuck me in the ass, Frenchie."

Jean Reynald shrugged his shoulders. "It's true. You're a name. A placeholder. You're the focus of his divinity. Without him—"

"Without him, none of you'd be here today."

West grumbled. "Stop this shit."

Sapphire and Jade Jennings West sat on either side of their "father." Like almost all of the others, they'd been retrieved from the enemy line just before the hells Paul had written. They both made to speak at once, both looked at West, both let mouths close and fingers interlace.

West, the twins. Jud and Reynald. Honeybear and Banana Tits. Arik Mandela, a circle of a dozen others, each noting the echo of staccato fingertaps across the chamber as Jud thought.

"He's falling apart."

"He knows we're here right now."

"Don't be too sure of that. He never saw the Delta crossover coming. It was—"

"If he'd looked hard enough, he'd have seen it."

"Stop." West rose, paced. A thought and the A/O line appeared at the center of the table. "Only thing that matters is that it happened, we're trying to fix it, and the focal point of our existences is losing his fucking mind. We can't get a solid lock on Delta within fifteen points. We can't—"

"You sure that's not just the loss of your maths girl?" Reynald considered, turned to Alina. "No offense intended, dear."

"None taken. I suck at 'maths.'"

"How many times do we have to do this? Without even knowing how or why? He hasn't told us nearly enough for us to succeed once he—"

"Once he loses it completely," Jud sunk farther into her seat, "We're dead. You know that. Simple as that. Once he forgets us, we're gone."

"Then what's the point of this?" Alina looked up from troubled brows.

"Killing time." Reynald cleared his throat. "We're just killing time."

❧

"Lights."

West's whisper echoed out across the liquid expanse, his bootsteps following not far behind. The chamber door snicked shut behind him, adding to the building bounce of sound. He tried to walk quietly, but doubted it really mattered.

He sat down on the pool's elevated lip, triple-checking his seals before making any contact. His atmosphere chilled; he could see his breath attempting to fog his lookers.

They'd started harvesting as much silver as they could filter from the combat zones. Paul hadn't been taking many trips out of Judith ME. A lot of people had died to bring him his silver in drips and dots at a time. He thought there was an answer in the machine ocean; West thought it was a pointless indulgence.

Paul's nose was the only thing breaking the surface of the pool. He didn't appear to be breathing, but upon closer inspection, West saw the faint ripples of exhalations. More and more often, he'd find the young man here in the silver pool, his patented hawking Hughes Nose the only indication that he was there.

West knew Paul knew he was there. He needed no words; the tug and release was enough.

Paul lifted himself to a sitting position, swung forward to a crouch, the silver sliming from his nude form. When he stood, the fluid pool solidified under his feet, a mirror field. Trailing rivulets of the invasive metal dripped down from Paul's ears, nose, eyes.

He always scared West after his swims.

"How's the meeting?" His eyes were silver, were motion, were mud hazel. The last of the silver evaporated (absorbed) from (into) the tangles of his chest hair, pubic hair.

West shrugged, popped his seals and removed his helmet after the silver was gone. "Not a lot of faith."

"Fuck faith." Clothes over flesh. "Give me time."

"That's the thing, boy. We don't have time."

"We—"

"You've been in here more and more often. People are starting to talk. They think that shit's getting into your head. They think—"

"It's already in my head. Where do they think it came from in the first—"

"We're ready to strike. With Reynald in now, good leads on Zero-Four and the Windhams—"

"That's the wrong way to approach this."

"That's the only way we *can* approach this."

"I just need more time."

"I know." A tender, fatherly gesture: a reassuring grip of Paul's shoulder. "But—"

"Tell them I'll be out soon. Rest up."

"Yes, sir."

Paul grinned. "Don't call me that, old man."

Alina shifted in the sling from right to left, from sleep to wake. Sandwiching her, the West twins inhaled in unison, a slow, tentative feeler into consciousness quickly overruled by collapse back into dream.

She didn't know why the girls were so drawn to her.

Their extraction had been unpleasant. The Mara had been deep within a fleet of shredded and disabled Judas vessels, a horde of Enemy projections flashing in and out and through them. Jade had been a simple grab from the exterior; Phire had had to be pried from the can with Arik Mandela's deft touch.

Paul hadn't helped on that run. He was taking a silver bath again.

Alina wondered if he

and stopped.

She guessed they liked her because she was the only really approachable human female operating in the inner circle of Judith ME. Jud certainly wasn't nice to kids, and that's what they were, a decade younger than her twenty-five standards, a year younger than their respective enemy line deaths, Jade uploaded into Program Seven, Phire taking her own life just before the first Jag war. They couldn't have known, so she never told them.

They were both so skinny. Pale. Children of the space between stars and times.

Alina was losing her Ft. Myers sunwindburn.

Each night, they'd cuddle with her in Sam's command chamber, away from the cold halls of the ME, the sterile rooms and flayed god, the birthing fields, the libraries upon libraries of catalogued nevers.

They'd never known West. Although he tried at first to communicate with them, he was nothing more than an alternate to the father they'd left behind with their silver mother in a swarmed When. He eventually gave up; he'd never known their West, their Patra. His yesterdays were

Abigail and the farm and the war, a different war, silver skies and children.

They inhaled as one, exhaled as one. Al had never before seen a twin bond so tangible, such a blessing. Such a curse? She could tell them of histories of loss, of ruin.

It was better that she just hold them both in the sleeping egg until morning came, bringing with it new insertions, new faces.

They were safer in her warmth, in what little comfort and solace she could provide, knowing what they'd been extracted to do, knowing what tomorrows would bring to shatter that gentle breath of dream.

Alina fell back into sleep.

∽

If the Self is defined in its interactions and oppositions to and through external stimuli, and those stimuli are grouped in contextual accordance to the shifting nature of existence, we can define the Self as the opposition to environmental stasis.

How can we delineate and nominate that particular stasis? What collection of sensations and memory compose a being? How do we define Home? Is it the place where one exhales and doesn't fear for the next breath? Is it indeed easier when nowhere and no one feels like home? Is home a place, a collection of interactions, a veil of memory constructed solely within?

To Maire, the concepts of home and pain were one. When something such as the concept of home, something so traditionally regarded with quiet desire, respect, even reverence becomes intrinsically linked with a deep, inherent negativity, things happen. As we now know, things happened to Maire.

It wasn't that her planet was a bad home, but in the vast scheme of intergalactic destiny and solar-systemic politics, bad things happened there.

Sometimes a species outgrows its collection of rocks.

Would she have defined home as I did, as a loose collection of images and sensations, centered on those who inhabited that same space? In the sterile cool of the ME, I tried not to think about home. Tried. Hard. Didn't work.

Home was unappreciated farmers, those sixty- and seventy-year olds still working eighteen-hour days, permanent sun across noses and cheeks, burst vessels beneath the skin, white whiskers poking through until the weekly shave before going into town: a new fencer, ten rolls of sisal twine, doses of Today and Tomorrow, defined not as divisors of time, but by the product names of dry cow and fresh cow treatments, slow visits by neighbors, sharing forecasts and anecdotes, busting through frozen bolts, tearing flesh on rust, the scent of sweat and hay and milk spoiling from where it spilled on ancient jeans ten hours before, then exposed those ten hours to sunlight, to humidity, to manual labor. Grease guns and kittens, hay hooks and goldenrod and vetch.

Home was the desolation of a post-industrial world, abandoned paper mills, a population displaced from suburban hold by the necessity of the commute in too-big pickup trucks, status-symbol sports utility vehicles, the embarrassment of the family mini-van, the occasional Freudian commentary that was the convertible, men who'd drive to service jobs, mill work in other towns, re-education as a mid-life crisis when plants closed, environmental regulations tightened, their wives taking jobs, nurses and day care providers, pathetic local politics of heightened local importance.

Home was hick bars and dirt tracks, girls knocked up before high school graduation, sexual assaults in the nearby barracks, Canadian dance clubs, the polarization and fragmentation that the adolescent clique system embedded: some spoke with accents, some struggled to excel in sports, some wore only black, fancied themselves gangs, just white kids with access to drugs and knives. Four had stabbed a middle-school friend half a hundred times; I'd sat at the other end of their lunch table: the outcasts, and later, some would embrace the mythos of bisexuality, homosexuality, painted nails and dabbling in their own sex, as if it were the popular thing to do, anything to distance themselves from tradition: jocks and cheerleaders, band geeks, farmer's kids, racecar drivers and those who chewed tobacco in the parking lot, spitting brown into the previous weekend's collection of floormat beer cans, the cheapest yellow shit marketed widely, and there were the sneakers, by brand they judged worth. I wore Voits.

Home was bonfires in the woods, cool kids fucking in Daddy's sedan; they never escaped those early designations, and as such became a part of home: unchanging, stagnant, dead already, those who never wished to escape, those who never tried.

Maire's home? Interwoven with that particular brand of revision that torture induces in the tortured, it came to me in razor-edged shards, horrible images, many without a suitable vocabulary with which to describe them.

Maire's home? Just a rock, far out from One, far enough so that the first machine wars had barely scratched its surface, but close enough to experience the desolation of the century-long Silence during which the victors re-engineered the inner worlds to suit their desires, abandoning the outer worlds to their own devices: the horrors of famine, drought, pollution, a cultural and political isolation so devastating that planets burned out there, their own squabbles raging into limited conquests, subjugated populations put to the sword, the light, the dinner table. Taboo became norm in that vast starvation, that vast cesspool of decaying genes, mutation and stench, moons spun out of orbit in desperate gambits to win wars the underlying flashpoints of which no one any longer remembered.

Hunger has a special memory of its own.

Home to her was the taste of livers. Her own baby sister, dead just hours, put to the carving knife. What precious little flesh left hanging from the emaciated form roasting over one of the encampment fires, the smell and sting of bubbling fat giving voice to her empty stomach, rumbles inaudible under the night sky of combat. When the fuels ran out, even that fell to uneasy silence.

Fuels and missiles, bullets, poisons: none were renewable there, the planet just a mining outpost, the only ore of value shiny and gray. Craftsmen had worked it into jewelry once.

Tender and juiced, an arm pulls from torso, skin splitting and black. Chewing and swallowing: a denial of that child she'd held when her mother had died, attempted to nurse from pre-adolescent breast buds. The animal farms had been raided long before.

Those base desires in times of hunger and blood become base realities. She'd been a viable replacement fuck for her father and brothers after her mother's death. She'd killed them each eventually, wondering what of her was left on them, in them, of the four babies she'd given them, the last a screaming mistake that had entered the world just long enough to exit in blessed suffocation. She'd wrapped its umbilicus around its neck and killed it to stop the noise. She tossed the lump of flesh to the eager onlookers, even helped them coax the afterbirth from her; some lapped blood from her lips and thighs.

After she'd first bled at age ten, she'd never stopped.

Home? For Maire, it was pain.

∽

They knew he'd see them. It didn't matter which he; he did. They all did.

The bell on the door rang from behind to signal their entrance. The patrons of the Cafe Bellona went about their business of coffeehouse intellectual discourse. There were so many of them. All blended and faded, became distinct, swam back into the moments. People overlapped.

Berg was the first to release the necksnap of his hardsuit. Leif and Roman followed his example, followed him to an empty table at first, then populated by two, three, seven for an instant. They sat and ghosts flickered. They became the sole customers of that table.

"We're locked in. ME tether's steady."

Roman was the first by a blink to notice his new apparel: white lab coat, thick glasses. Clipboard on the table before him. Is this really how they looked to him?

"It's amazing." Leif, the youngest by a decade, let the eagerness and wonder of his age leak through.

"Not amazing." Berg grumbled the words out. "Just a merge. Let's get to work."

Berg, Leif and Roman were the three best quantum-X physicists Judith had left. They'd been promoted and pressed into service after Benton's death. They'd been kept a secret from the author because of the what and how of their inquiry.

The answer was, of course, Seattle.

"It's true." Leif poured over data presented to him on the papers bound by his clipboard. "It's right here, right now, all of it, converging."

Rumble from the sky; Paul, Benton and West ran past the front entrance of the coffee shop. The phase flak needled from the sky. They were just blocks from Helen Windham's small apartment that she shared with her son and his teddy bear.

"Let's get some samples." Roman's hand went into the air, a signal to the proprietress. She smiled and walked to their table.

"Sorry, didn't notice you come in. What can I—"

Leif grabbed her forearm and stabbed it through with a metallish instrument he'd withdrawn from his lab coat. She gasped and exhaled, built up to a scream and

"Got it. Checking for—"

"Let's get some coffee." Roman's hand went into the air, a signal to the proprietress. She smiled and walked to their table.

"Sorry, didn't notice you boys come in. What can I get for you?"

"Three coffees, please." Berg's eyes met hers. She was warm; her smile caused a bullet-hole dimple. "Worked here long?"

"About a year. Have I seen you here before?"

"I don't think so. Are you a student near here?"

"Yeah. Art major at Cornish, just down—"

"Sample confirms. Let's get some coffee." Roman's hand went into the air, a signal to the proprietress. She smiled and walked to their table.

"Sorry, I didn't see you come in. What can I—"

"Know any authors?"

Her smile dropped. "Excuse me?" Exquisitely sculpted eyebrows furrowed.

Leif looked over the people in the shop. An older version of the proprietress came out from the back room with a small package wrapped in gift paper. The man sitting at the counter unwrapped it: Marlboro 100s, now banned decades.

"Don't look around, boy." Berg shook Leif from his voyeurism. "Bad for business."

"Let's order some coffee." Roman's hand went into the air. A spectrum of proprietresses smiled and walked to the table, smiled and wiped the counter, frowned and ignored him, walked toward him, walked toward him and tripped, tripped and laughed, tripped and died, walked out the door, started screaming, aging, dying right there, then and then, a spectrum of everyones.

"Want some coffee?" The young blonde with the dimple put pencil to her pad and anticipated.

ஒ

Paul saw them. He realized that Judith would assemble a crew of quantum-X kids to figure out that great hole in his thought.

He didn't know why the Cafe Bellona had forced itself into everything of substance he'd ever written. Now that Judith had brought him in to repair the forevers he'd broken, he'd had to sit down and think it over, which is what he was doing right there, a cup of black coffee on the table, an unread newspaper and two packs of smokes in need of an ashtray.

He knew Berg, Leif and Roman from the hidden chapters of his existences. They were the team who'd eventually unraveled the silverthought lattice. Far in the future, they'd been able to crack the deadlocked omni-DNA code residue left behind in a ship named Gary after the second War of the Jaguar. A beautiful young brown man named Michael Balfour had based his forevership design on the Berg/Leif/Roman Lattice.

Paul watched them, all of them, across that dive. At the counter, older versions of himself and the coffee shop owner held hands. A mid-twenties future-version of the waitress served BLR coffee. Joseph Windham got down on one knee to propose to his Helen. Maggie Flynn and Simon Hayes talked shop over *Demian* and *Deus ex Machina*. Judith and god talked shit over Formica. There were others, so many others, but they were hidden to him, just blurs, all a spectrum of silver. He averted his eyes from the brilliance of that overlap.

The door jangled and he saw the enemy, in present form, a scruffy drummer with corduroy pants, Kente cloth sewn up the seams. Paul swallowed hard, scrambled for a smoke. The enemy kissed the young waitress. Paul smoked, looked out the door into the rain, into the sunset over the still water, over the lances of phase flak and the sight of himself and West and Benton running.

It was that moment, that moment, that moment forever, all moments in one, all thoughts pressed together into a tangible damnation. He reached into his pocket and didn't find a marble. He did find some cash, which he placed on the table. He found a handful of silver coins, which he placed on the table. He found a wooden puzzle piece in the shape of Michigan. He found a pin: World's Best Wife! He found absolutely nothing at all.

He had had enough of the Bellona Merge. He waved half-heartedly to BLR. They returned the gesture with guilt. They knew he hated being watched.

As he opened the door, she called to him from behind the counter: young again, standing alone, wiping dry a coffee cup. He saw paint stains on her hands, knew that on one finger he'd find a scar from when they'd removed a tumor from her bone, knew her scent from across the cafe, mixed with rain and smoke and blood, that spectrum, that spectrum, and for an instant, he remembered the way she tasted. Then it was gone.

"Come again!" Her smile widened to be polite, fell from her face when she realized who he—

Paul shut the door behind him and

❧

threw the door open to Jud's chamber.

"Stay out of my fucking head."

The twins were there, Alina, the bear: a symmetrical arrangement: Alina flanked by the girls, the bear on her lap. Jud Indian-legged on her chaise; her words ended upon his entry.

"Guess you saw the boys."

Paul scoffed, paced beside the window that looked out upon the birthing fields below. "Lab coats? Yeah, I saw them. Stuck out like an ingrown toenail. Try harder next time."

"Sorry."

"Fuck you. Bring her back."

"You know I—"

"Bring her back!" Alina and the children flinched at his voice. The bear's smile faltered. "You expect me to work with these?" He indicated the silent onlookers.

"Hope's dead. Her code's lost." Jud shrugged. "Sorry."

A breath and he was over the god. Lifted. Strangled. She grimaced, her face turning black from her suffocation. Paul walked her to the window, slammed her against the frame. A slizzle and his blades leapt forward, opening her chin to pubis, through flesh and bone.

He tore the silver ball from her heart and threw the corpse through the window. Glassish shards fell miles below to babies, babies.

Screams: Alina and the children.

He squeezed the marble in his right hand. It started to blacken.

"Find a way to bring her back."

He tossed the marble to the chaise and stormed from the room.

Al did her best to comfort the sobbing girls. Honeybear frowned to himself.

The thick gurgle and flicker of silver, flesh, blood. The Judith ME sculpted a new body over the marble. Flash, snap to grid: Jud stretched and sat up.

"He's broken."

❧

that savage transition back to the merge, the tickle and strain, dull beating behind my eyes, the pins and needles stippling up the spine and neck, around my head to settle at my temples, and West was there, all shoves and fists, beating me to the pavement, a knee on my chest: I felt ribs crack.

"Don't you ever fucking do that again." He got off me, extended a hand. I accepted and he pulled me up.

I wheezed through blood. "But—"

A swift crack across my face. Index finger extended. "Don't do that again. I don't care. I miss her, too. But it's not Jud's fault, not Alina's. Not my daughters'." He reached and wiped blood into the front of my shirt. "I loved her, too."

We stood in a silence. The merge had flattened for the moment: one existence, no fragments or echoes. I knew it had been raining; the sidewalks reflected the emerging moonlight.

Jingle. Jangle.

I pulled West into the alley beside Cafe Bellona. I knew the door had opened and was now lazily swinging shut. She laughed, and four feet tapped paths past our hiding spot.

West's eyes narrowed. He looked from the couple to me: lock. He'd known them.

"Welcome to the merge." I felt my whisper had been too loud, but they didn't seem to notice us.

"Simon and Maggie?"

"Yeah." I looked out from the alley. They were much too focused on each other to notice me. "Let's get out—"

"Quiet." He pulled me back. "Listen."

Another set of footsteps. A different sort of sound.

I felt it: that lance, that extraction, the energization of the metal now coursing through my blood, the place where my heart had once been, and I knew that Maire was there, somewhere.

"Close your eyes."

"What?"

"Shut 'em. You're glowing."

I shut my eyes and heard her draw closer to us. The footsteps stopped at the alley entrance, just a pause, but pause enough that I sensed West's heart beat faster, knew he wanted to inhale, but like me, he'd retreated to silence.

She started walking again. When she'd passed, I opened my eyes.

"Let's go."

∽

the theory that the self is the only thing that can be known and verified, the theory that the self is the only reality: solipsism.

He was solipsistic. He knew rejection, and that knowledge forced him within. That knowledge forced him apart.

She knew this because he knew this.

And children, and werewolves, and piano, and cheese. She'd never heard music. She'd never learn to sing, to dance. She'd never smell lilacs or taste Pabst Blue Ribbon. These things were good.

She'd managed to distract the girls from Paul's break with a runtime environment resembling a beauty school dropout's bedroom. There were giggles. The twins played with rouge. The blush brush tickled Alina's cheek; she attacked them with bright-red lipstick, drew a smiley face on Phire's forehead, a moustache above Jade's mouth.

Confident that they were engaged enough in the trappings of teenybopperhood to relent the gosling imprinting with which they'd taken to her, she slipped deep into the Judith ME.

The source of that plague, that collective of shadow and doubt: she thought through the entry guardians and walked without footsteps into Paul's refuge. She wasn't good with maths, but she knew intuitions and rejections. The silver pool chamber was colder than she'd expected; her breath danced, and each painful inhalation, each wheezed exhalation echoed, bounced, and in return to her ears, heightened the loneliness of that place.

Reaching into, out and through: she knew their senses.

The silver should have killed her, lapping at the edge of the pool, exposed as she was, but she'd always known from that first breath after virgin birth that she wasn't like the others. She wasn't a fragile construct of flesh wrapped around bone; she was, and just was.

He'd made her to precision specifications, a fine silver blade hidden within a despised and uncertain framework.

Alina leaned over the pool's edge, saw her shadowed face in near-perfect reflection, her awkward long neck drawing the eyes down to prominent collarbones and pendulum breasts, nipples erect from the chill and something deeper, darker, pointing parallel to the silver's surface, and she cupped small hands (long, lithe fingers) and plunged in, retrieving, and she drank deeply of that metal, that mercurial fire, the burning like ice, carving through teeth, tongue and gums, into and down her throat, gasping, coughing, a flare and seizure of cold

though i know we be but dust

and she rolled into that mirror, let the metal pour into her, a frigid embrace, an inclusion and wrapping, and in that metal horror, she felt him, knew him, surrendered to that silver and that man, because that's all he was: silver, and as the surface hardened above her, fine crystalline suffocation, she screamed without sound, her fingers plunged into her, frantic and yearning, her liquid, his liquid, all silver, all silver and

It wasn't love, but it was something as painful.

When she was done, satiated, the surface released with crackle and splintering. She stood from the pool, let the rivulets of silver, of him, of loss and ruin retreat from her entries. She wrung the metal from her hair, for once a semblance of control, spiraled curls then escaping and drying, frizzing, accusing outward.

"You'd think," Jud half-whispered from the edge, "he'd have told me about you."

Alina jumped at the voice.

Snap and a towel. Jud flickered, threw the towel to Alina. "Dry off."

"How can you—"

"The real question, I suppose, is how can *you*? It's simple for me. Disposable body. ME's cycling me through about sixty thousand Juds a second. That silver's a bitch to withstand. But you're different. You're built from him."

Alina stepped out of the pool and stood on the edge. The towel hung unused at her side. The silver dried by itself.

"Mr. Hughes is full of surprises." Jud's fingertip traced from Alina's bottom lip down over the outcrop of chin, the valley of throat, between the fraternal twin peaks of her breasts, the gentle swell of her belly, and farther down to settle between and within the vegetative growth on her cleft. Settle and stammer, caress, drape, rupture, rend, rive. Split, cleave. Jud removed her finger, shining with silver and cum, hungrily licked it. "And so, it seems, are you."

"I didn't—"

"Shhh..." Jud put her finger to Alina's lips, cut off her speech. The mouth opened, tasted. "We can use this." A touch without touch: *we can use this.*

They left the silver pool.

❧

those tenuous lines of commonality, and West wished that he was wrapped in a giant robot, a naval destroyer, one of the deep-black hatchets a different West had once used to carve apart the space between times and stars.

West thought Paul was having fun with it, but the concept of fun in that moment scared him more than the woman, the woman, the man, the man. He felt like he was intruding at a dance, the kid in the leg cast sitting on the sidelines watching the jocks grope his secret crush, plotting revenge, a bad eighties slasher film.

A controlled descent into madness: West felt his smile; spiral, spiral, uncontrolled, madness.

That city. That fucking city. Seattle. Seattle by moonlight. Couldn't Paul see that it wasn't real? A Seattle like that had never, could never have existed. His romanticized vision of a city he'd never see, a purposeful avoidance regardless of opportunity or adolescent dreams of visiting Kurt's bridge, *something in the way* and that something was her, dead now to everything outside of the Merge, that spectrum of broken tomorrows, and it was like he wanted that pain, wanted to go into that shop and steal just a strand of blonde, a lip print from coffee cup, steal anything as proof that he'd not dreamt that life (he'd neither yet nor ever would live that), but proof? What proof could that place give them?

He hunted her.

From the cafe down dark streets, grunge lilting from afterhours bars; the streets were too dead, a perfect moment for her, but too dead: unnatural, as if the buildings lining each avenue barely contained a dream of life, as if the avenues themselves drew them into the center of the maze, and West knew Paul felt it, that merging, that convergence around Delta, around the witch Maire, her shadow form dancing between streetlights and footsteps: they followed the two (three).

Hesse and *Deus*. They were a cute couple, those ghosts. Maggie Flynn and Simon Hayes traced the edge of the city's knife; by moonlight: a fog lifts as the desire and thirst of a madwoman descends.

Mr. Hayes, I—

Call me Simon.

That would have been her ultimate victory, to take them from the Enemy line. Paul had been proud of those characters, fucking around with their names until he got them just right in the tenth or so version of the book, that first book, nothing so presumptuous or gaudy as "Hunter" or the troublesome "Lilith." Read into that what you will, but Paul liked them, liked their names. Simple names.

Maire made her mistake.

As the young couple walked innocently down East Roy, 714 (he knew the subtraction of four, the exact and precise number, but because of concern, lost love or stalking, but because he was thorough, *solipsistic*, self-involved and self-aware to a fatal flaw, and if we're taking the story there, take it there, a reminder of loves wasted and loss, a ruin of a building now, if a building could signify a loss, [he never knew: bricks of what color, consistency, texture? some research is beyond safety and the ability of reuptake inhibitors to allay that desire]), Maire struck out, or tried, but his hand met her fist, and she spun to him.

It should have killed him, that touch; it didn't.

And the city wiped away, a smooth transition to the non-space he projected. West was there; the couple wasn't. Paul had saved them from Maire and brought West along for the ride. Maybe he needed a witness.

The horror of him, the astounding horror of him: becoming silver. West had first seen it on the ice, then in the pool, now in a muted substrata of the dead city. He could taste it, smell it, hear its screams; Paul stood before her, her small fist grasped easily in his hand. His face was empty. Eyes gray, then silver, then

And he'd mastered the laws of metaphysics and quantum maths, bent sciences and witching sight; he'd become more of her now than she could ever be. It was everything, everywhere: the crush of his mind as he grasped all probability, sent time and space down channels of non-exist that only he could envision. He'd trapped her, that sometimes child, that now-woman with the raven swathes. She snarled and hissed as she tried to tear her hand from his grip.

Simon and Maggie were safe. Gone. Maybe he'd erased them.

"You," he whispered, and it was like tears, "never were."

❧

there's a place in france where the naked ladies dance
it was a beautiful hand
the dust was thick... nothing had been touched since she left.
rupture

rend, rive, split." Kisses grew frantic. "Cleave." She pushed Alina down to her chaise.

Below, she was born again, a million new Judiths, a million short-term possibilities.

"Is this..."

"Shhh..." Lips drag. "It's perfect."

so textural, so sensual. inviting, but distant, the strong contrast of the white of the panties, human-made, human-patterned, to the natural bristly texture and dun color of the flowers, implied scent: the queen anne's lace to the cotton to the gentle musk of skin

A tickle of something; she ignored it in favor of the tingle of fingers around and into and within.

Trapped for so long: god. Not that she minded the ancient housed inside of her, now one with every fiber, now one with every bioelectrical impulse, every desire; hers was a life shared with forevers. She remembered her first meetings with god fondly; she'd been chosen as a Medium at a young age, raised among her flux siblings in generation chambers beneath One's surface, miles beneath, those first meetings with gentler deities: angels and saints forced into the slumbers in the time between machine wars, and that last time, the time she became one, only one with god through that tainted host body, the instant of realization, the burning of merging, merging: omniscience. Omnipotence. Enveloping, encasement, purge. The dark night of silvered space until rescue: Hannon.

Another book: another line.

To be resurrected: the boy author, in his subconscious collision of realities, his unknowing manipulation of probable realities, brought her from the deep of non: JudithGod, even before Benton and West were sent in to retrieve him. What pathways of thought, dream, and fear constructed this? What innate and incomprehensible combat of the soul had taken place to allow the forging of broken tomorrows from the space and times between bound paper?

Surprises, more and more: his immunity, his immaculate conception of the silver-proof Alina. Banana Tits could be her vehicle.

Judith's was the Mind-Essence; she forced universes of analysis into motion. Galactic networks of circuits, planet-sized nano-pathways of bent energetics: a whim, a thought, and it was done, bursts of zeros and ones carved from continental shelves, zero, one, and the spectrum of realities contained between: her mind was forever, and the answer, not a city, a scent, a hair pulled from teeth, was silver, silver, and had always been silver, that ocean of machines, that alien viral agent, that scourge: an answer.

Alina had been born without the sin of risk.

It was extortion, excision, removal, usage. Sticky, honey-sweet, like blades, that union, her host, her hostess, as she'd been for too long, as *take it from me, from me* she'd been forevers. Jud seized at those cycling selves, new bodies and souls (or the precipitous lack thereof) flickering through the spacetime she grasped. That quickening, that shuddering as their bodies entwined; she felt it: silver, reaching, tearing from flesh to flesh. Alina above her, spread, outstretched, tissues stretched, her face: those arched eyebrows could have signaled pain, ecstasy, and they did, her mouth chewing on nothing but air, heated from their exchange. Her breath smelled of Judith.

Bleeding, gushing, neither red nor clear nor viscous: silver, coaxed and urged from her, across the bridge between skins, from every pore, every entry; it crawled into and through Judith, and it was fire, ice, a swift smack on the ass, a kick to the throat, a feather across nipple, and it was silver, tomorrow, everything, agony.

They became one.

❧

Maire laughed.

"Never was?" She slapped her free hand down upon Paul's, crushed. "Never *was*?" Her face morphed between grin and grimace. A hiss escaped between clenched teeth as her grip forced the author to his knees. They could have been the same age. Weren't. West heard the crackle and splinter of metacarpal, phalanx. "I've always been."

A flash and he'd swept her legs from beneath her, his hand still locked in an improbable vice. Maire was on the ground; he straddled her from above, his free hand flickering: silver: his eyes now burned. Hers matched his: free hand and eyes.

Strength he'd never suspected: she threw him off, over. He rolled, snapped up to a crouch. She matched his ready stance.

So it would be combat between them.

And it bent, everything, and it was beautiful for a moment, that bend. It wasn't Seattle, had never been Seattle; the sky was gauze, and above it, something swam, that something black and writhing.

She'd summoned the Enemy.

❧

entry: transgression
function: noun
definition: violation
synonyms: breach, contravention, crime, defiance, disobedience, encroachment, erring, error, fault, infraction, infringement, iniquity, lapse, misbehavior, misdeed, misdemeanor, offense, overstepping, sin, slip, trespass, vice, wrong, wrongdoing
concept: error

❧

Buffer Overrun:

An attack in which a malicious user exploits an unchecked buffer in a program and overwrites the program code with their own data. If the program code is overwritten with new executable code, the effect is to change the program's operation as dictated by the attacker. If overwritten with other data, the likely effect is to cause the program to

⁂

crash cart in here!"

"Hold on. Just fucking hold on!"

He heard, tasted the panic, felt the array of warming steel probes, that copper aftertaste, the scent of smoke displaced somewhere in front of his eyes, the sensation of warm water, warm red water. His fingertips sparked, he thought. He thought, but metal intrusions forced new pathways, new avenues of

and there was the hitching of chest, bubbling of what he assumed was blood from beneath a facemask: citrus, giggle, two or four tears escaped. Fists slammed; ribs broke, and he was

⁂

falling from the veil of silk, the upload generator struck the surface of the false city, dug, righted itself. Enemy warships swarmed.

i am silver, weaponized silver, humanized silver. i am

Alina appeared.

Mousy hair, weird knockers, a complexion that wasn't sallow, wasn't glowing, but was just intensely *normal*, and her eyes, colorless eyes. Breeder hips, a little beer belly, a connect-the-dots of moles, freckled shoulders, angled nose, big cheeks. She was the kind of girl who wasn't hot, wasn't really beautiful to anyone unless maybe they loved her. Cute in a way that felt like home. And there she was, suddenly there, somehow different, suddenly somehow different there.

Maire snarled at her, more animal than human, but then again, she'd never really been a human, had she?

"You again?"

"Us again." Her voice embodied a confidence Paul had never heard in the girl.

Maire inhaled; lip corner upturned: grin. *Judith*, the realization melted into, swam through her breath. It'd gotten cold.

"Judith?" Paul stood. Confusion.

"Get away from her, Author." Alina pointed. "Run."

"You're not shielded. Not shifted. How can you—"

how can you use that shampoo? the children who saw that it was blue, their dreaded hair beyond repair, ate nectarines on submarines.

"You wrote me." Al turned away from Paul. A splay of fingers and Maire slammed to the ground. "West?" She didn't look. "You shifted?"

"Yeah, girl. I'm up."

"Hold your code."

A flicker in the line, a snap to grid, and she was above Maire. The silver witch flinched as Alina struck her with a haze of metal. She jumped up, tangled with the girl. Another time, another place, Paul would have expected mud or jello, but there in the non, everything was gray, flares of static, that hum and tug of mercury. Their two bodies merged into a disgusting, flopping mess of limbs, hair, screams.

Maire tore away from Al, the sound of twisting metal.

"Why, Miss Alina, you have a secret." Maire mimicked fanning herself, southern accent. "Do tell, honeychile."

Alina swung, her hand silvered, but Maire dodged.

"What's this about hope?"

Another swing, another easy dodge.

"Or is it— 'Hope'?" Grin.

"Shut your fucking mouth." Paul knew that voice: Judith, but it came from Al's throat.

"What?" Paul. Almost a whisper. His face whitened.

"You didn't know? She didn't tell you?" Maire simpered. Giggled. "Oh, now *this* is rich."

"What about Hope?"

"Don't." Alina breathed it as much as consciously said it.

"How long's it been since our petite soiree in that cave? Days? Years? And you never figured it out? Some author you are."

Paul shimmered.

"She killed her. Little ugly Allie killed your darling Ms. Benton."

"It's not true."

They circled, the three of them, this slow dance of shimmer and merge. Paul stopped.

"You killed her, Maire. You—"

Flicker and thrash: he flew backwards, landed ungently on the non-ground. Maire didn't stop. She shifted into and through Alina. Al shattered, dusted, re-formed. One hand to balance, one hand between breasts at the cardiac shield, she gasped for breath.

"Sam above, Allie within. Lots of soldiers to kill my children. Lots of shots. One wide shot. Guess where it went. Give up? Ms. Benton."

"Paul," she choked through wheeze, "it's not true. I swear—"

And the sky opened up: incoming Judith fleet. They slammed into the Enemy horde, strafed the upload generator. Sam dipped down, tipped his nacelles. He swam back into the fray.

"Don't believe me, Author? Who'll you trust? Why don't we ask Hope?"

Maire spun and wasn't there. Wasn't there, but she *was*. Not her, but her. The voice was different, the body splintering to a form West had etched behind his eyes long before they'd brought the author in, a form he'd met after re-birth from the Forever Dust: Hope. The body fell, meaty slap on non-pavement, but she wasn't dead. Couldn't be dead, because she gasped an inhalation.

Alina: "Don't touch her! Jesus fuck, it's not her, it's—"

Paul, more lips and tongue than sound: "Hope?" He went to her, cradled her head in his lap.

"Paul—" Alina pleaded. Hands to fists to hair: frustration, weeping. "It's not her. Don't touch—"

And Benton spoke, if such a ruined form could speak. Paul's mouth moved over the impossibility of sobs. She spoke.

"You're letting your hair grow out." Semblance of a smile. "But I liked it short."

"Hope—"

"They're all dead here." Fingers interlaced with his. Her voice was becoming echoes, static, and "What'd you do to her? Why'd you write? Why...?" Two tears, more blood than water: "You've killed us all."

Such ferocity barely contained in the sky: the upload generator shattered; a thousand vessels carved the earth.

He stroked her hair. "Hope, I—"

"There's no Hope anymore. No hope. Nothing. But she's with me." A smile so bright from assemblages of flesh and muscle: impossible. "She's saved me."

"I'll save you. We'll save you!"

"Paul..." She pulled him closer, whispered. "The Purpose will be completed."

He hatcheted an inhalation. Her eyes were silver.

He threw the body to the ground, clambered away and to his feet. The body shattered into blood and silver rivulets, dissipated with haze and static. Where Maire had been, where Hope had been: nothing.

The wind picked up.

Sam appeared above again. He folded from his vessel form, all shivers and digits, landed with a few stumbling steps as his human form.

"Allie? What happened? We got a beacon and..."

She didn't answer. Wasn't talking, wasn't moving, just stood there beside Paul looking at the place where Maire had been.

"Paul?" No answer. "Adam?"

Silversens registered negative. West shifted to normal. "We found Maire. And Hope. And—" He shook his head. "I don't fucking know."

Alina looked up at the author. Caught his gaze down. A small hand grabbed a large hand. Just for a second, West could have sworn he had seen a merge in those hands.

HEILIGENSCHEIN

HEILIGENSCHEIN

Δ

[login]: query((?))

[username]: **Hocking, Peter**: [variant trace: **lock**]
[password]: *******
[verification]: [sample approved.]

[login]: success.
[/login]

[search]: query((?))
[search]: [[**Paul** + **Hughes**] + [**silver**]]
[search]: [run]

[/run]

Δ

[run]: [system: **override**]
[run]: [command: **interject**]

[/run]

Δ

[run]:
[read]:
author: *la biblio["o]mnithèque universelle* agent 66.14.7.050.
title: of loss, of ruin: An Introduction.
publication: *Ein Journal des Instituts für die Erforschung des Heiligenscheineffektes.*

[full text]:

Thank you, [**Hocking**, **Peter**], for your interest in [**Hughes**, **Paul**].

As you know, *la biblio["o]mnithèque universelle* is still recovering from the effects of the Forever Dust. As such, results to your initial query may be incomplete or irretrievably lost. We are working to refine our recovery methods, and we assure you that the best teams of quantum-X string theorists are making valiant efforts to contain the loss of our database and re-integrate the mind-essence of our host soul caches.

[**Hocking**, **Peter**], your inquiry regarding [**Hughes**, **Paul**] presents several unique difficulties in that access to biographical elements of that particular string are severely restricted due to [[**security** + **protocols**] + [**threat** + **matrix**] + [**containment** + **Forever** + **Dust**]]. We hope, [**Hocking**, **Peter**] that you will understand our concerns when [(*excerpts are expurgated due to aforementioned security concerns*) + (*incomplete data retrieval prevents total output of designated inquiry elements*)].

We hope that you find [(designated output): [**Hughes**, **Paul**]] helpful and informative.

Sincerely,

agent 66.14.7.050
primary avatar re: [**Hocking**, **Peter**]: [inquiry **#77.75.140**]
la biblio[“o]mnithèque universelle

[/read]
[/run]

Δ

[run]:
[read]:
author: *la biblio[“o]mnithèque universelle* agent 66.14.7.050.
title: of loss, of ruin: An Introduction: **technical specifications [re: search results.]**
publication: *Ein Journal des Instituts für die Erforschung des Heiligenscheineffektes.*

[full text]:

[**Hocking**, **Peter**] [trace:(lock: **68.166.235.153**)], your search re: [**Hughes**, **Paul**] was generated [Q3:0**7**.**14**.20**64**] by temporal servers [B.0-B.6] [Sedna Core Information Archive: tight-beam encrypted transmission] outside of the plague zone quarantine demarcation [refer: **Forever Dust**]. *la biblio[“o]mnitheque*, in conjunction with *des Instituts für die Erforschung des Heiligenscheineffektes*, maintains quantum computing facilities [Omega-point hyperthreading techbase reverse-engineered from target Whens (salvage law compliant)] utilizing the best semantic web search engines available [B-LGoogle @ 147zettabytes/sec.(147x2^70mb/sec.) on MS/Halliburton™ dedicated a-zero servers].

This report represents the best assemblage of non-deepblack declassified intelligence fulfilling your designated search parameters [**Paul** + **Hughes**] + [**silver**]]. Due to ongoing security concerns regarding your line of inquiry, our engines have limited output, in cases removing sensitive passages and expurgating entire documents. This report embodies the most complete analysis of [**Hughes**, **Paul**] available to the public at this time. Due to ongoing concerns this Institute has [re: security clearance: **Hocking, Peter**], your access has been limited. You may re-query the database at any time after [Q3:0**7**.**21**.20**64**] given bandwidth availability and continued access rights.

For your convenience, physical report [re: inquiry **#77.75.140**] has been printed on week-dissolve fiber. Your access to the digital output will expire [Q3:0**7**.**21**.20**64**] to conserve resources.

We hope that you find [(designated output): [**Hughes**, **Paul**]] helpful and informative.

agent 66.14.7.050
primary avatar re: [**Hocking**, **Peter**]: [inquiry **#77.75.140**]
la biblio["o]mnithèque universelle

[/read]
[/run]

Δ

[run]: [hack]
[hack]

[display]:
author: *la biblio["o]mnithèque universelle* agent 66.14.7.050.
title: untitled.
direct/direct: [**tracking lock**]: [**lock**] [ghosting: **subset**]: [**ghost**]
[full text]:

direct: [**Hocking**, **Peter**] re: [**Hughes**, **Paul**].

Well, you have balls, I'll give you that much. Listen, I don't have much time, so I'll get right to the point. I've hacked the backend of Ib'otu to send you this message and give you special access to your search results. The sysops would usually time out your connection and draft a threat matrix asap, given last year's lockdown. I'll let you in for as long as I can. Consider me your guardian angel.

You're not unique. Everyone wants to know why he did it and where he went. I ran a search on you, and I think I know why you're asking. I'm putting my ass on the line for you, not that I expect anything in return, but it's information that needs to get out. Read it. Spread it.

If you're looking for answers, you might not find them here. Much of it's there, the influences, the actions, but as for intent... Who knows? We can fumble around the edge of his intent for as long as we'd like and never get to the core. It's obvious he was troubled. He thought that he wrote worlds into existence. Given the forty billion dead across seventeen charted systems, given the silver infestation, maybe he did. I'm not a religious man, but he's the closest we've found to Omega.

Fuck this, I'm out of time. You're safe for now; I've shielded your transmissions i/o Ib'otu. Look around. Try to find meaning. As meticulous as he was at analyzing himself, you think he'd have done a better job analyzing his creations. He spent twenty-seven years undermining existence, and we're still suffering the aftershocks and still trying to find intent. Lawyers love this case.

This is the last you'll hear from me. I need this job. Good luck. Purpose be.

agent 66.14.7.050
primary avatar re: [**Hocking**, **Peter**]: [inquiry **#77.75.140**]
la biblio["o]mnithèque universelle

[/hack]
[/display]

Δ

[/search] complete:
[display]

search results: [[**Paul + Hughes**] + [**loss + ruin**]]: [translate: **standard**]:
author: unknown.
title: "An End of Us: An Ontological and Epistemological Discourse on The Forever Dust."
publication: *Ein Journal des Instituts für die Erforschung des Heiligenscheineffektes*.

[recovery team notes signal shatter; text incomplete.]
[*la biblio["o]mnithèque universelle* confirms textual probability to statistical significance +/-33%]

...] deny that the Forever Dust was the defining metaphysical and cosmological event in the history of the first universe, the least of whom, those charted survivors. More than an historical crux from which we delineate the major eras of humanity into pre- and post-argent, the Dust is an evolution, a chimera of [...

...] far lower than first believed, the ignition point of the silver catalysis experiencing total sub-spatial anchor diffusion consistent with first universe crossover. The magnitude of the primary [...

...] found that contrary to their initial fears, the consumption line of the dust zone experienced a near-predictable transition to clean space.

...] hadn't been for the discovery of the untainted genetic code of the arc female (later identified as Patra Jennings West, Enemy line -FD), the continuation of the species would have almost certainly relied upon XY splitting and double-X recombinant techniques. Viable male codes were plentiful; the pre-Dust attacks on Sol-3 (native: standard: Earth) and Alpha Centauri AB (Proxima Centauri destroyed in native civil war only twenty years prior to loss of binary system: AC A destroyed by Sol-3 forces. AC B hidden by native forces in a megascale system enclosure, later the site of the Dust trigger.) had in effect eliminated the female of both species, due largely to metallurgical contaminant's ability to destabilize double-X codes via chromosomal synch/dislodge.

The discovery of the arc female allowed primary expansion of both species. Cross-pollination difficulties resulted both from basic atmospheric requirements (nitrogen active agent in AE-line humanoids; oxygen active agent in Enemy-line humans) and sub-genetic differentiation. Silver un-process rates for affected sample: AE: 99.9>%, E: 0.00~47.1%. *

The arc female's voluntary life partner, one Enemy-line Adam West, was [...

* **refer**: "La Séparation L'argent et la Poussière: Une Analyse d'Improbability des Existences Auteur-Créées," *la biblio["o]mnithèque universelle*, FD+MCDVII.

[/display]

Δ

[run]:
[read]:
author: *la biblio["o]mnithèque universelle* agent 66.14.7.050.
title: of loss, of ruin: accomplices [re: Hughes, Paul]
publication: *Ein Journal des Instituts für die Erforschung des Heiligenscheineffektes.*
[full text]:

[**Hocking**, **Peter**] [trace:(lock: **68.166.235.153**)], your search re: [**Hughes**, **Paul**] includes supplementary information to your primary search string [[**Paul** + **Hughes**] + [**silver**]]. This supplemental information is intended to provide a context for the crime and suggest possible accomplices. It is unlikely that [**Hughes**, **Paul**] was the sole catalyst for our current socio-political desolation [refer: [[**post** + **Forever** + **Dust**] + [**Heiligenscheineffektes**]]]. As such, we at la biblio["o]mnithèque universelle have included a partial analysis of possible [(**influences** + **inspirations** + **peers**) + (**accomplices** + [**Paul** + **Hughes**])] that might have [participated/precipitated] the tragedy of 2050 [refer: "An End of Us: An Ontological and Epistemological Discourse on The Forever Dust"].

We hope that you find [(designated output): [**Hughes**, **Paul**]] helpful and informative.

agent 66.14.7.050
primary avatar re: [**Hocking**, **Peter**]: [inquiry **#77.75.140**]
la biblio["o]mnithèque universelle

[/read]
[/run]

Δ

[/search] complete:
[display]

search results: [[**Paul** + **Hughes**] + [**forever** + **dust**]]: [translate: standard]:
author: [...] Dela[...]unay].
title: "of His loss, of His ruin."
publication: *Ein Journal des Instituts für die Erforschung des Heiligenscheineffektes.*

[recovery team notes signal shatter; text incomplete.]
[*la biblio["o]mnithèque universelle* confirms textual probability to statistical significance +/-45%]

excerpts:

...] and upon his disappearance in 2005, on the eve of his twenty-seventh birthday, friends and family simply assumed that he was hiding from his long-before prophesied death, perhaps on a beach, perhaps on the road. He'd spoken of it all the time, that ouija board prediction; few knew just how much it had terrified him.

Those of his immediate circle who had actually read his books might have recognized in his disappearance the opening theme of his third speculative fiction novel.* Solipsistic, self-indulgent to the extreme of alienating his potential audience, he'd gone into hiding after its completion. He somehow felt responsible for the deaths of fictional characters, whom he seemed to believe actually existed, actually lived and died in nearby parallel existences.

By 2006, people had stopped looking for him.

By 2010, his books had started to come true.

*refer: Hughes, Paul Evan. *broken*. New York: Silverthought Press, 2010.

> broken: Alpha: 1.4.0: 17 December 2002.
>
> *He'd disappeared.*
>
> *They searched, friends, family, the authorities. There was no evidence that he'd been to Panama City or Charleston or the writers' conference. They waited, but there was no word. No body. In time, many forgot.*
>
> *He'd disappeared.*

[/display]

Δ

[/search] complete:
[display]

search results: [[**Paul** + **Hughes**] + [**criticism** + **posthumous** + **negative**]]: [translate: standard] :
author: Thara Ruskin.
title: "[re][dundant]: PEH Pap in the Age of Transgressive Interdisciplinarity."
publication: *NY Times Book Review*, 08 February 2010.

[recovery team notes signal shatter; text incomplete.]
[*la biblio["o]mnithèque universelle* confirms textual probability to statistical significance +/-27%]

excerpts:

...] (Hughes's) writing grates, indeed, *chafes* at the spirit of modern speculative fiction. Steeped in the post-Delany aesthetic, the author's latest (and presumably last) offering is a confusing, dissatisfying and ultimately offensive collection of "transgression."

If we are to assume that P.E. Hughs (sic, henceforth) is in fact dead, then the literary world should rejoice that we will no longer be subjected to such self-indulgent rubbish. It is painfully obvious to even the casual reader that what Delany handled with such skill in *The Mad Man* (1994) and *Savage Bent* (2007), Hughs maims. Is *Broken* truly the gift he had intended for his sf idol? Doubtful. Delany, were he dead, would be screaming invective from his grave.

Essentially a string of space-suited dykeouts intermixed with the post-post-modernist ramblings of a mentally-ill young man from upstate New York, *Broken* is transgressive only in implication... What else would we expect from a self-published author? What he lacks in talent, he makes up for with vivid descriptions of sexual encounters, cannibalism, brutality. In essence, exactly what we don't need in a novel.

A message to Mr. Hughs, if he is reading this from an island populated by other victims of the age-twenty-seven curse: stay dead. Our slushpiles are already filled with similar pap.

[/display]

Δ

[/search] complete:
[display]

search results: [[**Paul** + **Hughes**] + [**criticism** + **posthumous** + **negative** + **response**]]: [translate: standard] :
author: SE Colmey.
title: a response to "[re][dundant]."
publication: *NY Times Book Review*, 14 February 2010.

[*la biblio["o]mnithèque universelle* confirms textual probability to statistical significance +/-14%]

full text:

To Ms. Ruskin:

I guess I'm partly to blame for the book that so upsets you, Paul Hughes's *Broken*. I found the manuscript in an old cardboard box he had willed to me should he disappear. Inside the box, there were photographs, letters, cards, things that meant nothing to anyone except him and me. At the bottom, I found a cd-r with the novel on it. Sorry that I disappointed your precious literary world so much. I just thought it was a story that should be told.

What's your problem with his book? That he wrote things that made people actually *feel*? That he had a following, people who would read everything he wrote just because of the way he had of drawing us in and making us think we were part of the book or his life? Some of us loved him. I understand it's your job to read books and write reviews, but your commentary wasn't a review of the novel, it was an attack on someone dear to many of us, someone who had more love to give than he knew what to do with. He knew how to write the things that most of us could never even begin to put into words, and his words were beautiful, magical things. Some of us regret letting him go.

And yes, I'm the Seattle girl in the books. I'm sure that taints your view of me. I'm too involved in this to see things clearly, right?

It's now been almost eight years since I saw him, five years since anyone else saw him. I just hope he finally found what he was looking for somewhere out there.

In closing, fuck you, Ms. Ruskin. It was a good book, better than anything you ever could have written. "Pap?" Nice word. Do you feel proud that you have a big vocabulary? Get over yourself.

Sincerely,
Mrs. SE Colmey

Chair, Fine Arts Department
Cornish College of the Arts
Seattle, WA

p.s. There's an "e" in his last name. Use it.

[/display]

Δ

[/search] complete:
[display]

search results: [[**an** + **end**] + [**forever** + **dust**]]: [translate: standard] :
author: unknown.
title: "An End of Us: An Ontological and Epistemological Discourse on The Forever Dust."
publication: *Ein Journal des Instituts für die Erforschung des Heiligenscheineffektes.*

[recovery team notes signal shatter; text incomplete.]
[*la biblio["o]mnithèque universelle* confirms textual probability to statistical significance +/-33%]

excerpts:

...] post-Judas anthropological teams from Sol-3 (14.7+) found little to suggest that the agent actually arose from "Black Space," that area of the AC system most affected by the destruction of Proxima Centauri. Intervention posts listening from the edge of the timeline reported no significant evidence of remaining industrial centers, much less the planetary production system that the creation of silver would have necessitated.

Perhaps it should be noted here that the anthro teams did eventually compile a comp/cont report on the status of the AC system pre- and post-war. That report is fundamental to understanding the conditions in that system that most likely were contributing factors to the madness of subject Maire and the Forever Dust she caused.

...] remember that teams arrived mid-war, and even under the cover of [...

...] major shipping lanes closed, and some evidence suggests that orbiting war platforms enacted a planetary blockade that forced the starvation of over ninety percent of the population. We can only imagine the desperation that the survivors felt while quite literally under the gun of the blockade platforms. Added to the lasting effects of biowar and engineered climate changes, the [...

...] without doubt tortured.

Torture is that most effective of appropriations: the victim in essence becomes the transitional commodity of the process. The information gathered during torture is only secondary in importance to the "owning" of the victim by the perpetrators. The process is one of excision. First, the victim is excised from her normal environment. Second, the victim's language is excised. Torture enacts a regression within the victim; it takes away the ability to communicate as one always has and instead replaces it with those first forays into verbal communication that we make as infants: cries of pain and fear. Third, the perpetrator restores just enough verbal ability to excise the required information from the victim.

Torture is an insistence. Without the benefit of [...

[/display]

Δ

[/search] complete:
[display]

search results: [[**Paul + Hughes**] + [**criticism + posthumous + negative**]]: [translate: standard] :
author: Thara Ruskin.
title: a response to SE Colmey.
publication: *NY Times Book Review*, 15 February 2010.

[*la biblio["o]mnithèque universelle* confirms textual probability to statistical significance +/-27%]

full text:

My dear Mrs. Colmey,

You are the *last* person I would have expected to write to defend the late Mr. Hughes. My apologies for misspelling his surname. Truthfully, I couldn't be bothered to care when I wrote my review; fact-checking is the responsibility of interns. Let us for the moment set aside personal differences (I am familiar with your painting practice and your work at revitalizing Cornish, and for that, I applaud you as an admirer) and analyze your involvement in PEH's books.

We all know the story of the manuscript at the bottom of the cardboard box; please don't insult my intelligence. I commend your willingness to seek the publication of the third novel in the *silver* series, given the unflattering character summary of you young Paul wrote in both *an end* and his online journals. I commend your willingness, yet lament it at the same time. What you've given the lament it at the same time. What you've given the literary world is a horrid tangle of self-serving scribble hardly worthy of a hand-written diary entry. Empower yourself, woman! Can't you see what he was writing about? You. He wrote about you in the most selfish, vain way possible; your side of the story has never been represented. All the readers are left with is but a shadow of whom I assume you truly are. That, in and of itself, is unforgivable. Had I been you, I'd have burned that cardboard box and been rid of that man.

We can only forgive so much to mental illness. I hope someday that you see what you've done. *Broken* will only serve to inspire future generations of conceited young authors.

Ms. Thara Ruskin,
associate editor
NY Times Book Review

[/display]

Δ

[/search] complete:
[display]

search results: [[**Paul** + **Hughes**] + [**personal** + **journal** + **2002**]]:
[translate: standard] :
author: Paul Evan Hughes.
title: "hovering."
publication: 28 June 2002.
[*la biblio["o]mnithèque universelle* confirms textual probability to statistical significance +/-50%]

full text:

through it all, i'm still crazy

this veil of dream i weave around myself

moon behind gauze: walk, because. that's all there is. stumble. through tripping grass, barefoot. thistles, prickers. shred. flesh. but at least i can feel something, anything. not him, not now. he's asleep.

stumble into black, smoke inhaled, exhaled, tears under gauze: moon. walk: because.

if this is a test... how much more can you take from me? how much more before i am broken completely?

whispers into that night. shards of a song. two songs. more. words run together, thoughts: none, because. there is this, but it isn't stillness. there is defeat. replacement. there are silences begun, and

all i ever wanted was forever.

there was happiness in those months, happiness in those years. in that life. in what existed between us and between Us. i've lost. so much. and. the mind. it consumes.

i've considered locking myself away in a place where chemicals will wash the blood from these wounds. for a while. just to get away. from this. from

and i trip, fall into a rut, grass, stems: gouging pathways into palms. mud. water. wash my face with this dirt, rub mud into those wounds so that they'll scar and i can be reminded someday of how far i once fell.

things will be okay. not now. not for a long time.

and tonight someone seemed genuinely concerned. thought i was joking at first. when i told her that i've slipped into a deep depression. slipped? falling, falling, feels so much like i'm still falling and there's no end in sight. subtractions. how could anyone ever love this? broken? man?

it is better that you've escaped me.

take

take me

take me to

take me, too.

[/display]

Δ

[/search] complete:
[display]

search results: [[**Paul** + **Hughes**] + [**MFA**] + [**Goddard**] + [**advisor** + **response**]]: [translate: standard] :
author: Pam Hall.

[recovery team notes signal shatter; text incomplete.]
[*la biblio[“o]mnithèque universelle* confirms textual probability to statistical significance +/-50%]

excerpts:

...] [I] feel pressed to note and name the “tone of voice” that runs through these pages. Paul, you have such a powerful (and yes, engaging, seductive, inspiring...) “positive” voice. I cannot tell you, as both your advisor, and as hopefully, a friend, how fine it is to share it and the energy that it carries... energy, which, yes, is also *in* the work and thinking and just kind of leaping out of everywhere[...

And here I want to take a small stab at pulling out what I suspect might be an important thread of practice even though it might be obvious. This shift in your voice, (and I suspect in your eye)... this joy, this more active attitude, represents for me what I have meant all along when I share my little platitudes about “practising your joy” or rigorous play. As artists, almost everything we do depends on our “seeing”... our gaze, our perceptual “attitude” or stance. Our work in the world begins with how we “see” the world, yes? With how it excites us, makes us wonder, invites our curiosity, or interrogation, or awe, or even anger... So it seems to me that part of our “task” is one of making ourselves, keeping ourselves in a state of sharp-eyedness... raw receptiveness... “good looker”... yes, “see-er/seer.” This is part of practice... fundamental I think to the next step or layer... which leads us into “making” or “poking at” meaning. And, if this little “theory” might have some truth, then it makes a profound difference “where we look from”, i.e. our Point of View, our stance, or what I call the “attitude of the gaze”. And we *need* more than one.

The gaze of “beginner’s mind”, of child enchanted, of pissed-off cynic, of broken heart, of deep despair, of wild, erotic heat, of heart in love, of brain on fire... are just a few that we might bring to the way we dance our work into the world. And just as I would argue for diverse vocabularies for expression, different strategies for different discourses, so would I argue for diverse “attitudes of gaze” or perceptual stances or POV’s[...

...]It really *is* the “eye of the beholder” that creates the thing “beheld”.

...] can we become fluent enough, flexible enough, skilled enough to select our lens, to call up that stance or attitude most needed by the notions we are dancing with, or are we victimized by a single purpose POV forever, and cursed to frame a lifetime’s vision from within a single “attitude”?

...] there is a fundamental thing afoot here, Paul, a “quickening”, a new way of “seeing/looking”... and it is beginning to sing through you... Pay attention to it. Find out how to call it up when needed[...

[/display]

∆

[/search] complete:
[display]

search results: [[**Paul** + **Hughes**] + [**music** + (**John** + **Cage** + **Farley** + {**middle** + **C**})]]: [translate: standard] :
author: Brandston, Ken.
title: "The New Cage: The Experimental Revival from Cornish to Prague."
publication: *Journal of the American Musicological Society,* February 2010.

[recovery team notes signal shatter; text incomplete.]
[*la biblio["o]mnithèque universelle* confirms textual probability to statistical significance +/-33%]

excerpts:

...]and consider the following journal entry recently decoded from the private writings of self-styled wunderkind Hughes:

> *...]newfound love of john cage's music now forever tarnished by biographical research. you should know why unless you're completely ignorant of cornish alumni.*
>
> *MethodStructureIntentionDisciplineNotationIndeterminacy InterpenetrationImitationDevotionCircumstancesVariableStructure NonunderstandingContingencyInconsistencyPerformance(I-VI). —"Dream": In a Landscape: John Cage.*
>
> *there has to be a reason for these webs.*

Mentor and ethnomusicologist Dr. Michael Farley presented an intriguing posthumous analysis of Hughes's musical mentalities:

"The Hughes boy... He was a different kind of young man. Please don't take that the wrong way. He just thought too much. The kind of thinking a person does when they can't sleep, but they also can't stop listening. Not hearing; it's not an issue of hearing. He couldn't stop listening.

“He told me once that he’d figured out that that ringing in his ears was a ‘C.’ Took him a while, since he wasn’t the kind of technical musical student I usually get. I asked him to play middle C on a piano once in my Musics of the World class, but he couldn’t.

“His dad had tinnitus, too.

“But he said that that sound, that ringing, it was a ‘C,’ and I played it on the piano, and he just nodded his head.

“He had a theory, said it came to him one night when he couldn’t stop listening. He thought that maybe people were drawn to music that featured the note of their natural resonating frequencies. He told me he’d gone through dozens of songs that had touched him deeply at some level, and ‘C’ was a prominent tone in each of them. He was convinced that those songs literally resonated with his heart.

“There’s a thing called a seiche wave. It’s a wave that travels on the surface of a lake, or any landlocked water. Barely discernible. Sometimes it takes minutes, sometimes hours to oscillate completely. It’s the natural resonance of the earth.

“That boy got caught in a seiche wave. Maybe he heard a ‘C.’

“That’s why he disappeared.”

[/display]

Δ

[/search] complete:
[display]

search results: [[**Paul** + **Hughes**] + [**personal** + **journal** + **2004**]]:
[translate: standard] :
author: Paul Evan Hughes.
untitled.
publication: 12 February 2004.

[*la biblio["o]mnithèque universelle* confirms textual probability to statistical significance +/-35%]

full text:

i am complicit in my own desolation.

no matter how brilliant they say you are, how sweet, charming, intelligent, no matter how innovative your work is or your theories are, no matter how all-around great they tell you you are, the cold, hard truth is that you fall asleep at night alone, and in the end, there will be no one to hold your hand and watch you die. there will always be someone prettier, more interesting, more spiritual, closer, bigger, better, faster, to fill the time with flesh and sound.

there is no enlightenment.
there is nothing left to enlighten.

[/display]

Δ

[/search] complete:
[display]

search results: [[**Paul + Hughes**] + [...signal corrupted...]]: [translate: standard] :
author: [...signal corrupted...]
title: [...signal corrupted...]
publication: [...signal corrupted...]

[*la biblio["o]mnithèque universelle* confirms textual probability to statistical significance +/-50%]

full text:

dear jacob,

i've dismantled my life completely in these two weeks.

dear jacob, i know i haven't spoken to you in a while—it's been difficult. it's been the happiest almost-year since you left, and i apologize for substituting contentedness for communication. i owe you more than silences. the time i visited you, just before the dismantling began in earnest, i didn't give you my full attention. i was selfish. i didn't listen, didn't really talk. just looked at a rock and wondered what's left of you.

dear jacob, i know you would have loved her. and i know you now know everything i've collected of her. and i know that i would have been the one sobbing at the fire.

it's now been a year since that first kiss, and i think i've lost her.

forever is a difficult word. you know that better than i can until i'm there.

i'm leaving this place, and i've started to box things up. the dismantling has ruined me. i can't apologize enough, because i don't know what to apologize for—it's me, just me, all of me, and i don't think i can get it right.

dear jacob, i understand the how and why now, and every day for weeks has been dissuasion. it's been a fog. i've slipped back into so many habits. you know—the drinking, forgetting to eat. 176lbs now for the first time since you left. i've spiraled off into productivity, but what products could substitute? i shouldn't have driven home.

god, i wish you could have seen me this year. almost-year.

because i'd never had a partner, never given myself so completely, never loved so deeply, and now i think i've lost it all. and the worst part is the maybe—maybe she still loves me, maybe there's a chance, but i can't operate like that. i have no great goals of getting back into the game—the thought of being with anyone else makes me sick. the thought of her being with anyone else makes me want to stop breathing.

i've started stuttering again.

if you could have seen us—

i don't know what to do anymore. it's all broken. there is no home, and i've substituted moving away for any semblance of trying to improve my situation. you know the friends—they're gone now, married off and busy. no one's visited since may. i'm always the one to drive to visit. and home—how do we define that? the farm has gone. under new management. and the constant—every day for almost-a-year, she was my constant, and maybe i shouldn't have ascribed that responsibility to her, but i thought that's what partners were. now it's lost, and i stay awake at night wondering if i'll ever see her again, if she'll ever love me again. because i can't imagine a lifetime without her.

if you could have seen me that night—you would have known.

dear jacob, i'm on the edge, and i know how it must have been for you. at least i can suspect.

but i won't be visiting anytime soon. i'm sorry and not in the same breath.

i'm so lucky to have been given the time with her i was. few are given the opportunity to love like that. i know i'm greedy and selfish to want more, but i don't know how else to be. i'm so lucky—do you understand that? to have loved like that—to continue to love like that, even if it's only me.

i can only hope that something remains of this almost-year.

dear jacob, i'm fighting right now. i know you understand. because even with you gone, you're still the one who listens.

i love her.

let me broadcast that with everything i have left—i love her. and if that love is resigned to echoes and sunrises, if it's only a box of plastic or a folder of postcards, let it be known that my heart continues to be hers. and i'll hide away from the world. i'm done with the game. i'll rebuild in a ghost house and make a bonfire pit. i'll set and overmeet goals and my heart will be hers, as flawed as it is, as broken as i am, because i've never wanted anything more than this. anyone more than her.

i've lost my best friend.

dear jacob, i'm so tired, but i'm fighting. there's no room for surrender.

a year ago... i can't write through the tears anymore. so much of me has been excised.

and i know words are weapons and this broadcast could ruin further, but i can't keep it inside anymore. it would have been one year today since that first kiss, since i started to fall the best fall. i'm so scared to tell her how i feel, and i can only hope that she knows, beg that she remembers. because i gave her the best of me i could, and i don't think i did enough. it's a startling realization to know now that my best will never be good enough.

dear jacob, i'm coming home.

[**signal faded.**]
[/display]

∆

[/search] complete:
[display]

search results: [[**Paul + Hughes**] + [...signal corrupted...]]: [translate: standard] :
author: [...signal corrupted...]
title: [...signal corrupted...]
publication: [...signal corrupted...]

[*la biblio["o]mnithèque universelle* confirms textual probability to statistical significance +/-50%]

full text:

...] [i] know you told me to go to bed, but there was editing to do and i wanted to write to you before i tried to sleep.

i'm sorry i haven't called. i know it's ridiculous and i can call and leave a message and i know i should, but i don't want to interrupt and i want to talk to you when you have time and i know you have time for sure. i don't know how to do this. i think i've been doing a bad job, and i apologize.

...] [i have had] dreams of you, and i've looked through england pictures and all the other pictures. missing you is my constant. and it's something i don't want to get good at. i don't want to be good at missing you. that's why i'd really like to see you on saturday. i don't mind driving, and i wouldn't presume to spend the night, anyway. i'd just like to be within a distance of you where i can feel you there. i don't know if that makes sense. i never imagined that you'd feel farther away in vt than you did in england, but it's happened, and i know i have to deal with that. i miss my best friend, my lover and partner. i miss us. broken hearts can heal, but it's like the heart is made of glass. scar tissue can form around the pieces, but every time it beats, you can feel the sharp edges. i've never felt so lost.

...] people come into and leave our lives, but we keep going. i'm trying so hard to keep going, but i'd give anything to hold your hand again. i keep busy and do things that most people never do, most people never have seventeen authors excited over the opportunity of being published, and i'm the one offering that opportunity, but everything just feels like i'm going through the paces, sitting in front of the camera putting on a strong face and saying that i'm okay, but everyone knows that [i'm] lying. the cashier jokes playfully while checking my id and it makes me sick. i'm in love with someone i'm afraid i'll never see again. my dad says i need to find me a big indian woman to keep me warm in this cold old house this winter, and i know he's just joking, we have the same sense of humor, but there's no one else i want to hold on to. sisters hint at passing my number to really nice 36-year-old divorcees, two kids, like to read, and i feel like breaking. does any of this make sense? i know i'm tangenting. but i sit here and wonder what set of paints i could wrap for you, what little drawing with "never give up" on it. i looked for you my entire life. and if i could apologize for the times i hurt you, i would, if i could erase the stupid fights we had over nothing, i would, but that was a part of us as well, and erasing any of us would be to alter something that was beautiful.

so i say goodnight to you each night and i hold my pillow and pretend it's you and i feel the pieces of glass grinding. i'm making a living on words and these words don't even begin to approach what i feel.

i don't know. i don't know how to write what my heart's telling me. it's been so difficult, and i know you know that, it's just. i don't know.

i stood in the rain yesterday and replaced the broken clutch in my truck, just in case you wanted to get together this weekend. i hope we can, even if for a few hours. i know it'll be difficult, and i don't know how i'd be able to keep my eyes dry, but i miss you so much.

life's composed of moments. i think back, and it's so overwhelming. "cover my feet" and the way you said NO, seeing you from across antique shops, holding hands walking up the hill at the grange. sitting on rocks with you and eating cheese by the water, washing dishes, washing the entire floor's dishes while you cooked. running for buses and trains and standing in awe at paintings and just curled up together on my futon after you got to my apartment. the way you said my name. i've never felt closer, never felt safer. and it's so hard to let go of that—i don't want to let go of that, don't want to experience you through memory, because i've almost forgotten the scent of your hair, something i realized nights ago, and i'm holding on so hard to what i have left, the feel of your cheeks on my lips, the taste of you, the size and squeeze of your hand, the way we fit together spooned, or with your arm around me from behind. half asleep and waking up to *i love you, paul hughes, so much*, a kiss and you fell back asleep. how can i give that up?

i love you. this is a love letter—they all are, they always have been, and when i'm gone someday and all that's left of me is my words, someone will know that i was in love and my world was beautiful.

i love you, [...

[**signal faded.**]
[/display]

Δ

[run]:
[read]:

author: [Hughes, Paul]
title:
publication:
[system interject]: [**deepblack**]: [ops: **eyes-only**]: **DESTROY AFTER READING.**

Paranoid: Very High
Schizoid: Moderate
Schizotypal: High
Antisocial: High
Borderline: Very High
Histrionic: Very High
Narcissistic: Very High
Avoidant: Very High

Dependent: Very High
Obsessive-Compulsive: High

[recovery team notes signal shatter; text incomplete.]
[*la biblio["o]mnithèque universelle* confirms textual probability to statistical significance +/-50%]

recovered excerpts:

...][I], Paul Evan Hughes, of sound body and questionable mind, do this sixteenth day of March, 2005 at 10:14AM, write this document in my own hand, which should be considered a holographic confession of my misdeeds and the wrongs for which I wish to repent. A fundamental confusion and misinterpretation of my intents this last decade has solidified my decision to subtract myself from this timeline and attempt to repair the damage that I have done. What follows is a brief account of the circumstances that effected this decision and the course of action I have undertaken to[...

...]was a desire to create a virtual space where kindred spirits could gather. Of course, the kindred spirits drawn to such a place were[...

...]transgressing the line between real and virtual spaces, hoping to validate that which I had created in a space that was not a space, a world outside of time and[...

...]and how much farther, how much further could we transgress? Maybe if I'd chosen a closer semblance of reality instead of that blurred[...

...]unrest appeared not long after the return to the digital world. Those drunken collisions of flesh, those muted penetrations and slicks of sweat[...

...]was complicit in that process. I am complicit in my own desolation. To surrender to temptation, to bridge the virtual and physical worlds, to give in to that desire to[...

...]giving in to loneliness. I knew then that it would all change, that[...

...][I] had birthed new notions of virtuality. Dissatisfied, I took it upon myself to destroy that world.

...]began the dissolution of the[...

...]before reaching the breaking point. It wasn't long before[...

...]and yes, an ego the size of Sedna, an intense jealousy that at that gathering I hadn't found the relationship that I suspected might arise from that breach of worlds. There are differences between electricity and flesh, heightened by observation from feet of air, not fiber. How many young men create and destroy empires of zeros and ones? How many young[...

...]speech almost a decade before, I had prophesied what would become the core of my unrest, urging my school to focus on the students, not on the then-new invention of the "information superhighway." I sensed the impending societal shift from physicality to virtuality, and now, in these last days, I have seen the deadly results. Communicative technologies have created worlds that at first might appear to contain just as many inherent exceptions to truthfulness as reality, but I am now convinced that[...

...]asked me to define my concept of transgression. Is it my recurring practice of acquiring and exploiting others' words and actions for my own purposes? Is it the desire to breach and destroy? Or is it perhaps the willingness to let strangers so far into my heavily-guarded, subjectively-constructed notion of history and "reality" that they can't ever completely escape? I have no answers. I realize that I have lied, cheated, and stolen, as painter Jack Beal insisted I do in one of my first studio art classes in 1996, if I ever wanted to become anything in life.

...]virtual world that I began and ultimately killed was one of intricate deceits.

...]that I have maligned and fabricated my art from subjective memory filtered through a rapidly-dissembling mind. What memories have I constructed of my best friend? "Best" friend? Is that because he was truly my best friend or just because he's dead now and can't disagree? What shames have I subjected her to? I loved her, but was that love as strong during our relationship as recall would have an audience believe after she left me? How much of this is a lie? I can no longer tell the difference between past and dream, and I fear that as long as I invite viewers, readers, strangers into my soul, I'll never be able to discern truth. So much of me is performance now that[...

...]stealing words, shattering memories, placing words into strangers'[...

I don't know who I am anymore.

...]know what I have to do, what I've known for years. I will take this jihad to the[...

...]if I can only secure this reality, if I can only guarantee that this soul, these lives[...

So I confess these transgressions. I will reclaim reality. I will[...

It begins now.

[/read]
[/run]

AUTUMN'S SCION

AUTUMN'S SCION

Alina screams. She sobs, throwing herself against the display until her tiny hands wilt. West hears flesh split, fingers crack. She keeps beating against the glass, keeps beating, keeps screaming, even as he pulls her away, the stubs of fingers smearing that image with bloody letters; hers is a language written in despair.

West holds her tightly, but she still struggles, her crumpled hands pressing against him only jarring loose more of that loss; she seeps through his shirt, and he feels warm copper run down through the hair on his chest, pause to circumvent his navel. She eventually relents, slumps into him, allows herself to bury her eyes under his jawbone, anything to force away the screen, to erase that image.

West watches it all, even as he holds Alina so she can't.

❧

Inhale: no lung, no mouth, but why the sensation of drowning, of choking, the scent of burning flesh when there is no nose, no body?

All around him, silver. Waves still came back to slap at his shallow corpse, near-corpse. It burned; it froze.

He struggled to sit up and remembered that things were no longer attached to him in the way he remembered. His starboard nacelle lazily rose, slammed back into the silver ocean, stirring the metal again, angering what sensors he had left operational.

The nacelle crawled through half-crystallized mercury slurry until it met his main chassis. He was disturbed but not surprised to find that his pelvic fin had been shattered on the impact, and his caudal fin was twisted into an array of broken metallish.

s

paul hughes((?))

come here ((?))

cover my feet ((?))

rupture rend rive split cleave

Maire had pierced through his chest, heavy silver armor cracking and splintering before her. Reflex forced his head back; agony kept it there as spasms wracked his entire form. The hole in his hub was slick with his blood, mechanicals, the shimmer of venting containment chamber exhaust. He finally settled in the shallow silver, nacelles digging into the flooding ground.

Too tired to move his port nacelle. Too broken.

Starboard nacelle feels around the hole. The wingtip snaps off, falls to his belly, slides into the silver.

Focus, but

It's flooding, that alien, that lifeblood. Choking, gasping. Somewhere, a line of code reminds him that there's a human buried inside that ruined sculpture of metal.

i'm sorry

i'm

His nacelle falls back into the ocean, the wingblades now useless.

i'm

❧

and the ten years after the Unravel Moment saw the birth of a metageneration.

In his divine wisdom, the Episiarch Paul Evan Hughes, beginning with that day of flights and flames, engineered a corridor into Upwhen, bringing order to all improbability.

❧

"And if your heart should wander, if someone more interesting should come along to fill up those places that I couldn't reach with a bigger dick, a bigger brain, or a bigger heart, go to him; follow him to the place you'll call home. Live in that new love, breathe him into and through yourself, cover your past in new memories and sights, new tastes and nights without sleep, just your gasping, grating, puddling, and love him; love him as you'd loved me, but deeper, faster, harder. Love him as if he's forever, as if he's home. Forget this... *everything*, this person, the moments we breathed as one, when I entered you and we felt fire, that tide, that blood. Love him with ease and joy, overwhelmed and filled up. Love him entirely, because know that someday I'll find you."

He squeezed and felt her voice try to escape from beneath his thumb. Her neck was so thin.

"Know that I'll find you."

❧

There are of course connections that imply a verifiable cosmology, a totality of phenomena constituting all of time and space. Beyond theoretical physics, string theory and the anthropic principle, there is a fundamental symmetry to existence that is better described through a defined set of characteristics in the known megaverse embodied in the form of a particular set of children born in the summer and autumn of the second year of the third millennium.

At the St. Elizabeth Regional Medical Center in Lincoln, Nebraska, early on the morning of August 16th, 2002, a boy was born to Tyler Jennings and Jessamyn Smith. He emerged screaming, bloodied from the tear he had rent in his mother. His parents named him after his paternal uncle who had been killed eleven months prior: David.

A midwife delivered a daughter to Judeh Hassan, widow of industrialist Antonio Cervera, at the Cervera estate in Los Angeles on September 9th, 2002, almost a year to the day Cervera had been killed. The couple had tried unsuccessfully for seven years to have a child, and fortunately, enough of Cervera's semen had been cold-stored at a fertility clinic to allow an in-vitro fertilization to finally take place. Judeh Hassan named her daughter Antonia, in honor of the child's father.

At the Hyannisport Compound on September 15th, 2002, Kara Anne Kennedy and Michael Allen announced the birth of their third child, a daughter, Abrah Allen-Kennedy.

Rhonda McClure gave birth to a fourteen-pound son on the night of September 16th, 2002 at the Keweenaw Memorial Medical Center in Laurium, Michigan. Rhonda had narrowed down the possible fathers to two suspects: Robert Hodge and Ray Shore, two members of the Harkness, Michigan high school baseball team. Her zippers had dispositions that forbade distinctions. She named her son Robert Ray McClure. She called him Buddy.

Hank the Cowboy flickered to life in the mind of Los Angeles screenwriter Les Harris at 2:00am on September 17th, 2002 when the lights came up at the Dresden and Harris realized the girl he'd been talking to was a transvestite prostitute.

Honeybear Brown's final stitch went into place on September 21st, 2002 at a sweatshop on 7th Avenue in New York City. Creator Desree "Sugar" Williams quickly bundled him into a DKNY rucksack before her co-workers could steal her design.

James and Destiny Richter's first son arrived in the world on September 11th, 2002 in silence, his skin pallid, a caul covering his face. His parents were not allowed to hold him until three months later after extensive reconstruction of congenital birth defects to his respiratory system. Finally able to breathe on his own, his parents took baby James Richter, Jr. home to a suburb of Phoenix, Arizona.

༄

"How're they taking it?"

His wife, or the photon sculpture thereof, shrugged. "You know. Everyone had expected it for a while."

"Wish I could be there."

"I know."

"Tell them. It's nothing personal."

"I know, hon."

"Caroline was a great woman. A great woman. The Council and Cabinet extends their deepest—"

"David—" Abrah Kennedy-Jennings reached out. "You don't have to get political."

He sighed, slumped farther into his chair. "I'm—You know what I mean."

"I know."

Even through the jittery, static-veiled avatar, he sensed a deeper trouble, scrutinized the way his wife's eyebrows begged a concern. "What's wrong? Not your aunt. Something else."

"David, I—"

The door to his office slicked open, lines of conversation emerging in mid-thought from the three, four men and women walking through.

"Mister President, we have a situation." How many times had he heard that these last few years? How many times had it not led to heartburn?

Breine Frost sat down without invitation, turned to the hologram link. "Abrah, I gotta steal your husband."

"Of course, Mister Vice-President." Jennings hated the resignation in the sculpture's tin voice.

"I'm sorry, baby. I'll call you back after these bastards are done with me." He smiled at his vice and secretaries. "Love you, Abrah."

He waved his hand to the cut wave.

"David, I'm—"

A carbon wedge severed the signal between Hyannisport and Washington.

"Okay, Breine. What's wrong now?"

From the communications room of her family's compound, Abrah Kennedy-Jennings completed her thought, a whisper; her hand unconsciously traced her navel.

"I'm pregnant."

"Refer to the threat matrix from thirty-one August two-thousand thirty-six."

"Nothing big. Some rumbles overseas, a riot in—"

"Refer domestic."

"Breach of security at LAX, mining accident in—"

"Bingo."

"Wyoming?"

"That's the one."

"Why's it even listed? No imminent—"

"It's imminent now."

Jennings frowned. "What's going on?"

Frost turned. "Tony?"

Secretary of War Antonia Cervera lifted what appeared to Jennings to be a model airplane. "This is a print from our latest scans."

"Scans of what?"

Frost took the model from Cervera. "Dave, this bird is in Wyoming. Buried under a mountain." He handed the print to the president.

"You've got—"

"Not kidding."

"And we're—"

"We've got Milicom teams cordoning off the area." Cervera clicked a data spinner into Jennings' table display.

Jennings exhaled audibly, his face reddened by the slowly-rotating image of a bogey buried under a transparent mountain, the path of mining tunnels overlaid in a pale blue grid.

"Where are we now?"

"We've cut an entrance. Found an access port. Took a hell of a beam to even scratch the surface. We have teams on standby, ready to insert at your go call."

"And we have no idea what this thing is?"

Frost shrugged. "It's not an airplane."

A tickle behind his eyes, not pleasant in the least.

"Send them in."

"They'll insert asap."

"Send the order and head to the bunker. Get my plane ready; I'm going to Wyoming."

"David—"

"No buts. You should know that by now."

Frost cracked a grin. "Sure I do."

❧

"But what if..." He sipped the fine Tempranillo, La Riota, vintage 2001. Full and rich in his mouth, a complicated density of flavor. "What if there's so much more than this?"

His date played through a stack of untouched dwarf asparagus stalks, swirling blood sauce into eddies, inadvertently scraping silver against bone. "Sorry." Blush. "What do you mean?"

James Richter wiped his mouth, draped the napkin back over his uniform slacks. His eyes, a disarming gray, swept left, right, focused ahead as he leaned over the table, closer to her, as if he were about to reveal a state secret to the girl his few friends had deemed "perfect" for him. At least his white friends had.

"Your Deep Eyes have shown us what we'd expected all along: this galaxy's alone out here, separated from all the other castaway birth matter of our universe by great deserts of—" Hands gestured, eyes squinted—

"Nothing. The Eyes have confirmed the insulation of galactic bodies by expanses of immense probability collapse. Our present tech doesn't even begin to approach traversibility survival. The distance between galactic clusters is so incomprehensibly vast... Our slowships would freeze up at the edge. Generation ships wouldn't make it beyond a million solar measures. There's just nothing out there to power on."

She enthralled him, this mathematician who worked for the Milicom Cosmotech. Hope Benton. He couldn't have conversations this deep with anyone.

"There's two types of galaxies, correct?"

"Spiral and elliptical. A few random distributions thrown into the mix."

"And how many has MC charted now?"

She laughed, not in jest, but at the answer she was about to give. "We're approaching a million billion charted galaxies." Sip of wine: empty glass. "What you laymen might refer to as a 'shitload.'"

"And in this 'shitload' of galaxies the Eyes have seen, has there been any successful contact?"

"Contact? With little green men?"

"Green men, white men, brown men..."

"Zero contact."

"Something happens to the signals."

"As they pass through the inter-galactic deserts."

"The signals bounce back?"

"They come back flawed. The message is still there, but it's distorted beyond translation. Something in the galactic barrier deserts fucks with our beams. Even our brightest, deepest lasers return to us sounding like underwater gibberish."

Richter raised his index finger. "Let me propose a hypothesis." Devilish grin.

"Here it comes." Benton shook her head, bemused. "More of your Omega dogma?"

"Maybe." He pushed his plate away. "Maybe in each of those galaxies, there's a system just like Sol's—"

Eyes rolled.

"And in each of those near-Sol systems, there's a planet just like Earth—"

"I've heard it before, James."

"And on each of those near-Earths, at the exact moment your Deep Eyes broadcast the SETI beam, their near-Deep Eyes broadcast their near-SETI beams—"

"Impossible."

"Not impossible. Your Cosmotech colleagues simply misinterpret the alien beams as garbled reflected transmissions. They try again, get the same result, eventually give up because there's this big mysterious impossible barrier surrounding our galaxy, a desert of heat death cold, in which our galaxy and a million billion other galaxies are simply oases. Can you just consider the possibility? What that would mean for the nature of our existence? That we're just one of a million billion trillion galaxies in which a million billion trillion of our worlds co-exist, albeit separated by cold, impassable distances?"

"I—" She studied her empty glass, moved to fill it from the dwindling bottle. "I can consider the possibility. But the signals aren't—"

"They're garbage. I realize. But with no common ground, no points of contextualization, how could you begin to recognize it as language, as communication? Of course your systems are reporting it as dicked-over return signal. Our machines jump to the conclusion that every attempt at communicating beyond the galactic barrier will fail because of an incomprehensible physical obstruction. But what's out there, between the clusters? Nothing. We can't begin to theorize why a beam of light would stop and come back to us. Doesn't it make more sense to conclude that it's getting through, that it's reaching someone, and they're talking back at us?"

"Or maybe their Hope Bentons are frustrated and coming to the same conclusions?"

"I knew I'd win you over."

"Win me over?" Her hand attempted to cover his, but his fingers still poked out underneath. "I said I'd consider it, James Richter, not that I'd convert."

"Once you go black, baby." Eyes crease with hard-fought lines.

"Oh, get over yourself!" A hand squeezes a hand. "Want to get out of—"

An alarm chimes.

"Shit." Richter reached for his link. "I have to take this. Sorry. Bee are bee." As he stood, the server placed the bill on the table. Richter pointed at Benton. "Don't pay that." He winked and left for the front of the restaurant.

He ducked into the coat room and flashed his Milicom badge at the attending employee. "Out." The young man blinked at the silver circle and trotted from the room, closing the doors behind him.

Richter activated his link, which blanketed him in a privacy wall constructed from flickering photon discharge. Within the cylinder, a smaller holo sputtered to life, confident in its recipient's identity after genetic identification and the glare of a biometrics heuristic.

Benton watched as her date nearly jogged back to the table. Something crawled behind those eyes, those gorgeous gray eyes.

"Sorry, Hope." He placed the bill and a debit slip into the table's scanner, at the same time ordering another bottle of the Tempranillo. "I gotta go, but you should stay. Call some friends. Put it on my numbers."

"But—Where are you—"

"Wyo—Fuck. Sorry, can't give you details." He stooped to give her an absent-minded hug, stood, then bent down again to kiss her cheek. "I'm sorry, it's work. You look beautiful tonight." He cradled her cheek in his hand.

"Okay, well, when will you be—"

"Don't know. Listen, there's transport waiting. I have to—I'm sorry. I'll see you soon, I promise." He turned and walked away, not thinking of anything but "work."

Hope Benton sat at the table until the bottle of wine arrived. The server poured her a glass, but when he'd left, she filled it to the top.

Wyoming?

She wondered if she would see James Richter again.

⁂

In the fall of 2021, some things happened.

David Smith Jennings, on leave from Milicom Arlington, visited the childhood home of his friend Gregory Bates in Roanoke, Virginia, with their fellow officers Antonia Cervera, Michael Balfour and James Richter. The Bates family home, a sprawling manse in the Neo-Plantation style, became the site of a weekend party before the Milicom soldiers had to return to base for a silver anniversary memorial. The Mayflower Hills Bates estate overlooked a tributary of the Roanoke River, and it was on those banks that one Robert Ray "Buddy" McClure attempted to rape young Lieutenant Cervera as the party raged on just behind them. McClure, a vagrant from Harkness, Michigan, who for almost a year had been hitching the east coast, making a living from itinerant roofing, and who had in fact been hired by the Bates family to renovate the roof of their guest house, suffered a fractured collar bone from Cervera's self-defense, but still managed to successfully sodomize his victim after knocking her unconscious with a rock.

Upon waking her hung-over colleagues the next morning and contacting the authorities, Cervera was able to successfully identify her attacker from a police lineup. McClure had been found and detained just hours after the rape by the Roanoke PD on drunk and disorderly charges.

Because crimes against Milicom personnel were federal offenses, the McClure rape case went before the federal court located in Roanoke. Judge Hannah Kilbourne oversaw the case. Attorney Abrah Allen-Kennedy acted as McClure's defense attorney. Allen-Kennedy, with the star power of her lineage and the sheer brilliance of her academic career, having graduated high school at age eight, Colgate at twelve and OU Law at fourteen, drew a crowd of several thousand reporters to the Roanoke courthouse. The proceedings were broadcast live on Court TV 1-7.

No one was really surprised when Allen-Kennedy secured McClure's release with a not-guilty verdict.

The once-close friendship between Milicom colleagues David Jennings and Antonia Cervera effectively ended once Jennings revealed that he was dating Allen-Kennedy, whom he had met at a Roanoke bar on the last day of court proceedings in the McClure trial.

Hounded by paparazzi as they left the bar, Jennings and Allen-Kennedy ducked into a toy store on the next block. In the back, stacked between displays of Let's Eat Meat Elmo and Mistress Beasley dolls, Jennings found twenty small stuffed bears. Their design was charming in its simplicity, and the lack of a plastic nose nub gave the toys a humble demeanor. Jennings purchased one of the bears for the giggling lawyer. Outside of the store, he ripped the Honeybear Brown tag from the bear's ear.

She held his hand as they flagged down a cab and returned to her hotel.

They watched the hotel room television under the preface of "just hanging out," but the show didn't hold either of their interests. They seemed more interested in exploring each other, and after half an hour, Jennings turned the "Hank the Cowboy" show off with the remote in his right hand as his left made the daring jump beneath Allen-Kennedy's black silk thong.

Network executives from CBS cancelled "Hank the Cowboy" the next week, citing demographic analyses that showed that even the rapidly-fading Boomer generation was sick of CGI retro-dramas. The program spent the next three years bouncing between the E!, Comedy Central and Sci Fi networks before being shelved for good. Unfortunately, all surviving digital copies and source material for the series were lost in the cave-in of a secure archive facility in Wind River, Wyoming, along with three original James McNeill Whistler paintings and an original paper copy of Paul Evan Hughes's *silverthought* trilogy.

These things happen.

❧

"Cunt!"

Les Harris, creator and former screenwriter for the "Hank the Cowboy" series, threw the framed photograph of his wife at the wall link. The frame snapped, the glass shattered, but the only damage to the link was a small divot the frame's corner had inscribed into the plastic face. Harris went into the basement, unlocked his handgun from its safe, and shot himself in the right temple because his wife had decided to leave him after hearing that "Hank" had been cancelled and CBS was terminating Les's contract.

"Cunt!"

Jealous co-worker Sandra Chappelle pushed Sugar Williams to the ground in an alley off of 7th Avenue and wiped Williams' blood from her swishblade with a used tissue. Chappelle remembered friendly discussions over hurried lunches about starting a new toy line with Williams. When Sugar took Sandra's "Honeybear Brown" design and secured a lucrative deal with Mattel, and when every tabloid in every newsstand in the city broadcast a photograph of Abrah Allen-Kennedy running from the photog with a Honeybear in tow, someone had to die.

"Cunt!"

Antonia Cervera remembered the word she'd spoken to Abrah Allen-Kennedy after she'd gotten rapist Buddy McClure off. Months later, Cervera saw Kennedy walking with David Jennings in downtown Arlington, their hands held. Already furious about the rumors that her former friend and that bitch lawyer were engaged, this seeming-confirmation of a relationship pushed her over the edge, and as the happy couple walked by, Cervera lashed out, swiping two deep, two shallow nail marks across the left side of the lawyer's face. Cervera flicked the tiny bits of face from underneath her fingernails and spit at Jennings, who knocked her to the sidewalk with a reflex right hook.

Fourteen years later, standing as Jennings was sworn into presidential office, Cervera saw the faint, poorly-concealed lines on the impending First Lady's face. She smiled. Forgiveness only goes so far. Abrah was still a cunt.

❧

The site command center was situated in a volcanic bubble seven miles beneath the surface. Jennings noted the fresh fill of quickcrete that composed the center's floor. Scientists, soldiers: the room hummed with activity, but that hum quieted to a tickling underwhine as he entered and three dozen people turned to salute.

"As you were." He approached the main display in at the bubble's core. "Show me."

Cervera nodded to three technicians. Lights dimmed and the projector spun to life.

"Jesus fuck." Jennings knew his whisper wasn't quite.

The design was simple: a flattened-egg hub connected two rounded triangular nacelles. The slowly-rotating display indicated breaches in the hulls of both "wings" where molten rock had infiltrated the form. The wings had presumably once pointed to sharp tips, but both had been sheared away in asymmetrical impact. Rock had filled the vessel with earthen cancer.

"How old?"

"Preliminary estimates? Sixty, seventy million years."

Everything we know is wrong; everything we know isn't.

"I get the distinct impression you've been hiding something from me, Tony."

She hesitated. The command center filled with glances, cleared throats, busywork.

"Tell me."

"David—It's superblack. Need-to-know. We don't—"

"Override."

"I can't—"

"Override, before I lose my temper. Named orders?"

"President Holmdel, but it's deeper than that. It's old."

"Let me guess... Truman? Eisenhower? Override superblack. Release. I assume we're all friends here?"

"They're cleared."

Jennings smirked. "Phantom government strikes again. Am I really the Commander-in-Chief?"

"David—"

"We've got a UFO in our soil. That's some serious *Chariots of the Gods* shit. I think that makes me need-to-know. Holmdel's dead."

Cervera nodded and gestured toward the display's touchpad. "Bloody up."

Jennings' eyes drew to slits, the line of sight between their eyes unbroken as he placed his palm on the machine surface. "Do it."

"System, add user: Jennings, David Smith. President. Authorization: Cervera, Antonia. War Sec. Run: Holmdel

Directive, re: Von Daniken, subsystems Peru, Bolivia: Nazca, Titicaca. Superblack release: mark."

Jennings gritted his teeth as the sampler scraped genetic confirmation from his palm.

"Learn something new every day."

"David—"

"Tell me."

❧

You want a story? I'll tell you a story. I'll tell you about Lago Titicaca, our HQ in La Paz, the three-chip whores just begging for a *soldado americano quente*'s company. Holmdel had been in office just six years when we found the pieces. After the annexation. Before the shit found the fan. Looking at that chamber under the mountain, I remembered. Why hadn't we at least tried to piece the puzzle back together? I'll tell you. Bodies. Dated to around sixty-five. Not age. Million years. Thousands of skeletons scattered throughout the lakebed, across the rocky plateau, between potato fields and Bolivia and Peru.

It's dry. Freezing. That helped us date and sequence the bones. A million bones, a thousand patterns, each clavicle, each femur, each rib not scavenged by the Pucara or the Tihuanaco for their war gowns, each bone systematically rewrote our history and dented my lifelong assumption that I, James Richter, was a descendant of the cradle of man. I knew then no such privilege; those patterns were in all of us, in each and every one of us.

Imagine the impact: that ship who knows how fast, uncontrolled, damaged already, from what we saw in Wyoming. It left pieces across Uruguay, a few in Argentina, and the jackpot in Peru. Never found bigger pieces north. Guess we didn't look hard enough. Or maybe shedding the pattern cache over Titicaca gave the ship just enough juice to try to escape. Didn't make it. Welcome to America, ancient astronauts.

I shouldn't tell you—Guess it doesn't really matter. The author will probably edit this out if he ever gets his shit together and finishes this, but remember Benton? She put the pieces back together. Not the ship, but the pieces of me, all of those convenient assumptions that'd been shattered by my time in Peru. How's a man supposed to keep a secret like that? Hey everyone, guess what. Everything you thought you knew about where we came from was wrong. There're people just like us out there, and sixty-fucking-five million years ago, they paid us a visit. Left behind enough survivors to start this.

So the first time I saw the light, I was reasonably unreasonably afraid.

Holmdel superblacked the whole affair. Non-disclosure agreements all around, not that they could've done anything about it, not really, not to a man whose parents were dead and whose gee eff had been briefed on the surfaces before they'd even pulled out. I don't think she believed it. Maths don't care about evolution beyond its opposition to creationism.

The point is, no one could explain it, so they buried it and buried our eyescatch under penalty of death. Big threat. I was born dead. No paperwork necessary.

The way I see it, the bird dumped half its cargo over Titicaca after starting to bring them back. That's the bodies. Imagine the biggest cemetery you've ever seen, but in this boneyard, the people were just thrown on the ground. No bodies at Diablo; I think they didn't have time, or the damage was too severe to do that wing. Just dumped one wing, that coned-out ball with the human-shaped depressions in the walls. Some survived. If they hadn't, we'd all be talking Kiswahili. *Si jambo*.

Jennings had Holmdel and his administration disappeared after the Populace coup. Buried under buried under buried. And after most of the southern hemisphere got glassed in the Quebec War (oops!), there goes a little thing called plausible deniability. Deniable plausibility? Not that he needed to know, but maybe things would've been different. Maybe the last centuries of my life wouldn't have been spent thousands of years in the future, trying to fix this fucking mess. Guess I could take the blame, but why bother? Purpose be.

The point is, there's more to this story than you'll ever know.

*

"The agent in charge—"

"James Richter."

"What?" A ghost rattled chains in Jennings' attic. "Richter? From—"

"He was on your list to disappear," Cervera paused, "but we took him off."

"Any other undeletes I should know about?"

"A few. David, we just couldn't—"

"I understand." He didn't. "We're bringing him in?"

"Called him up. He's in transit. I'm sure he'll jump at the chance to puzzle a few more pieces together."

A nobody chimed in. "Sirs, the entry team is prepped and ready."

"Nothing's alive in there...?"

"Nothing on scope. Just one big flickering power source in the vessel's core."

"Reactor?"

"Maybe."

"Bomb?"

"...Could be."

"Send them in. We have visual?" Jennings sat on the edge of an empty chair.

"Eyelines installed. Ready to roll."

"Tell them to go, then."

*

Assault Force A was hardly fit for assault, hardly a force, but they were completely qualified for the "A" position, a group of men and women impressed into Milicom after being particularly good convicts, patients, and ne'er do wells with nowhere else to go.

They weren't issued guns.

Moore Chavez rubbed his eyes with gloved fingers, for a moment obscuring both the signal from Eyeline-17-A and the two teardrop prison tattoos a man he'd later raped and shivved had needled into his upper cheeks. He added that murder one artist to the tally he kept on his right thumb.

A romantic at heart, Chavez thought the rock seemingly growing from the metal hallway around him was beautiful. He held his spotlight like a gun, so far outside his conception of reality now than any reassuring contact with metal helped his feet move.

A lattice of passages, he followed the other members of A down what appeared to be a main shaft, his rubber soles grasping for purchase on the canted floor. Whoever had designed this bunker had a bad eye for level lines. Maybe it was art.

Up ahead, the hallway ended at a swingdoor. He thought it'd be the end of the line, but he saw that douche Monagan successfully pull the door's halves apart. Someone had left it unlocked for them.

He watched Monagan take a few steps forward, his light back and forth, before he tumbled and disappeared, his shout of surprise interrupting the mortuary silence of the expedition.

People ran. A few more fell.

By the time Chavez got to the front, people had stopped falling, instead stood out on a landing within the chamber. The talking stopped even more.

"What's the—Jesus." He crossed himself.

The double-dozen spotlights swished around the chamber in near-solid lines. Even at the bottom of the room, the three men and one woman who had fallen were sitting up, their lights arcing forth and back across the expanse.

They'd fallen off the landing and slid harmlessly down a big metal bowl, slight depressions in its surface. Above, the room's ceiling was that same bowl, mirrored. They were inside a gigantic sphere, or "spear," as Chavez would have pronounced it.

At the center of the room, exact center, hung a dull gray orb. Free-floating. Just sitting there in the air. The four fallen soon realized there was nothing attached to that ball, and they tried to climb up the bowl's slick sides, lest it fall on them.

"Fuck," Moore Chavez said to no one.

❧

"Fuck," David Smith Jennings said to Antonia Cervera.

"Are we seeing this right?" She turned to an engineer running the playback. "Is that thing floating?"

"I—I don't know, sir." He zoomed. "Looks like—"

The screens became white.

❧

Moore Chavez quickly yanked the melting communications band from his head, tried to slap out a dozen burning holes on his uniform. His eyes stung from the blackened, smoldering plastic. He found himself on his ass, slammed up against the back of the railing rim.

The room was brighter. He realized that the new illumination was coming from the nearest unsteady light at the chamber's center, the floating ball of whatever the fuck.

He grappled with his own disoriented body and crawled to the edge of the walkway, looked down into the bowl. The four members of Assault A at the bowl's bottom weren't moving. Others around him were. More moaning and confused cries than moving.

"Hey," he barely whispered down the bowl, but still it felt too loud. "You guys alright?"

He'd never forget the look on the woman's face at the bottom of the chamber. Her mouth hung open and his beam revealed a wet line of spittle looping out. Her eyes were gray, and he wondered how he could possibly know from that distance, but

the floating ball flashed again, not as brightly, or maybe it was and he'd adjusted, but Chavez thought he saw a passageway open directly across the expanse, a passageway exactly like the one he'd used to enter the chamber. With the flash came a great tendril of energy that lashed out, down that passage. At the same time, the four people at the bottom of the bowl began to fly up. He didn't believe it, but they did, flew up, flew through the floating ball of purest white light, a thin stream of their constituent parts splashing out the other side, guided down that passage, and then he died as he was pulled in and through and

❧

"Assault A, come in." The command center was a fury of chatter. "Assault A, report."

"Eyelines are dead, sir." The engineer watched the last of the head-mounted cams blink out.

What the array of cameras had displayed after the initial white had been confusing at best: twenty-four displays suddenly savagely displaced as twenty-four people were knocked back. Eyeline-04A lolled as if its carrier's neck had been broken, but the image focused briefly on the center of the room, giving the assembly a brief glimpse at the floating orb, a swirling, building illumination, and then white nothing.

"Send in Assault B, god damn it!" Cervera had a way of barking orders that any dog would have envied.

"Tony, we—"

Jennings hated it when she narrowed her eyes at him, so she did. "We need to know what's going on down there."

"So we just keep sending in more troops? What happens when we run out?"

"You're safe, Mr. President. Send in Assault B." She repeated her command, and her underlings communicated wordlessly with nods and tappings. New eyelines snapped into life on the display. "Fancy up and filter that last transmission. And someone get me some fucking physicals! Are we in any danger here?"

"Physicals run, sir." Another nameless engineer stuttered out from his panel. "Normal across the board—radiological, chemical—"

"Any change, you tell me." Cervera had a way of gripping any situation and steeling herself. "Status, Assault B?"

"B ready, sir."

"Insert. Get this to Richter."

❧

Somewhere above the planet flying roughly over Nebraska on a wedge of composite and titanium, James Richter responded to the chime. He removed his link from his wallet; his heart jumped a little at the incoming superblack icon.

He was the only passenger in the compartment, indeed, on that flight, so he slid the link into his seat's display. He exhaled slowly, his eyes closed. He cleared his throat and opened his eyes to the second-long burst of data that flashed from the panel.

He gasped, his hand reaching instinctively to his heart as his latticed mindwork began to puzzle over and assemble probabilities and contexts. He thought the name *Holmdel* for the first time in one year and seven months, really devoted thought to Titicaca for the first time in three years and eight months. He'd learned to bury.

If it's true—

It couldn't be true.

But if it is—

He put his link back in his pocket and attempted to will the wedge forward to Wyoming.

❧

"You *what?*"

Jennings at least attempted a look of the guilt he genuinely felt. Cervera just met Richter's gaze and threw it back unused.

"We've sent more teams in."

"How many?"

Without hesitation: "Five. We're gaining valuable new data with each attempt."

Richter just scoffed in disbelief. "Don't we have robots for insertions in threat zones? You know, threat zones inside of *alien* fucking *vessels* buried underneath *mountains?* Little tank-tracked numbers, with instruments and cameras and *weapons?* Or did I just make that up?"

"Yes, sir. I mean—We have robots." An engineer, listening in, turned from his console, surprised at his own volunteering of an opinion in the charged atmosphere of the command center. "But Secretary—"

"*We* thought it best to get a first-hand look." A gofer handed Cervera another glass. She scanned it and threw it onto the growing pile.

"The Holmdel Directive specifically states—"

"There wasn't any indication that the chamber was—"

"You didn't think the big floating ball at the center might have been a threat?"

Neither Cervera nor Jennings had any response.

"No more." Richter shook his head and waved his glass to black. "Shut it down. We're not risking any more lives for something we can't—"

"You don't have the authority," Jennings said quietly.

"The Directive hands final authority over any encounter scenario to the agent in—"

"Holmdel's dead."

Richter considered the possibility of his own disappearance if he didn't tone down.

"Then at least slow down. Send machines into the chamber. Get a better idea of what that thing is before wasting any more people." Richter tipped a glass from the table. It displayed the torn, bleeding pile of what had been Assault B. "Take your time with this. The vessel's been buried for sixty-five million—"

"We don't have the time."

"You're afraid of War Four breaking out? Neighbors to the north?"

"How did you—"

"Everyone knows. They're up to something. And you want this alien technology—whatever it is—as a weapon. Then fucking research it first. Don't just throw men at it."

"And women."

"And women." Richter scanned through more images of bodies bent, twisted, pulped. "All I'm saying is slow down. We spent years going over every square inch of Titicaca. Give me a blueprint."

A holoprint image of the buried vessel sparked to life on the main display. Richter walked to it, studied it.

"This area," he pointed to the starboard nacelle, "is missing something. See the difference?"

Jennings and Cervera blanked.

"A smaller sphere. Not the floating one in the central chamber in the connecting hub. Note the conduits running through the twist points, the nacelle sockets." Reynald poked the holo, which smudged and rebounded. "That floating ball is directly between two similar chambers, one on each wing of the vessel. One of those connected chambers has a spherical slug of metal secured inside. The other's empty."

"Not following."

"We found what I suspect are pieces of that missing ball spread throughout South America. That thing shattered as it was ejected before impact. The ship is on a straight-line trajectory from the Titicaca site, and fragments of that shattered ball have been found from Uruguay to Peru." He slaved a hemisphere map from his personal link.

"Why didn't I fucking know this?" Jennings barely contained a lethal frustration.

"You didn't need to know this." Richter swiped a red line across the floating map, connecting the dots between Uruguay and Wyoming. "And I didn't much feel like volunteering any information after you put me on your kill list."

"Listen, James. All I knew was that you were close to Holmdel. After the Populace—"

"If you want my help, I'll need to choose my own team."

Cervera shook a no. "I don't think—"

"My own team."

"We can't just bring in anyone you want..."

Richter glared. "Cosmotech has a math egg named Hope Benton. Bring her in. And no more of these," he wagged the autopsy glass before them, "third estate types. Guinea pigs. Send in the robots, and then we'll talk about sending people in again."

Cervera and Jennings locked a look.

"Fine."

❧

"Me?" Adam West slid his only photograph of Abigail into his empty wallet. Milicom paid the bills. "Blood money. Early release from my contract."

"How long?"

"Eight years left."

The wheezing, jittery teenager huddled in the corner of the staging area. West saw the healing split of a lip. West saw the dusky haze of a Pearl addict. She shook her head. "World won't last another eight years."

"Sure it will. One last dance, and we're both out, right? Have to stay positive, kid."

She wracked a cough, enough to scare West marginally. Either she had been smoking three packs a day for the last forty years, or she was terminal Pearl.

"What's your name, Irish?"

She looked him up and down, the distrust of a life of trauma.

"Come on. We're gonna be here a while. Might as well get to know each other."

"I'm called Maggie."

West extended a hand, shook her collection of metacarpals. The drug had burned through her, leaving only a gaunt form topped with a blossom of orange curls, tied lazily back with a drab cord. The green of her eyes was diluted.

"Adam West." He was relieved, even after a lifetime of dealing with the brutality of his name, that the reference was lost on the Irish.

He could have constructed a conversation around her age, the fact that she was obviously an outsourced asset, or the Blood Army tattoo he saw crawling up the left side of her neck, but Adam West's parents had taught him tact.

He saw others among the group crawling over her, or wanting to, the dozens of eyes of the trapped coming to rest on a pretty young thing, vulnerable, slumped in the corner. He was immune to those restings. She was a cute little girl; he was a widower. He'd protect her, although he suspected that she needed no protecting. Each trace of the artist's needle was a kill; each slough of lung tissue was a testament to her steel core.

The staging area had once been an upper-level office complex for the Diablo Mining company. Now, fifty soldiers, all of whom West suspected were there for their own escape plans, to get out of MSI early, to make recompense for some transgression, to be promoted, all waited in various states of anticipation and fear. They were poor, scrawny kids with bobbing Adam's apples, a few with the lowbright slope of War Three's fallout, the non-coms and executives among them standing straight and proud, doing fine jobs of hiding their uncertainty. This job would come with a price, and no one knew who could pay.

The room held the hushed murmur of conversation that only waiting emits.

"You been here—"

West cut off as the door cycled open, cut off as one of the more eager execs stood bolt-upright: "Uh-tennn-HUT!" One hundred legs extended, one hundred heels clicked.

"As you were." The officer was a tall man, a dark man; his suit was tall and dark. He walked into the middle of the assembly, followed by two. "I'm James Richter, and this is Hope Benton and Michael Balfour. We're here to apprise you of the situation."

"Hope Benton, Quantum-X." She tossed a projector marble into the air, where it spun to life, splashing a neon blueprint into the air. The assembly silently oohed and ahhed as they studied the display. She'd done a good job of forging a schematic; the grunts would never know the difference. "What you see is the layout of the Diablo Mine, sector fourteen, subsector seven. You've been contracted for an important mission, one that will release you from all previous obligations to MSI."

There was a smiling anticipation in the air. People caught glances and grins. The fifty participants each had their reasons for obligation releases.

"It's fake," Maggie muttered under her breath. West heard.

"Quiet, please." Benton continued. She sparked a pointer to life and began to indicate places on the blueprint. "The Diablo Mining Corp called in Milicom because they've had an incident downstairs. One of their fat-bore diggers snagged a thread of an unknown metal, and that caused the core of the tractor to seize up. It went a little critical."

"This is a cleanup, plain and simple," Michael Balfour took off. "I'm sure most of you have experience with cleanups. MSI doesn't usually grant contract releases for mop work, so consider yourselves lucky. If you work hard, you'll be out of here by the end of the week."

"Sir?" A low-lev exec, probably accounts payable in some square-state branch, raised his hand. "What kind of core was it? I mean—Are we walking into a hot pop? I want to have kids someday, and—"

Balfour shook his head, chuckling. "No, no, I assure you all, you're in no danger. The engine was a simple—Hope? Help me out?"

"It was a pebble bed reactor. Just a big splash of pyrolytic graphite and helium. The hot pocket's halved down to almost nothing." She circled an area of the projected schematic. "We waited six months to bring you in, to make sure it was safe. Diablo just needs the human touch before they can get back in and start digging again."

West followed Maggie's gaze. She stared at Richter. West could have sworn that Richter was acting. Some people can't contain lies.

"The initial blast rocked the mine, so watch your step on entry. The walls and floors are a little tilted. You'll be issued protective gear, so don't worry about making babies." Hope looked over and smiled at the low-lev, and a nervous laugh sputtered to life around the room. "And so—" she motioned to two guards at the chamber door, who cycled it open. A line of gofers carrying crates of rubberized protective suits came in. "Everybody suit up, so you can begin. Good luck, Assault K. Stay safe down there."

West noted a glare behind Richter's eyes as he looked at the woman.

The display blinked off, and Benton caught the marble. The three left the chamber to the sound of squeaking rubber being pulled over street clothes.

⁂

"Michael? We'll catch up to you."

Balfour winked at Richter as he continued down the shaft.

"James?"

"I can't believe we're fucking going through with this."

Benton exhaled slowly. "There's no other—"

"There's plenty of other ways."

"The probes didn't tell us anything. We need human—"

"Rats. You need rats for the maze. We don't know what that thing is, but we're still sending people in to get slaughtered."

She bristled at the word. "The last two groups—I wouldn't call it a slaughter."

"Still ended up dead."

"No." Her eyebrows narrowed defensively. "Two lived."

"And then fucking died."

She started walking again. "Why did you even bring me here? If you don't believe in what we're doing?"

He grabbed her hand and anchored her in place. "Because you're brilliant. I thought you'd figure it out. I didn't think anyone else'd have to die."

"I'm sorry to disappoint you."

He let go of her hand in frustration, raising his own helplessly. "You haven't disappointed me."

"Will you still say that when the K group comes out dead?"

"I don't know."

She walked away.

⁂

Jennings had gone home. Apparently his wife was sick. Cervera sat in his chair. None of the engineers seemed to mind.

"It can't be easy for you, I know." She said, half-watching the eyelines begin to light up. "Being here."

"Hmm?" Michael Balfour turned away from watching a disembodied conversation between two of the fodders.

"It can't be easy, seeing those two all over each other." The unspoken implication.

"James needed help. You, too. It was the least I could do."

"Who would have thought, all of us back together again?"

"Not all of us."

The room was suddenly a torrent of chair squeaks and throat clears.

"You could have said no."

"No. I couldn't turn this down." *Couldn't turn him down.*

"Couldn't turn her down?"

She has no idea. Michael smiled.

"Speak of the devil," Cervera offered seats to the returning Richter and Benton. "Judas cow ready?"

"The herd's getting suited. The lead's been briefed. He thinks we're after gold. Enthusiastic sort. They'll follow him." Benton sat between Cervera and Balfour. Richter noticed. He took a chair as far away as the room allowed.

"Eyelines?" Cervera performed a quick survey.

"Allll—up." An engineer activated the last of the fifty.

"Good." Cervera leaned forward. She was starting to like this dance. "Send in K group."

❧

"No good," Maggie grumbled. "They're lying to us." She adjusted the tiny camera mount banded to her head. "And I don't fuckin' care if you're listenin'." She let the microphone boing back into place.

West grinned as he locked his bubble in place, the cool wash of canned air displacing his internal warmth. He grinned, but he felt it, too.

"All right, everyone. Ready?" The low-lev was a little too eager. West thought he knew something. "Assault K, move out." Authority fills a void, especially at the prospect of gold.

❧

Walking down canted corridors.

❧

The groan of a metallish bulkhead.

❧

"What the—"

The world became light, and Maggie fell to the ground.

Screaming, life in gaps, brilliant white light, brilliant white light. West knew he was screaming, knew it, but couldn't hear himself, the room was so light. A ball at the center, a light, and fingers, reaching, grasping. He didn't exactly have to throw himself to the ground; he fell beside Maggie. The last thing he saw was the light, that light, reaching out and through the fifty, K group, eyes open, lances of white erupting from the ball, the ball at the center, reaching, and

❧

"I'm going down there." Richter's chair tipped as he stood up. "This has to stop."

"James—"

"Don't fucking *James* me, Tony. We have to stop this." The door closed behind him.

"What do we—"

"I'm going, too." And Hope Benton did.

The eyelines were dying, one by one by ten.

"Mike, get on the—"

"Sorry, Tony. I have to stop them." Balfour ran.

Cervera wasn't going anywhere.

⁂

It was a heartbeat.

West thought he was still alive.

Blood. Gushing from his nose, thin, hesitant trails from his eyes. The worst headache. He rolled to his side and vomited across the composite floor. There were bodies around him, and something had changed. There were bodies around him, and one was alive.

Maggie coughed beside him, a wracking, horrible affair. He crawled the feet to her, the distance seeming miles. Wiped vomit and blood from his face as he touched her. She started to cry.

"Did you see it?"

⁂

Cervera stood over the engineer's glass, jaw dropped. There were lifesigns on two. Not flickering, strong. They were talking. Finally. A breakthrough. Two survivors who weren't squealing bags of smeared flesh and agony. Finally.

⁂

West nodded, nodded and sobbed, stroking Maggie's hair, wiping tears from her. He nodded. He'd seen the light. They'd both seen everything.

⁂

"James!" Her voice echoed down the corridor. Richter heard, but he kept running. "James, please!"

He came to the chamber door, slid to a stop across the slick, tilted floor. He could hear Benton running to catch up. He opened the door anyway.

༄

Two people looked up. Gray eyes. Forty-eight corpses around them. The light at the room's center throbbed.

༄

Hope slammed into his back, grabbing his coat and pulling him into the corridor. She shoved him against the wall, stood between him and the thrumming, screaming ball of light.

He turned to her, his eyes distant, his mind lifetimes away. He saw Balfour coming down the corridor, the hallway of an alien vessel, forty-eight corpses, two survivors, the light.

"James—

༄

A palpable thrust of brilliance tore from the light at the chamber's center. West and Maggie clawed into each other, the song of the trillions broadcasting above them, the light reaching out, out, out

༄

When Richter came around, one of the K group survivors was cradling his head. A girl. The other crouched beside Michael, whose head lolled toward him. Richter's heart stopped an instant when he saw Michael's cold gray eyes.

"Hope?" He coughed out, choking on something copper. "Hope?"

"She's—" The girl's cold hand was against his cheek.

"Hope?"

The man tending to Michael whispered something.

"What?" Richter tried to get up, found himself weak in the aftermath of the light, drained. Something was fundamentally different.

West turned around, a small motion of his head indicating the chamber.

Richter threw Maggie's hands from him, crawled slowly, painfully into the orb room. Made it to the edge of the drop into the bowl. Saw what remained of Hope Benton curled peacefully against the corpses of Assault K.

Something broke.

❧

There are of course connections that imply a verifiable cosmology, a totality of phenomena constituting all of time and space. Beyond theoretical physics, string theory and the anthropic principle, there is a fundamental symmetry to existence that is better described through a defined set of characteristics in the known megaverse embodied in the form of a particular set of children born in the summer and autumn of the second year of the third millennium.

David Smith Jennings died an old man in the far, far future.

Antonia Cervera was shot and killed by David Smith Jennings in Wind River, D.C..

Abrah Allen-Kennedy was killed in the Quebecois nuclear attack on Washington, D.C.

Buddy McClure broke his neck and drowned on the bottom of Lake Superior.

Hank the Cowboy was cancelled.

Honeybear Brown lives on, under the couch.

James Richter went into the future to find

AMONG THE LIVING

AMONG THE LIVING

was never known to command respect from his peers
was known to steal his fourteen minutes in fragments
was known to sometimes allow ashes to burn on his forearms and face
while waiting patiently for them to gutter out
because at least it was something nearing proof
that he was there at all

was never known to entertain such revolutions
but the autopsy was inconclusive
as to when and why he chose to
enact such validity
[then strike in my name; these are mine to erase.]
on histories
[if the self is defined as

[/there is nothing left to enlighten

wished he'd sky-wide hands with which to grasp the world;
such moss, the old-growth, teardrops of ocean:
the cellular towers would embed themselves in his palm like

fiberglass dust
as he squeezed a little too long, a little too hard,
neither burned nor blistered by the lukewarm blood.

considered himself an aggressive driver
considered himself a philosopher, a deep thinker, an author
behind the wheel
considered his thoughts the best when thought while driving, while wrapped
within a ton or two of green Ford, tan interior
so aligned with the subtleties of his landship that once
just north of the Mexico exit
when the number two cylinder coil blew and his truck
resonated new harmonics across grinding metal,
he promptly took the exit,
checked the oil,
and turned around to home because his father had once
fixed airplanes
in a life younger than his own.

defined himself in histories of who started hating him
when.
[the places between stasis are horror.]

was known to accelerate into curves
accelerate into downslopes
into relationships
was known to fear braking.

learned eventually
learned early
learned a little too late
that locating his happiness within the
broken puzzle pieces gifted in
the hope of finding purchase in the segment
he'd long ago torn from his own viscera

only forced the disbelief of soulmates and wondered him
wandering in search of so much more than this.

he'd invented his own mathematics to explain absolutely
nothing.

wished he'd a sky-wide heart with which to love the world:
[the world, to him, was always internal, never
and he'd hate cities for reasons.
sometimes pretended he could poetry,
sometimes neglected the laws that fed him,
always hated womyn,
always hated person's who couldn't tell the different between
websters plurals and possessives.

if it were possible, he'd use subjunctive.
if it were possible, he'd trade his ability to dream.

found inspiration at speeds above legal,
at acceleration,
at speeds in alternate states:
[New York drivers are so... aggressive.]
found something comforting in riding the edge,
the rumble strips calling out,
dead deer

at what point does animal
become meat
become carrion?
once took a mislabeled hamburger from the dining hall
heatlamp
to find portobello: wondered then if that was the taste of
coffins, memorials, garroted friends.
he'd spit out the first bite,
but took so many more after the voices.

how much now is left of you?
the sickly fascination with unstrung vocal chords,
rotted through, never again to
sing.

was once so
twice so
always so enamored by speed and swerves that the
rearview mirror delighted hindsight with the dopplered impact
of an orange construction barrel.
water.

was known to pick targets
when boxed in by tractor trailers
when the median gave chance
for a head-on collision.
drove like he didn't care to survive.

bumper stickers warned innocents.
an army seven-million strong by the time he was ready

would be nice if once
just once
or twice
we could stop hating each other so much
to honor that time
and maybe it's not really hate
but a succession of days spent wondering
through desert life
at stars
at breath
my decision of each inhalation tempered now
with the surrenders inherent to each departure:
i must hate you.

i must unlove you
unseat you from this tangent,
exponentially tangential,
scattershot into futures apart.

was unknown in brevity,
famous in obsession and little else.

multitasked his path to mediocrity:
books, pages, digitally-versatile
stubbornness borne on
[did you know he was actually allergic to donkeys?]

i don't know who i am anymore.

never tried a drug he didn't fear,
never didn't fear You, that base addiction
concreted, secreted in a night that he put his
hand over your mouth so the neighbors wouldn't bitch.
knew then that your flicking tongue tasted yourself on his
palm
from cupped foreplay: [this isn't cheating; this is friendship:
beneficently extended.]

synesthetic in that he could hear your smile,
taste your release.
synesthetic in that he could live
the shadows of you and die each time he felt for your
heart-beats.

ate aspirin like breath mints.

hostaged himself to yesterdays.
to three-times-nine,
to fourteen-seven:
to morning, afternoon, evening and night smoke.

once considered working on a bison farm
because "artists" need real "jobs" to pay for cable.

[your dark exterior masks a caffeine-driven activism/]
[you'll take up a cause and you'll get ugly to advance it/]

thought that maybe if he smiled hard enough, long enough,
his face would stick that way
[such childhood threats only work for negatives]
[and no one would know].

realized long after they'd left that they were gone
long before they'd left.

stole poetry from his inbox:
Under the cheese, reconciles a breezy stain.
Dresses by drugs, transmutates the acorn to guy.
Ruined by chariots, wipes the light to guest.
Transmutating, saying, transmutating, writing, stepping.
Counter had a spill, which was not at all a gut.
Tells cowardly, wordlessly, like keys yelling, allegedly.
Seasons like rocks go slyly but angrily.

lonely man: suspensory particularist falconine boil lonely
euangiotic

lonely man: wondered exactly when the future became a
time
when scambots used "euangiotic" to market
cum-guzzling tranny vids and
bigger dick pills [ripper cun7 open 2nite] and
the. lowest. mortgage. rates. ever.

was never particularly falconine.

synesthetic in that
the point is, i forgive you.

synesthetic in that
he never wanted an acknowledgement,
just silences

the suicide watch was long over,
the july phone call of an angry father
and halfhearted attempts to convince him
he wouldn't walk off the roof.

sometimes swerved into traffic.
sometimes ran into snowbanks on purpose.
sometimes pretended he wasn't home.

the catalytic reaction of palm to palm,
palm to breast,
wondering which geography hearts learn first.

his madness taught him that tinnitus
ringing through from first memories sang
a perfect constant note, an S note,
inextricable from musics that dredged and
driver units, fifty millimeters spanning twenty-
five thousand hertz were the most convincing evidence
that he wasn't in fact indistinguishable from god.

wrote such worlds into existence
with maths learned in base one
four seven fifty three forty seven fourteen
made no sense to anyone beyond the periphery of
his madness: for all we know,
benton really existed somewhere dying at
quantum light x and ghosts are nothing more than
unrealized lovers.

let's disappear.

wondered if the three seconds of static from
two minutes, twenty-two seconds to
two minutes, twenty-five seconds was
intentional.

have you remembered me as
he
fucks
you?

long ago forgot the ingredients of love if ever
he'd purchased them in the first place.
substituted distance for proximity and
water for milk.
burned the mess.

learned the result of making love is often
a screaming, dying pile of flesh
more self-inscribed suffering than infant.

the morbid lock with which he fantasized
an elegant entrance to their funeral cars
and the questions whispered by strangers, of strangers:
was he?
the one?
who?

such daymares unseat the hesitant security of decades.

revised his histories to include suspicions.
revised his memories to include evidences.
revised his life to the end result of conscious constructions
of begged pities and reassurances:

we are here for you
[based on truths we can never believe].

wondered what you were doing these days
with your hairs or if maybe every reimagining of self was
nothing more than a surface attempt to become present
while
underneath you knew the same battles
used the same metaphors for us
and plagiarized my hate.

surrendered more than once.

never had anyone travel so far away and come back to him.
[these things happen in threes.]

surrender
capitulation
without white flags.

put down payments on
too many others' emotional dowries;
invested too much of himself
in the gentrification of exiled landscapes:
he was the art kid they took home before
they met the safe one.

argued the non-pre-raphaelitism
of a proud antique-shop purchase and probably ruined all
chances of getting in good with mom.
[sure, it's impressionist. sure.]

waited for the other shoe to drop.
spent most days barefoot so he'd never break a heart.
was accused of ruining lives twice.
took heart in knowing that he'd not once made that accusa-

tion,
hated himself more for self-ascribing all responsibility
often broke plates and
stood on them by accident.

knew that once he began to associate music to specific humans,
they'd either die or cross the world to escape him.
never again wanted an our song,
but he did enjoy plural pronouns.

agreed with blair about ginsberg,
but still wrote this.

editor recommended the expurgation of
two shitty teenage poems from
his first book,
so he wrote a poem chapter in the third
of seven entries, all math internal.

[the lessons of the second are that i can survive,
and no matter how much you were to me,
i will use the us we were to pay the rent
if i can't use you as a pillow.]

drove in circles.

light bulbs lasted for durations of residence
because he preferred his work in the dark
and found that he couldn't proofread
when the songs had words.

rusted through most recollections
and lived as dust, wiped away more than once
but always returning, an exquisite layer

only visible under heartbeat scrutinies,
mostly shed flesh.
reserved a large percentage
of his willpower for a time when
he'd not likely need it longer.

divided and hid his past
[the electron flicker, stippled]
into convenient sub-folders
that only turned bold when someone actually needed him.

he hated bold folders.

preferred acoustic versions.

counted three grammatical errors
in his deepest inspirations.

marked his days
in the number of times
he emptied the desktop ashtray;
most days, three.
what a war mask such ash could inscribe.

marked his months
in the number of cartons, the handful
dozen career aspirations
and the nights they went to tully's;
had a specific memory of each booth.

marked his years
with ink lines on left forearm.
no. it doesn't scan.

gave more of himself up than he kept.
[it was a flawed campaign for a recalled product.]
first woke up

wondered what the end destination
for a course charted across freckles would be;
was satiated on a southern path,
and his tongue remembers.
they do leave texture:
he preferred that alternate smooth.

you don't need to know.
you don't need

wrote poems of war
in his own blood, vomit and shit.
such holographic wills are legally-binding
if properly witnessed;
i call you to bear witness.

burned all the steak-ums
and days later dreamt the gutter was filled with the war dead.

to walk across that desert to you...

convinced himself that he could pinpoint the
exact moments they'd erase him from memory:
11:11, 11:42pm, 7:41am.
he'd sometimes wake for no reason with an urgent sense of nothing.
resigned to the same status as the dead,
intangible.
wanted to write her into a book,
chose words for actions, phrases for breathing
the way she smelled at night.

hid the explosions of the midnight city
behind headphones, sirens bleeding through,
once watched them hose the blood from the street
and gasoline
after two vans danced around the corner, tangled,
the very spot the crazy man had shouted in dozens:
"Mayor Matt Driscoll is an asshole."
until sun rose, traffic drove over glass.

sat on the roof sometimes because
he loved the smell of sun on tar.
reminded him of his lung.

a spiraled coil, a field of red:
he carried within him delicious genetics
for heart disease, Alzheimer's, a predisposition
for children with inexplicable holes in their chests.
vowed that his line would end with him,
since his siblings did a good job of breeding.

reserved core terrors
for plural pronouns and the fear of substituting new names
into well-worn phrasal constructs.
felt disingenuous and watched ceilings
because he was so afraid everyone would see through his
skin.

underreported the number of cartons
overreported the frequency of meals
never told anyone of the hours he'd spend lying on the floor.

once rocked forth, back, forth after lighting
a candle now long melted into the rock fabric of
a birthday gift, a monkey sculpture veiled with dozens of
dollar-store candles

[once wrote a poem]
prayed the first and only time.
[these penance years

never restarted his computer when prompted.
allowed frost to build to ice in the freezer compartment
until he hacked the tip off his one good knife
and breathed freon enough to make him sit down.
the landlord paid because he lied about the affair.
not once used his toaster oven.

wondered if cats saw ghosts when
they looked past him at nothing, attentively intent.
wondered if cats talked to his dead.

fatigued by himself
but just wanted to try something different for once
in a life filled with static days.

the downstairs neighbor ran out to the street
to help what was left of the white van driver:
he stood at the window and counted the pieces of her
as he drank milk straight from the carton:
some conveniences come solely from a life without partners.

the end result of the total mathematical extrapolation of
the designed ignition of infinity:
collapse entire, cessation,
wanted to beat that compression of
all possible heavens by a record of
twenty, thirty billion years.

the next time, that would be it
because there's only so much a person can give
before recognizing such giftings deplete the
essential desires to remain.

had the mis/fortune of being an artist
born with a brain hardwired for logics and maths;
some chapters augmented his internal mathematics of desire,
her curves and planes and volumes.

slept nightmares drawn from futures forged
of the gutted nickel cores of rock seas, unbreathing.
woke too many nights to the recurring image:
the staccato tattoo of a war
without the possibility of surrender.

jog shuttle to pause, play:
rupture, rend, rive, split, cleave:

edited a past away.

what you thought would disappear
lies
and waits:

wednesdays are the days we fight.
i'd ask you to call, but i know money's tight
the true change of that transaction
still punched through your face
i'd call every day if i could, but we can't.

january cuts a deeper distance
and sometimes i can't taste the words you type.
you often remind me of just how fragile i try not to be but am.

once you told me i was asleep when you got out of bed,
asleep but i still asked you if you were leaving and
looked so sad; i've tried dying those reflexes to departures.

i wonder if i whispered;
it feels like i would have whispered it
if asked not in sleeping, if asking awake,
if asking you to stay.

once you reached for the light switch and
in doing so, a tear fell from your cheek to mine.
i never told you that because i didn't want you to know
how close you'd come to breaking my heart with that tear.

once we didn't shout over something about dinner
but it felt like it, and i apologize for not remembering the specifics.
i wanted you to leave the room so i could pull the bones from the chicken,
and stood there listening to the hot fat silently burn my fingertips
and hoping to hear you laugh at something the television could provide.

we've fallen, and we'll stumble, still learning this
and i know the insecurities have to be exhumed and waked.
i've buried so many of my loves, and you met me
in an interesting time, i'll admit.
i don't doubt you.

smoking my last cigarette
and the snow's too deep today.

"come here."
i remember the shapes of those moments, the
Modular Calculus
we figure each time we assert.

how “I’ll be right back” palimpsests
the variables with which i’ve measured times,
two minutes, five. thirty, after fifty-
nine, i shift to hours and trust you’ll be back
eventually.

others never inspired such trust.

i think the definition of a partner is
someone you always want near, but
you aren’t afraid to let them wander because
they come back.

our calculus is of additions:
cats, green radios, our bed, our house,
augmenting concepts of home with plural pronouns,
subtracting places and histories with a honed
methodological approach, methodically
approaching methods of subverting:
i’m a capitalist confused by your anarchies,
but i’ll learn you through them.

i read fascination into you.
all the internal conflicts and external dissatisfactions
i learned a collection of decades ago to forget;
you reopen convenient scars and ask me to look.

it helps that you hold my hand.

i can imagine your fingertips typing, those
same fingertips i cradle with my tongue, tasting us,
those tips urging words into action, the letters a confusion
sometimes that adds to my wonder of the way
your mind works.

our mathematics—
i want to learn you and buy our cat.

paul hughes, come *here*.

i'd ask the same of you, but your name isn't mine;
i've had dreams that part of it will be.
i've had dreams of entering that city in conquest with you.
i've had dreams of a coastal life.
i've

because i've never been loved like this.

but

a heart can only break so many times before
you start to lose the important pieces

the nearest unsteady light
the return of books
or the brittle desire thereof
t-shirts you will never wear again
pajama pants too big for you
too big for her

thursdays are the days we fade

a fist bundle of broken glass
beating, chiming sunrises
echoing, screaming loss
each departure a new crack
each departure a new opportunity
for scar tissue to encapsulate
for the appearance of normalcy
but the grinding of the heart's edges goes on.

the nearest unsteady light
a burn barrel that wouldn't accept the flowers i bought you
the oven that ate the pumpkin pie
i've put the rest of you in a box
when are you coming?
when are you coming?

please don't ask if you don't want my answer.
please don't ask if you don't want me
because i'm assembled from memories that could be lies
missings so muches and i love you toos
and i think of you all the times.
maybe it's because you taught me how to play checkers
in bed
and i beat you the first time.

maybe only a poet could ever deserve to love you.
but i tried to learn your language
the subtleties and nuances of you
and there were great plains of you i never saw,
but i wanted to with everything i had.

which edges were lies?

that there are people who will wander the world,
never knowing the path of damage they leave behind,
always convincing themselves that it's okay to walk away.

that we are downgraded.
that he hoped that someday, someone would feel for him a
fraction of the love he jettisoned into the world.
that there are people who deserve your touch more than i
ever could.
that there are some trips you have to take alone.
that i am faithful to dead causes.
that there are no second chances and barely any firsts.

that we can be cheated of futures that were never ours.
that i will never forget the airport.
that i put holes in my body.
that we ran through a city and we were in love.

that i'd go around by Doney's
to see you once more.
to laugh at that.
with you.

you told me where i stood.
i fell down.

to learn that language, to speak with your tongue
i've forgotten your taste but only mostly.

you were imprinted.

you've given me a window
to count every fiber of my being,
and every one agrees:
my worth has an inverse relationship to proximity.

maybe if i were a poet,
i'd give my life for yours.
i'd walk those streets with you.

calling all certainties forth to question: think, miss, love.
the heart's sudden inability to unravel memory from lie.

we had a song.

the way a jaw works over words that won't form
the way the chest hitches as the devastation soaks in
the gasping, flailing loss underlying disbelief.

of course you'll see me again.
of course you'll see me before i go.
of course i still love you.
of course.
of course i miss you.
think about you.
dream of you.
of course you'll see me again.

of course
i've never seen any of them again.
of course.

because i would come to you
over the water
through hills and memory
i would come to you,
i promise.
through the fragile web of the distances between us
accelerating into turns
never looking back,
i would come to you.
i would run.
i would promise.
if you asked me.

i'd run alongside your code forever
girding for wars of desire without end.

was never known to command respect from his peers
was known to steal his fourteen minutes in fragments
was known to sometimes allow ashes to burn on his forearms and face
while waiting patiently for them to gutter out
because at least it was something nearing proof
that he was there at all

jog shuttle to pause, play:
rupture, rend, rive, split, cleave:

edited a past away.

what you thought would disappear
lies
and waits.

it wasn't love
but it was something as painful.

OF SPLENDOR, OF MISERY

OF SPLENDOR, OF MISERY

If we're going to do this," Jean Reynald paused to snuff out the unfiltered cigarette between his fingertips and the ashtray glass, "I want my ship back."

"That's.. impractical." Cellophane wrapper crumpled in Paul's hand. Next, foil. These late-time strategery sessions were bronzed with a nicotine aftertaste. "We've looked for—"

"Maggie or nothing. That's the deal."

"I can't just—"

"Paul."

Eyes lock across distances deeper than a tabletop, a war machine. "Fine. We'll get her. Any other requests for your strike team?"

"Only two more. Relatively easy."

"Let me guess—"

"Simon."

"And pilot?"

"Michael."

"Of course."

Reynald's silvered eyes narrowed as he sipped the last of his monkey-picked oolong. "Son, I know there are places you don't want to go, and people you never thought you'd be asked to bring in. I wouldn't ask you this if I didn't know that we need them. That's the cold truth of this: we need them."

Flick, scratch, click. Paul inhaled, talked through the smoke's exit. "I know."

❧

"Why?"

"Hmm?"

"This place—Why'd you bring me here?"

The wait—The weight of being whole draped the winter plains with a tougher skin than dustings of snow could provide. He'd dreamt worlds into realities, and this was how he now regarded the ghost space: more Minnesota January than Michigan February. He'd been to neither place, now never would.

The work-shined leather gloves were warmer than they'd ever really been. The realizations of ghosts were in the details of perception. There were trees on those edges, timothy spines interrupting the cadence of the frozen ground's rises and falls. Grabbing and tearing one of the winter hay stalks without gloves would have been painful; the way timothy snaps, inserts itself into the palm when grabbed, when dry. Under gloves' pressure, there was no danger, a buffer between red-stitched palms and infection. Ground those now-weeds into chaff. Alfalfa barely broke the snow's surface; it was pliant, without will, bending to the white pressure and hiding until rising again, desiccated, in the thaws.

"If we're going to make this work, there are things about me you have to accept."

Alina walked to his side, faced the small snowed stone, one of dozens (hundreds, thousands?) across the ghost space. Glove reached for glove, but his hand was slack, not returning her attempt at reassurance through pressure. That place contextualized a particular, peculiar fear: he's gone already, no hand in that glove; this is how distance feels, tastes of wind.

"Say something."

"What do you—"

"Anything. Something." But in that expanse, silence seemed the most appropriate discourse.

"I—"

"Not that, not here. There's no way you could, not here."

"Get out of my head."

It hung there.

The glove under her grasp grew a framework of bones and action as it pulled away. He knelt before the stone, swept away the sugared surface. She thought of childhoods she'd not known spent building forts in the snow, a sunny day lying warmth, hardpack bleeding into snowpants, numbing knees and afternoon hot chocolate before suppertime. Snotty noses frozen solid. What semblance of a childhood she'd survived had had alternate definitions of forts, bleeding, and freezing.

"Know this: this man beneath me, this boy, he died because I chose typing over listening. Stayed home to finish writing a book and never looked at his warnings. Spent years trying to convince myself it wasn't my fault, but I know... If I'd listened—"

"Paul, you—"

"And this one?" His bad knee locked upon attempts to rise, limped with a dragging right diagonally one row, one column. "She wasn't nearly as passive a departure. Forced her away, murdered her in time. There's a murder that allows the victim to persist. And persist," he wiped the rock face, "she did, never knowing that she'd died. From the inside of a life based on lies, it's easy to confuse continuation with happiness."

"You're—"

"A *god*. A fucking *god* here."

Stumbled over two, up one.

"Paul, it's—"

"She," wiped the face, his own, "died in my arms. Do you still want this?"

"—not your fault."

Pulled the gloves off, clenched hands to fists, smashed both against the ground. Compound fractures, each finger. Echoed across skeleton trees. The wind had stopped. She'd felt the impact across twenty silent feet.

He stood, dribbling blood and flecking fragments to the ground. Steam. One simple flash and his claws had repaired. Grabbed both gloves in one hand.

"I refuse to be the end of you," stood in place, yet she walked toward his speech, "but if we do this, there's no other way."

"You can't know that."

"I can't," another line burned across his temple, "but I do. I'm asking you to leave. Right now. Don't be a part of this. I can almost see your face—You're becoming integral."

Proximity. Saw silver crawling behind his muddied eyes. Alina thumbed the new burn, allowed her palm to rest against the unshaven cheek. "I'm not leaving."

He grabbed her wrist, considered removing her touch, but held her hand closer. Mouth played over appropriate sentiments, found none to voice. Some communications are solely internal approximations of external poetries.

Love is, after all, sacrifice, whether borne out in bitten tongues, arms wrapped around and stifling fears, nighttime combat over sheets and vying for higher percentages of a bed's square footage. No one will admit to the fraction of hate rippling under love's frozen surface, because to acknowledge that dichotomy would undermine the hesitant interplay that defines desire. Love is, after all, defined by loss.

❧

Staff meeting.

West noted the unfamiliar, growing steadily more-familiar, silence whispering out of the stillness of the birth chambers. The ratcheting and slams of a million billion artificial canals had been replaced by the echoing nothing in which you could park the moon, if you were in fact driving it, ever since Judith had—

fused with Alina, the new woman walked in and took her place at the table. She still answered to Alina, Al, Cap'n Crunch, sweetness, but she was more. The god Judith had found home, and that home was somehow less mousy-haired, less banana-titted. She'd grown freckles for every transgression that she wore mostly on her shoulders and the back of her neck, a scatter across gently-angled cheekbones under upturned eyes. As she slid into her chair, utilitarian (the chair, completely, the woman, mostly), Reynald cleared his throat, and she raised her hand to preempt.

"Boys."

And they were. Veritable sausage-fest. West, Reynald, Hank, Sam. The twins were elsewhere. The bear lacked balls.

"Where is he?" Reynald accented over the three words, the tension materializing in the acute angles of his fingers.

"Detox." Her term for the silver chamber. Quickening, they all knew. More and more time in the mercury sea, leaching out, leaching in, a Chinaman's attempt at karaoke. "Let's hear it."

"The Lettuce Brothers report A/O lock at eight under, hovering on Delta." West let the glass tink the tabletop. Things were falling in the space outside of time.

"New sights, new sounds?"

"Fairly certain Tunguska, 1908, fourteen-seven."

"Good. File under 'sneaking suspicion.' Next?"

"Bleedthrough tertiaries on 1994, 1998 lines, fourteen-seven."

"Interesting, but no surprises. Next?"

"Lunar meteor impact, 2047."

"Fourteen—?"

"Thirty-three."

"Extrapolations?"

"Didn't touch our target. Fucked thirty-three over, though. Moon collision. Sixth extinction."

"Kink... Forget it, let's run the nineteen naught-eight probables and feed it to the maths. Get on it asap. Target completion—"

"Wednesday is the day we fight."

"'Thursday is the day we fade, to live a life unfiltered, mirrors of the ways we smoke to graves, we are ghosts,' et cetera, et cetera. Don't quote him. Not here."

A rubber can only hold so much, and Hank finally came. He slammed his palm down on the resin tabletop, pulled off his hat, looking strangely pathetic given the tousled strands of surviving white hair sticking straight up from his head, falling in slow motion back into place, a high red rudding his nose and cheeks. His jaw working up to: "Goddamn it, just *stop* this shit."

"Problem, Mr. Cowboy?"

"Yes there's a *problem*, Jud. Al. Whoever the hell you are today."

"Care to bring it to the group, or are you just going to smack my table around some more?"

There is an uncomfortable dynamic that develops when dams break, when dikes leak, when a group of people share something and must present it to an uninitiated brunt oblivious to the conflict. This dynamic evidences itself in diverted eyes, sudden attention gifted to the mundane: a hangnail, the right angle at a paper's corner, evidences in the until-then suppressed urge to clear a throat or cough.

The assembled hierarchy of Judith Command, at least those possessing balls, now all looked to Hank while Alina leaned back into her chair and interlocked her fingers with a confidence that could only have come from Judith herself.

These men were not cowards; know that. They just didn't know how to tell god she was wrong. They were each fictional characters, but they left it to the fictional character twice removed from reality to voice their concerns. Hank, as a character within a television show within a novel, had a disconnect that they couldn't.

His gun hand shaped itself into an all-fingers representation thereof and pointed at the young woman at the table's head. "You," he chose words just before speaking them, crafting each into viable concepts, "need to get that fucking boy out of the silver and into this room."

"Miss him?"

He scoffed. "We all do, girl. But more than that—That shit's getting into his head. He ain't no good to us in there. If we're gonna—"

"I believe he met with Reynald yesterday...?"

"He did." Jean Reynald's voice wasn't nearly as unafraid as he'd hoped. "It was... I don't know."

"That ain't the point, and you know it. If we're gonna finish this, he needs to be a part of it. Can't all be worked out by you two."

"We," Alina's face stuttered over a smile, "have things in hand." A jump cut reduced to a fraction of a frame, for an instant, Hank saw Judith looking out from Alina's eyes. "Don't you trust us?"

"'Us?' No. Alina, yes. Paul, yes. Jud, you scare the shit out of me. He wrote me. You're just along for the ride, and I don't rightly appreciate you taking over while he's swimming."

"Listen, Hank... I'll try to be better about this. Try to get him in here and—"

"You do that."

She paused. "He needs to get his shit together. That's why—"

"—he lives in the silver? It ain't right, girl. He ain't right no more."

"We're working on it."

❧

He'd never learned how to swim.

He'd never trusted meditation, relegated it solely to the province of those unshowered *non-Western* types who embraced yoga and feng-shui and ate Thai to make themselves feel worldly. He didn't meditate in the silver pool; he thought, too much, simple as that.

He grew angrier with breathing.

The pool seemed deeper in those final days, and not being able to swim (or float—even with the requisite remainder beer belly, he had a hard time floating), he walked into the tideless, tideful mirror lake until the surface tickled his lips, plugged his ears and slid into his nose, his eyes above the surface until the alien crawled into and through, his too-long hair a shawl on the silver, grasped and pulled under by a trillion trillion reaching robots, giving himself to the pull and disappearing under the sealing, untouched glass.

After that first breath, he sometimes forgot to take another.

It wasn't meditation; he wouldn't allow the word to stain him, so imbued with past hatreds and connotations of loss. He thought. Tried to wrap his mind around a solution: they were slowly losing the war. Maire's nightmare forces, combinations of silvers, bleeds into all realities, were gaining non-ground quickly, urged forever onward by the great archives of knowledge stored in Hope's and Whistler's stolen patterns. Forts were burning, out on the periphery of core reality. Maire was strong, getting stronger. He was weak. She was coming for him, cutting straight for the heart of him, and he was tripped up more by his insecurities than a shattered knee he'd not yet lived through. The silver was the only place the outside non-world didn't scream at him; his children, the trillion trillions, whispered, sang in voices beneath perception. It was a cold embrace, but it gave him purpose.

The singing, bodhisattva drones, the tender tickle as they erased farmer tans, tweezed an ingrown hair from his jaw, twisted cancers from purchase in his lung and prostate, tenderly, tenderly aligned a spine, sloughed dead cells, slowed a racing heart, closed ducts and reassured, the singing, the drones.

He felt a hand.

Paul spun, lashed, feet pushing the bottom away, rising above the surface in motion, slowly, noting the returning droplets of the splash, the drone lapsed. He gasped, fearful that he wasn't alone, treaded toward the shore, hands shifting and eyes burning at the prospect of combat.

Another back breached the surface, the body arcing from one edge, familiar, unbeautiful and fundamentally same. A scar across the chest, code burns on left forearm, the white mark of Cain blaring less obviously from the right temple.

The figure stood, bent to the right: shattered knee. The figure stood, slicked with silver, unnaturally-large hands, hardened sculptures of bone and obtuse angle, brushed the liquid metal from arms and chest. The teeth were the same. The jib was cut more of brass than silver. It extended a hand.

"Shake my hand, brother." And he thought of the cold war of the end of his youth, a father extending a hand to a brother, the same admonition, met with refusal. "Shake my hand."

Fundamentally same, but.

"Come with me."

❧

They sat at the edge of the silver pool, Indian-style, both slumped forward for the weight of their torsos. They'd once been described as unique constructs: chicken legs, barrel torsos, the longest arms and biggest hands. Not well-designed. Unique. Pieced together from leftover parts. Mistakes given life.

Paul looked into the newcomer, had questions but didn't ask. The older version had answers but didn't offer them.

Whereas Paul was an image of a specific point in history, the post-college unraveling of muscle, a jowl, a gut, hair past his shoulders (he'd let it grow out since Hope had—) and a beard, full, (he'd let it grow out since Hope had—), the other was a study in evolutions and counterpoints, the face better-defined under taut skin, the hair cropped short, now lit with a disconcerting array of pure whites on the side, a clump, Whistler-esque, growing in at the line. Deeper canyons flanking the eyes, the mouth's edges forced a little deeper down by years. Two gray flecks marring the brown-green surface of the right eye, rendering it blind. The torso wasn't smaller, the arms not shorter; the legs were still chicken. Gray insinuated new patterns into the chest.

"Upgrade?"

"Paradigm shift."

"Office talk."

"Realism."

"Huh."

"Call me your Omega."

⁂

"Is this better?"

The silver pool had disappeared, replaced with the Cafe Bellona. Paul noted a sign on the counter: UNDER NEW MANAGEMENT. A bus ground to a halt at the stop down the street. The brakes sounded like screaming.

"Not better. Different."

The coffee shop was empty save the two time-offset versions of the same man. Paul thought he heard a rustling behind the counter, through the door leading to the inner sanctum, coffee filters and the cash box and mops. Presumably, New Management was back there. Those hidden sounds were more frightful than they should have been, the creak of a floorboard, the swish of fabric, the clearing of a throat.

"Where is everyone?"

The Omega let the question hang and fall. He gestured toward the great windows at the shop's front. There were people passing by, eyes as downcast as the day was overcast, no one diverting attention to Bellona.

Something crashed in the back. Paul jumped.

The link was dead. It was supposed to show the president.

Most of the tables' chairs were still turned upside-down on their tops. The lights were off. Maybe it wasn't open yet? Maybe Bellona had new hours of operation? The chair legs obscured the corners in dozens. Paul noticed that theirs was the only set table.

"Supposed to be people here. Simon and Maggie, Joseph and Helen, S—"

"Don't."

"How does it all end?"

"More with a bang than a whimper."

"No." Paul struggled over concepts. "Me. How does it end?"

"You developed a germinoma around your pineal gland at age twenty-four."

"Brain cancer?"

"You died of an overdose of anti-seizure medication at age twenty-seven."

"And you?"

The Omega smiled, an expression that reminded Paul of war. "That's me."

"I don't understand—"

"—and that's the problem. You're sitting there setting all these events into motion, having to retype the number 6 because your keyboard's broken, not as badly as you, and I know, I know that you saw those things, never did the research, fought with the fact that no one believed you. I know you saw things before they happened and wrote them down, uploaded them, and everyone thought you were looking into places you shouldn't, that your predictions were just snooping or luck, the falling towers, a hanging, a wedding, the silver. I know that.

"You've written things into existence, and I know you've struggled, tried to undo the damage done. And I know you'd sooner waste yourself away, surrender, than hurt the ones you loved again. I know you've seen the terrifying weaponry, the holland and hills, that you've walked beyond return to that edge, and you've tasted it, looked over and wondered. I know that. You've spent countless nights replaying the scenes in your head, wars fought between the worlds, great machines built of silver and light, the savage echo of billion-barreled shatter arrays, the silences, and there aren't words for what you've seen; no typing can convey that.

"I know you were basically a good man made bad by the departures of others, unable to grasp the concept that you weren't integral, were never integral enough to include, and the mathematics never worked: you wanted to be constant in a variable existence. You wanted—maybe deserved—a new calculus you never invented.

"You scared people.

"You're scaring people, and that's why they leave.

"I know you tried to fix it, the distance and the pills, hiding from the world while broadcasting the substance of their fear, flirting recklessly with their expectations of you, pushing away and surrendering, again, to your hate. You are a creature of hate. No forgiveness. When the world reacted negatively, you worked to dismantle it and rebuild it in your image. You fell into a place where no one could ever begin to understand.

"You weren't a sympathetic character."

Paul had been studying the city outside Bellona. People dissolved between ghosts. The sky darkened, an upload spire crashing to purchase in the distance, farther off, the orbital gun rising from the water, firing blinding phase slugs into the future. The sounds from the back settled dreamlike into a rhythm, a pounding heartbeat. A shiver worked its way up his spine, settled along his jawline.

"How do I fix it?"

The Omega shrugged. "You were a flawed machine, and it only ended once I—once *you* decided to silence the misfiring synapses. It'd been getting worse, the shaking, the thoughts at night. You were consumed, consuming yourself. A spectrum of innocent histories dredged into existence, trillions dead. Because of you."

"You're asking me to—"

"No. I'm just the end point of a statistically-significant percentage of histories. I'm not asking you to end yourself. You constructed characters, turning everyone whose hand you shook into fiction. You unlearned presence. You wrote people into plotlines and barely registered their realities. You filtered everyone through pasts. I'm asking you to recognize that you're not the episiarch, assembling realities. You're a character who doesn't know how the book ends. You're distracting what limited audience you have left with flowery language, never offering substance. They want resolution, a dogfight, a gun, not self-analysis buttered with delay tactics. Write the fucking book. Get it done."

"You're confusing them."

"And that's why I'm dead now. You don't have to be. If I could take it all back, the vengeance, the worlds shunted into existence, I would. What you have to do is separate your realities. These characters aren't the people you love or your mailman or the cashier at Price Chopper. Stop living inside of your book and start finishing it."

It manifests itself in one side of the face, the body, the head turning to the right, that side's eye clenching as closed as a fist, the subtle, uncontrolled flail of an arm against the table and its retreat to the lap, the foot tapping, not a symptom of boredom or nervous energy, just a manifestation of the worm that's gripping his brain.

"Some lives are cursed." Teeth gritting, speech barely escaping, a graveled whisper.

"Paul, you have to—"

"Let all—" a stutter, frustration flaring across the edges of attack.

"Paul—"

"L-let all Earth buh—" A simple, passionate fury.

"*Paul.*"

"Let all Earth be a *grave*."

Slow, sad. The Omega shook his head. "All Earth? Or just the exile city?"

Paul snarled inadvertently, the clenched jaw and upturned lip baring a V of teeth, giving him a decidedly deranged glare. Half a person shook with rage.

"You might be interested to know, you have a lesion in your corpus callosum, a precursor to the pineal growth. Should have stopped smoking, son." His smile was a mixture of pity and resignation.

"D-Don't call mmm—"

"Such lesions can lead to the infamous 'alien hand syndrome.' It cleaves the mind, ruptures, rends it in half. Splits presence. Gives voice to id."

Paul's right hand swept over the edge and slammed the tabletop.

The Omega regarded it blankly. "There were compelling studies that suggested we have little control over action, that the body begins to take action against stimuli before it decides to tell the brain what's happening. Not just reflex responses, burning or injury, but more complex reactions to a range of situations. Our sciences proved our divinity. Your flat affect was nothing more than an emotionally-autistic withdrawal response to precognition. You had a reach and couldn't deal with it. Stuck in a feedback loop.

"You want an answer for the loss? Want a target? Don't blame the boy who killed himself, the girls who left you for the exile city. And don't blame the city, Tzee-tzee-lal-itc or Sealth or Seattle, the little place where people cross over. Fitting title, considering the when and where of my crossing. Want a target?"

Paul nodded. It was a gesture pulled to one side.

"Maire."

Noise roared from the back room.

"You couldn't write her out of the picture if she got to you first. She does, eventually. She was there, whispering into an ear the day before your twentieth birthday. She pulled a love away from across three thousand miles. Helped secure the noose. Walked a step behind you each moment since the day you first typed her name. Extrapolate exponentially: in a Red Mount laboratory thousands of years from now, in a place that was once the focal point of your hate, a fourth-generation clone of a man named Michael Balfour, a former L-level Styx, will build a machine that will ensure the survival of the species. Maire will find it. She'll use it to unravel everything. You're responsible, having typed her into existence. She owes you a fundamental debt, but she'll do anything to stop you from writing her out. She'll do anything she can to widen the Delta bleed, to merge these two realities. She'll combine the strength of the Purpose and the silver, and you'll never be able to stop her. This is where it has to happen, right here, this innocent point of commonality between all possible realities, a little city on an insignificant rock in a backwater When no one cares about."

"She's been behind all of this, the betrayals, making people leave for—" his eyes looked out across Seattle—"this?"

"She's bringing the pieces home. She hopes you'll follow."

Paul shook his head in rejection. His fists settled into a bleak and horrifying surrender.

"Hunt her down. You've quite a group of friends waiting out there for you, fictional and non."

Somewhere along the conversation, the shaking had calmed.

"And—"

"Alina?"

"Yeah."

"She started pure, until you started writing into her. Can't take Jud out now, but you can prevent something deeper."

"How?"

"Don't you dare write reality into her. Keep her here. Don't see another in her. If you do, Maire will get her claws into her, and that's it. Three strikes. You can't control your real future. Just live with it."

"You didn't."

"Paul, I'm just a character in a book. A meditation. I'm the alien hand, or maybe the lesion, or maybe the tumor. But I'm not here to hurt you—just to keep you alive long enough."

"Long enough for what?"

"To win."

❧

Grasping, reaching, screaming.

love is the nearest unsteady light;
a heart can only break so many times before you start
to lose the most important pieces of yourself.

"I'm sorry."

The statement didn't so much flop as leap to the floor and grope around, seeking meaning.

"That's it?" West's face was steel and stubble.

"I don't expect a simple apology to—"

"You're damned right you don't expect. You've been in that fucking silver for so long, we didn't think you'd ever come out. Didn't think you'd ever finish writing."

"West." Alina reached out.

"And don't *you* start, god damn it. Every minute he's spent in that pool is another minute we've lost a ship, lost a fort. The bleed's picking up speed, no thanks to the hours or months or fucking years he's spent swimming."

"We can fix—"

"Alina, the Delta's at ninety over. Maire's gained a lot of ground since the last confrontation in Seattle. Since we lost Hope and brought in the Lettuce Brothers. We need new modular calculus. She's had a lot of time to infect both the Alpha and Omega lines. The code's spilling everywhere." Reynald pushed his glass forward across the table. It glowed with Delta gains. "We might be at a point where nothing we can do can—"

"Judith can show us the way."

"She can show you the way, inside looking out." West studied the window looking out onto stagnant birth fields. "And truth be told, I don't trust you any more than I trust him." He pivoted his head toward the author, met his gaze with no apology. "Hope was just the first to go. We can't fucking find anyone out there anymore. Hunter and Lilith? Whistler and Hank tried sniffing them out for months. If anyone could lock those lines, it would've been them. But the Whens are emptying out. Everything's blurred. Silver."

"What do you want me to do? How can I make it up to you?" Paul spoke through clenched teeth. "You think I was in there for the hell of it? You think—"

"I don't know what to think, boy."

Reynald cleared his throat. "I think what Adam's trying to say... We've been sitting here too long. Losing too many good people to Maire's armies. Waiting for a miracle to walk out of that pool. You. We've done what you asked, looked for more characters to bring in, reinforced the lines. We've done everything we could to seal off the merges. But none of it's been enough. We've been waiting for a miracle, and you've been swimming. We've lost faith."

"Alina has been a good commander?"

"She's done her best."

"And you've expected more from her?"

"I've expected more from you, Author." Reynald was cool. "Fewer words and more action. We've held the line as long as we could, but we're losing. Maire's only growing more powerful, the more her forces consume, with each break between the lines she finds. Her forces are pouring through, and the war's not just out there. We're all fading. I don't know who I am anymore."

"That neat little battle we saw at the initial bleed?" West remembered Frost's fleet, the beauty of their easy victory over the Enemy assembly. That insertion had been the first hint at something fundamentally flawed in the timeline, the Judas and Enemy in a time and place they shouldn't have been, a fragmented, shattered procession of reality from beginning to end starting to collapse upon itself, a blending of at first two distinct universes. "We've been losing steadily since. No matter who we bring in. All the main characters, all the forgotten plot points. None of it seems to matter. We're out of options. No more fresh meat to bring in." He picked Reynald's glass off the table. "Delta's propagating out of control, and we need to stop it now. We're only holding on to ten percent of existence, and—"

"Eight percent." Reynald's fingertips dropped from his subdermal.

West just shook his head, and Paul could see the wetness of frustration glinting in his eyes. "Eight fucking percent. What's that? Another three forts along the timestream? Another hundred fifty vessels?"

"Adam—"

"If you have a miracle, now's the fucking time, boy. If you learned anything in the pool, you better teach us right fucking now."

"I did."

And he was silver.

ஒ

Maire was pleased.

She realized she'd lived a lifetime of lie and hypocrisy. She'd embraced everything that formed the core of her hatred and attempted to manipulate it to her own ends. After the revelation, after encountering Michael Zero-Whatever in the Seychelles Drift, the tiny machine of night with its encoded civilizations that she could have held in her broken hand, after learning the nature of silver, she'd taken that possibility and used it to initiate the Forever Dust. She remembered Hannon's collapsing vessel and a war machine named Gary and the gorgeous dissemination of silver powder throughout everything, everything, but perhaps the most poignant memory as her body ungrew, as she stood a child dissolving into infancy, was the sight of Hunter Windham and his gun, that beautiful gun so like her own, and the phased slug that had sheared off the side of his head, leaving his body to collapse next to the love of his life, the spent and murdered Lilith. In that moment, she'd experienced the base loneliness of the final survivor of her existence, but she knew it wouldn't last. The child Maire, the infant Maire, grasped the Zero-Four probe in her palm, thought it to life, ushered it into silent expansion, gave meaning to loss and ruin.

They whispered through her now, the trillion trillions of uploaded souls, merging with her, feeding yet sustaining, outside of times and places. She was a galaxy; she was everything.

There had been a moment of abject solitude in the wake of Hunter's parting shot. She struggled against her child mind's instinctual reaction to sob, to plop down on that barren plain and grind tiny fists into the open sores of her eyes. She suspected that his body had held the possibility of immortality, if she could have gotten to it in time. Lying dead on the dust as the vessel collapsed around it, the corpse mocked her ambitions. She suspected a grin if there'd been enough face left to sculpt one.

Great slabs of metallish flung down through the silver cloud, drawn gravitationally toward center, against the outward tide of her eternity of tiny machines. The hunks of vessel frictioned red and shot apart with rends that burst her eardrums. The child Maire calmly toddled to Hunter's body, to Lilith's. A slick lost in that cacophony, and she split Lilith's chestplate, gutted her down. The child reached into the still-warm torso to her shoulder, searched, finally withdrew her crimson arm, her fist clenched around a tiny silver marble. The child smiled and grew up.

She knew there were survivors. Had to be. The universe is too rich, too fecund an expanse to allow the extinction of it all. She remembered heaven and Michael: *"I need you to kill a god."*

And she had—she had, but she knew that it hadn't been the god Michael had intended. She'd used the ocean of tiny machines to wage her war on Judith, and she'd succeeded, for the most part, but she'd left her existence a barren machine plane. She hated the stink of internal betrayal, the way she had used the machines to erase their darling, humble Jud. A wash of unreality and she heard in every fiber of her a word that meant nothing: *Kilbourne*. She felt an affinity, a sisterhood, with a concept she could never understand.

To kill a god. Yes. Another. The god that gave voice to all others. Divinity is layered, and at the bottom, the Author.

Because you must understand that her life of war had been lived with the distinct ambition of escape and manipulation. She had survived torture to exact revenge. She had forced herself to continue for the sole purpose of taking back all that had been lost to the machines and their collaborators. She'd seen the silver of the trees, the great black forms in the Drift, and she had known a higher purpose. Some people are the focal points of histories, and that realization was what had kept her always forward, always struggling. Weaker creatures would have given up, but hatred inspires. Maire was the embodiment of an intricate vengeance, a network of possible outcomes overlaid on an empty universe. When given the opportunity to take her jihad to the stars and across time, she welcomed the Enemy into her hearts, fusing them, reshaping her entirely, becoming something distinctly alien and alone. She felt a stronger Purpose than any those simple souls could dream.

She would be their Omega. She would give voice and drive to their hive desires. They wanted to upload every possible When; she wanted an end, of sorts.

And now it was happening. Those first forays into Alpha had whet her appetite; she'd eaten Hope Benton's soul and had seen the break in the author, that god, that target of her new war. After his mental collapse and retreat, her forces had raided the timeline, pushing Delta further, slaughtering Judith and Judas before them. With Paul awol, it was only time, only *time*, before Maire rewrote all of existence, every possible, fragile strand, in her own image. And then— then she could rewrite the Enemy in her image. Delete.

She had gathered an infinite number of strands and pulled them together into a cohesive plan of action. She had tasted the pattern cache, sampled its inhabitants, judged them beautiful and given them voice. She was more powerful than a god. She was

❧

silver hands before them, flickering and yearning. A flash, and they were his hands again, simple, too-big hands of callus and hangnail.

Nobody said anything. The fear in the room was palpable and cloying.

"I've absorbed it. The silver." Something crawled behind Paul's eyes, something dark and brilliant, in sum horrifying. Alina's hand had gone to her chest, as if simple flesh and bone could have protected her from her lover's silver. "I've overcome it."

"Paul..." West was as disturbed at the display as any of the others, but he was the only observer brave or stupid enough to speak. "The silver's inside of you?"

The author shifted again. "No." His hands sparkled to translucence, and the fade crawled up his arms. His transformation was a visual assault of static and stark, frigid light, a billion frames a second. "I *am* silver."

"But it's—" Reynald had leaned back in his chair, as if six additional inches could protect him. "We're unshielded. Why isn't it—"

"I've surrendered to it. I let it in. At the first Delta bleed, we saw I could kill it. And now it's a part of me. I can sustain it. It can sustain me."

Nobody responded to his smile. They weren't used to smiles of any sort from him, and that smile was particularly disconcerting, one of madness and barely-controlled fury.

"I surrendered to it. It's so beautiful." His form shifted further toward total mercury. The static became audible, the more the silver consumed him.

"Paul." Alina whispered, her fear soaking through and emerging through colorless eyes. "Come back."

"You asked for a miracle," he growled. "Now you've got it. Afraid, Jud?"

"No, it's just—"

"Don't lie to me." He walked to Alina's side, crouched down so that his face was at her level. "You're afraid. You should be."

"Paul, please." Alina blinked back something. She recoiled from him, as if his touch would be fire, the coldest fire, one assembled from zeroes and ones, old gods forged from gold and alloys, universes of souls. "Come back to me."

He reached to caress her cheek, his hand shifting back to flesh and bone before surfacing. She felt its warmth, its utterly normal, familiar warmth.

"I never left you." He stood, palming a glass from the table as he walked to overlook the birth fields. "Assemble the remnants of the fleet. We're assaulting Delta."

"It could take time to recall the forces containing the—"

"Bring them home. Bring them all home."

"Yes, sir." Reynald went through the motions of belief.

"Now." Stern.

Reynald and West stood and walked from the chamber, West casting one backward glance. Paul nodded without emotion. He knew there could be no understanding.

He was left alone in the room with Alina. It was the kind of occupation that rooms don't forget, the tangible fear and confusion of impending battle or love gone tragically wrong.

"I know what I have to do now."

She didn't respond to him, just pulled her top closed over banana cleavage. There was a winter fuming from him. He turned to her, and she studied the black glass on the tabletop. She had nothing more to say.

Because even the most passionate, ardent loves become unseated from passion and reality, replacing the underpinnings of possibility and hope with fragile experience. To see him shift—something had changed more than the underlying molecular layout of his physical form. Hearing his voice was like listening to every voice ever uttered screaming. They were inside him. He was plural. He was lost in the silver, the archive of lives he'd written into existences. Her fear manifested itself in an inability to speak out loud. His new, silver form resonated through the space, and she didn't know if her fear was her own or purely Judith's, if she was reliving a million Judith deaths or simply precognizing her own.

"I do love you."

He wasn't looking at her.

"I know."

She didn't.

❧

staring, but not seeing
thinking of the thought (itself)
breathing, but not living

He stirred his coffee.

What are the odds that we'll find the right person out of six billion people? What are the odds that we'll find anyone at all?

There was a quiet desperation to his madness, as quiet as the rhythmic clink of a stainless steel spoon against ceramic can allow. The sound was lost in the chaos of the place, orders shouted and steam escaped, the various startup beep-boop-beeps of laptop computers and the omnipresent tide of cell phone rings. Maybe a talent strummed a guitar in the corner. Maybe the world was falling apart.

Sip. He spilled some coffee as muscles twinged.

It was the wrong coast, the exile city, the embodiment of that place within us all, that darkest and most hidden place, the snarling, echoing graveyard hacked deeply into the most shielded hearts. He lit a cigarette and no one noticed. He hadn't written them to notice.

He felt the silver crawling through him, the ocean of machines still replacing flesh with metal. The body is strong and reluctant. It fights to the final beat.

But he suspected that there was a measure of surrender in his being there, Cafe Bellona on those days and in those times, the intersections of impossible histories, the unbelievable coincidences. He had to see. Had to know. Maybe he didn't know how to live if he couldn't tear himself apart. Maybe it's not really living if the heart is intact.

He was beginning to feel the approach of the ending, knew that soon the machines would have finished their purpose. He wanted to see the bleed before it was gone. Needed Seattle, that coffee shop. Needed to know. Needed something, anything, to show him that this war was worth fighting.

Reached into his pocket for his lighter and inventoried the contents, a glass ring, a blue, cracked marble, a tiny wooden puzzle piece shaped like Michigan. A silver bracelet he could no longer wear, couldn't because he needed no gripping, constant reminder of loss.

Lit another cigarette and stirred the coffee again.

President Jennings was on the link. Joseph Windham walked in from the rain, brushing the wet from his black leather trench as he surveyed the establishment for Helen Lofton, who waved to him with one gloved, shielded hand. Simon Hayes was engaging in a lively discussion of Hesse with Maggie Flynn. Michael Balfour read the entertainment section of a newspaper. A headline: *Hank the Cowboy Gets the Boot*. A child walked by, carrying a Honeybear Brown. Helen Lofton looked up and through Helen Lofton, holding Hunter's hand, Hunter's hand holding Honeybear. Uncle led a parade of little boys; angels escorted the shielded Lilith child. James Richter and Hope Benton paused outside, long enough for James to point down the street and recommend a restaurant. Simon Hayes stumbled by, almost knocking into Hope, his mind working over one word: *Brigid*. Jacob guitared in the corner. Susan and her drummer came in. Her pants were covered in paint; his pants were stitched with Kente cloth. She grabbed a job application from the basket on the counter. Susan stood behind the counter and smiled at her. She merged with the poet, who stood behind the counter, who walked in, talking to old friends from Sussex and someone new, a stranger Paul couldn't see but hated with what he had left. There would be a slam. She would win. Alina stared at him from behind the counter, and his heart was broken.

He saw himself run by again, run by with West and Hope, on their way to locate the bear. Honeybear was under the couch. Hunter and Helen were dead. Hope's cry echoed from a cave a world and lifetimes away as Maire murdered her. Alina grasped his hand.

We are machines of a horrible beauty.

Love is, after all, sacrifice, whether borne out in bitten tongues, arms wrapped around and stifling fears, nighttime combat over sheets and vying for higher percentages of a bed's square footage. No one will admit to the fraction of hate rippling under love's frozen surface, because to acknowledge that dichotomy would undermine the hesitant interplay that defines desire. Love is, after all, defined by loss.

Suddenly you're looking back and a week is gone, a month or a year, five, a decade, a lifetime, and it feels like a lifetime, a decade, five, a year or a month, a week, a day, hours, minutes, you're here, seconds, you're here and we're together, instants, you're here, moments, here, now, you're here, now, here forever, here, walking together down thin paths into broken futures and todays and

They'd all left him, all ended up here eventually, and he knew why, now. The bleed was palpable, the merging of everything he'd tried to write, from the adolescent crap a decade on to his last book. There's danger in writing reality into fiction. It was time for him to unravel it all.

Dregs. He still stirred. The rhythm and consistency of the sound just barely grounded him to that reality, a faint beacon as everything inside split apart and rewrote itself.

And it was gone, the people and cell phones and hissing machines, and again the Bellona was the silence it had been with his Omega. The wind picked up across the empty city outside, and something was in the back room, scratching and crashing and coming.

Everything he'd built, everything he'd erased, it'd all come down to this imperfect solitude. He thought of the poet and Alina, tried to separate the two, failed. He'd written her into fiction, or, worse, into nothing at all. Silences, silences. And in the perfect silence of the cafe, he knew how he'd end those universes of war.

An instant, a perfect moment of sound, the echoes of the dead, the enemy and the end, all those he'd let inside, all those who'd left. He heard their voices and knew that madness is beautiful.

Alina's door spiraled open. She knew it was him.

"Can I come in?"

She walked from the door and slinked into her chaise. Paul could differentiate the habits of the women combined in Alina.

She looked on in silence.

"Let me talk to Jud."

Alina looked hurt. "Something you don't want me to hear?"

"Just let her out."

Alina's eyes narrowed a huff, but she relented. A static flash, and Paul knew she'd been buried under the god.

"Good to see you're out of the pool, Paulywog." Jud grinned with Al's rabbit teeth.

"I need a pilot."

Jud nodded slowly. "Well, thanks to your time taking a dip, pilots are in short supply."

"I have one in mind."

"Nobody's been able to find Naught-Four or Simon."

"Not Michael."

"Hunter? And Lilith? Not exactly Judith *or* Judas material, kid."

"Alina."

Jud sat up at that. "Me?" She was suspicion and frown. "For why?"

"If we're going after Maire, I need someone to pilot—"

"You'll have your pick of the rides, Hughes."

"—me."

She let the statement soak in. Alina's face broadcast Jud's incredulity. "*Pilot* you? Pilot *you*?"

No sound, no motion.

"Unless I missed something being underneath Miss Becky Bananaboobs all this time, I don't follow."

He grabbed her hands. The shift was frigid and instant, the silver working out through his pores as it rolled behind his eyes. Jud hissed an inhalation as Alina's hands grew colder, pins and needles, the screaming, reaching need of the machine sea. The silver latticed up his arms and paved his shoulders, neck. He was growing. Increasing. Multitudes. Plates of metallish slammed down to define lines and planes. His form melted into something shiny and terrible.

"I need a pilot." His voice was static and distortion. It was still a growl.

"Paul..." Jud's voice was calm, and he could feel pieces of Alina shouting through.

"I can use Sam's shell. With Al in the pilot's chair, with you there..."

Jud stood up, pulled her hands from his with a tacking slurp. Head shaking, arms wrapped securely around herself, she walked to the window that looked out on the vacant birthing fields.

"This is your chance to kill Maire." He shifted back to skin and hair and scars.

Jud scoffed. She couldn't look at him.

"You deserve that."

Another bark of scorn, this time, the edge of a sob. "Deserve *what*?" Her hand swept out across the fields. "This? What kind of a life is this? Cycling through millions of bodies just to survive—" She wiped her hands on her sides and thighs. "Just to survive that fucking silver. And now you've let it in. I've already died once, kid." She finally looked at him. "You're killing yourself, and you know it. Nobody deserves this fucking life. And you've become everything we brought you here to destroy."

"I never meant for—"

"I know." She swallowed back the rest of her words.

"Help me."

"How? Follow you on this crusade? Watch you lose yourself in that *metal*?"

"If that's what it takes."

"She loved you."

He didn't have a response.

"And a part of her still does."

"She was never mine." The heart is unable to unravel memory from lie.

"She was yours, but the silver got you."

"You got her."

Jud bit back disappointment. "We merged so I could protect her."

"From me?"

"From you. And the silver. Should have never learned to swim. She's safe with me. It's always been there, the silver, and it's always worked its way through you. Writing people together. Should have kept her safe. You had a god damned obligation to keep her out of your head."

"I tried."

"Not fucking hard enough. Couldn't you have seen her for who she is, just Alina? Such a sweet, kind girl. Half-crazy, sure, but. Maybe not much to look at, but beautiful. But the second you started merging her with others, that's when you really lost her."

"Then give her back. Come with me. Be my pilot."

Jud stood silent. A billion empty birth chambers, a billion lives now impossible and fading. She'd been a god once, buried at the center of a planet. She'd been a god once, consumed by the silver contagion. She'd never felt so helpless.

"Come with me." Paul put his hand on her shoulder.

Jud nodded.

༄

The Judith Mara smashed lazily into the winter plain, shearing both nacelles from its superstructure. The control hub bounced twice, three times, came to rest in a mile of drifted snow.

Maire smiled. *Continue the assault.* The willing enslaved populations of the Enemy mind-essence obeyed.

Her war was big. Across the solar system, galaxy, across the entire universe of the Alpha line, Enemy forces spidered on silver webs, consuming every soul that had been left behind. She had been hoping to catch one of Jud's inner circle, but this kill would taste just as delicious.

A dozen Enemy were already on the hub, cutting, prying apart the smooth black of it. They stood aside so she could clamber in. The hole was tight; she ungrew a decade until she was in the command chamber. She smoothed her jet black swathe of hair behind her ears.

Sapphire West lay half crushed underneath the gauntlet interface chandelier. Loops of sputtering silver web draped her.

"Children waging wars," Maire said as she walked closer to the mess and grew back to her choice age. "They're really running out of options, aren't they?"

"Fuck you." Sapphire coughed a mist of blood. Her chest was crumpled under metallish black. Her left hand still hung in the air, suspended by her gauntlet. Maire tenderly released the mechanism and helped Sapphire's arm to the floor. The girl was tangled in interface web.

She reached immediately to her cardiac shield, fingers skittering over the surface, trying to pause and log out. Maire swiftly crunched down on Sapphire's hand, feeling the bones of her break beneath. The girl didn't scream, but two lines of tear were coaxed to the surface and out.

"He's sending little girls to do his job for him." Maire bared her silver fangs as she crouched down to Sapphire's tangled pieces. "Don't cry, child. You'll be with your sister soon."

"Don't you fucking—"

"Too late. Jade's droptroops were among the first to go."

"You motherf—"

Maire tore into the girl, her claws slicing into the cardiac shield and cleaving her breast into halves. Sapphire lurched, but she was trapped under the weight of the dead Mara's umbilicals. She tried to scream, but a simple flick, and her vocal cords were split. Maire gutted her, the foul internals steaming out into the frigid air. She reached into Sapphire's chest, groped around, and plucked a tiny silver marble from its resting place. She admired its design and saw movement from the corner of her

Honeybear Brown smashed the side of Maire's head with a hanging interface line, but teddy bears don't have much strength. The impact elicited a quick jolt of pain and a bark of surprise from Maire, who whirled on the toy. He jumped at her throat and clawed there, but his paws were plush. Before she could throw him off, he scrambled down between her breasts and wrenched Sapphire's marble from her hand. He landed on the floor with not much of a sound at all, tumbling to rights and activating his shield.

"You mother*fucker*." The bear sparked to static and disappeared back into Judith ME.

Maire howled with rage.

Children and toys.

The war continued.

*

"Does Adam know?"

Paul nodded.

Sam sipped tea, replaced the cup and leaned forward, hunched with arms hanging limply over his knees. "Did you ever think it'd come to this? That it'd all fall apart?"

Paul didn't have an answer.

"You had to have some idea that this was coming. That Maire would use everything Hope knew. That she'd incorporate it into whatever Program the Enemy's on now—Seven? Fourteen? Fifty-fucking-three?"

"I wasn't thinking."

"Neither was Alina." He hadn't meant it to cut, but it did.

"I should have known, but... We forget the basics when we're broken. Maybe a part of me knew that Maire'd upload Hope's ME. Maybe I was afraid to think of what could happen when she did. That everything Hope knew, about our forts and maths and Judith Command, all of it would suddenly be crystal-clear. Maybe I didn't want to believe that Hope could be the end of us."

"Maybe you were too busy locked in your chamber with Al to notice."

"I'm sorry, Sam. Sorry that I took her away from you for so long."

"You don't need to apologize for—"

"But I do. It wasn't fair. We got tangled up in each other. But now, well, she's all yours."

"I don't understand."

"She's yours for the assault on the Delta bleed. I want her to be your pilot. Our pilot."

"Am I missing something, Mr. Hughes?"

Paul's face was caverned and ancient. His eyes looked nowhere. "You know I've looked up to you for as long as I can remember."

"I assumed that's why you brought me in."

"You've been a mentor, an inspiration. You listened even when you didn't know I was talking to you."

"Go on."

Paul's right hand shuddered violently. He put it under the table. "If we're going to end this, we need to merge."

"Are you implying—"

He coughed a laugh. "Not like that."

"It's the silver."

"You have the vessel structure. I have the silver. Together, we can... Maire will never have seen anything like it."

"Do I get to stick around for the drive?"

The hand pounded against the underside of the table. The echo bounced in the empty construct. "I think it's time you get out of here, Sam. Maybe it's time for me to take over. To let you rest."

Sam sipped slowly, and the motion evolved into a nod as he lipped tea from his mustache. "I was wondering when you'd make this decision."

"It's not that I want you to go. Alina loves you. Everyone does. I do. But maybe it's time that I stand on my own for once. Everything you've done for me—I can't pay that back. But I can set you free. Let you out of this. Maybe it's time for you to go home."

"You sure about this, son?"

"No."

Their combined laugh was sad and knowing.

"Well, then," Sam stood and walked around the table, "no time like the present."

Paul stood. He shook with the fear of letting go. He extended his hand, and the solid shake became a bear hug, all slapping and gripping.

Sam pushed him back and grabbed his shoulders. His gaze was direct and forever. "You do this. You win this." His hand went to Paul's stubbled cheek. "And you take care of Al for me, okay?"

"I will."

Another hug, but it was something deeper; Sam's beard tickled as Paul shifted into the silver, reaching out and snapping Sam's phase tethers, the intricate web of memory and possibility that held him securely in the construct. Paul shook and coughed as he consumed Sam's pattern, the silver coursing through the broken collection of them, the oceans of machines dismantling and uploading the strands in a flash, in static, and silence.

Paul fell gasping, alone, to the floor, silver spilling out of him, a splash and a rebounding recall. He lay there into the night, categorizing and learning the complexities of the vessel. At some point, his breathing slowed. At some point, he pretended to sleep.

When he woke up, he missed Sam, but he knew that there are some trips you have to take alone.

❧

He had that cigarette musk in his mouth. The touch, the feel of cotton wads jammed into his ears with a pencil tip, straight through into the decay. He had that taste of blood wrapped around his tongue, the muzzy veil of waking up. He had that indistinct disconnect that only comes from revision and abject fear.

He cycled open the door to Jud's chamber, saw Alina on the chaise, comforting a sobbing Honeybear Brown. His heart sank as his eyes slid to another silver projector marble in the bear's paw.

He half expected West's blow, and that half allowed it to connect, knew that it had to. His jaw rocked away, feeling unhinged, locking as he reeled a stumbled step or three, righted, met Adam's second swing with a steel grip and threw the larger man to the floor. He stood over the fallen soldier. He worked his jaw until the grating of bones and intricate workings released. A tooth was loose, three. He pried them from sockets with his tongue, let them fall to the floor as new grew.

West's chest heaved; his teeth were clenched in a snarl to match his eyes. Paul walked to the conference table, joined the remaining Judith Command. West stood slowly and sat across the table, kneading his hands back to feeling from the impact.

Alina sat next to West, rolled the marble across to Paul.

"'Phire?"

"I couldn't get Jade's." The bear spoke as he settled into a chair. "There wasn't much left of the droptroops."

West's eyes reached across the polished wood with an unabridged fury.

"I'm sorry, Adam."

"You're saying that a lot, lately."

"They knew the risks."

"They were my—"

"No." Paul let the word echo. "They weren't."

"Just another merge." Reynald spoke from behind a stack of glass. He threw them to the table, a faint crack splintering the bottom display, a triangle of it spinning lazily toward Paul. Before it sparked out, he read: *elta bleed 96-over. [A/O reports 04%*. "Not his daughters, no. Not from the AE-line. Does it matter?"

Paul snuffled back a drip of silver. His hands were under the table. He kept turning to the right.

"Any luck finding your ship, Jean?" Alina had pulled Honeybear from his seat. Her arms were around him, stroking his sweatshop plush. His cardiac shield barely contained his broken heart.

Reynald's code burns flickered and rearranged across his temple. He barely noticed anymore; Maire's siege of the Timeline rewrote histories faster than they could be lived. "We've not been able to survey deep enough. With all the traffic in the stream, we can't get into the target Whens without Maire knowing. Hope was a close reader."

"You don't need Maggie."

"She was part of the deal."

"The deal doesn't matter now." Paul lit a cigarette and let the smoke cloud the stillness between them. "They're gone, Simon and Maggie. Hunter and Lily. We all know that. We would have found them by now if they were integral to the calculus. That leaves two possibilities—either Maire's found them already, or they were never really the focus to begin with." He ashed.

"We'll need as many ships as we can—"

"We're taking one ship."

Smoke drifted, not enough to conceal the shimmer.

"Have to be a hell of a ship." West reached to steal a smoke. Maybe it would help the moment.

"It will be." Inhalation, exhalation through words. Paul wiped a line of argent blood from the corner of his mouth. "Trust me."

"What are you planning, son?" Reynald took the cigarette from West's offer, coughed through. He knew already. "I see Sam's not here."

"He's here." An instant, a stark flash of reveal, and they saw Sam pressed into Paul's eyes. An illusion, a lie, it was gone before it registered.

Alina fumbled with the box of Marlboros. The battered gold Zippo ignited. She smoked as if she had before. Jud looked through her eyes but said nothing.

These veils of dream we weave around ourselves, never knowing for certain, but knowing enough: this is all we have.

"I'm flying. Al's my pilot. Everyone else, you'll be there for the show. Don't worry."

He lit another smoke. Eventually, they all did.

~

"You can go home. All of you. If you want."

The birthing plain pods were retracted, the sea of openings now closed forever, the expanse not worthy of a pin drop: a million or a billion, more, a trillion, more, everyone, everyone was there, all the possibilities he'd written, everyone who was left. Some near him sat. The shifts from foot to foot in anticipation alone was deafening, added to the murmur, but when he spoke, they heard.

He shook. Wracked with coughs. The silver blood, once a trickle, was now a torrent. He wrote a faded blue handkerchief into the dream and mopped the corner of his mouth.

West and Reynald flanked him. West's hand rested in wait on his back.

Another ripple passed through the assembly and a few thousand characters screamed away in bursts of silver. Somewhere out there, Maire's army was reaching for them. The spaces filled in.

Paul watched the empty. Alina grew concerned; his eyes were somewhere long ago. He was bending, collapsing. West held him up as silver pattered to the closed lid of a Jud cocoon. He regained his footing, wiped, straightened.

Her hearts—her heart sped a rhythm she resented, but it's not easy to forget better times and versions.

"You can go home," he whispered, but it carried. Another staggering ripple, seven million more disappeared. He could feel Maire out there, the grip of a projector marble slicked in blood, the windswept ice of the merge.

“We’re collapsing the Timeline,” Reynald shouted across the metal and dust. “Dismantling this foothold. We’ll use the last resources of Judith Command to fuel one final assault on the Delta bleed. Anyone who doesn’t want to come with us, your time here is done. Go home to your Whens and wait it out. You’ve all made a remarkable sacrifice to be here. We can’t expect more of you. Go home to your families.”

“What families?” A voice spoke out from the mass. “Most of us have nowhere to go!”

A rumbled assent. Paul felt them slipping, all of them innocent, each soul the work product of his madness.

“Then run.” West growled across the plain.

Whispers, multiplied. The middle C of uncertainty, a resounding seiche wave of fear.

“Those of you who choose to go with us,” Reynald continued, “will be loaded into a pattern cache aboard Alina’s ship. Our combined mind-essence will power the largest silver vessel ever...” he looked sideways at Paul, “assembled.”

One ship? The unspoken concern was tangible.

“Just one ship. Me.” Paul’s chest hitched with his body’s rejection of the silver.

The cries of outrage drowned any hope for hope. Alina gripped herself tighter, feeling it all fall apart.

“We’re taking the war to Maire. One last shot. One ship. As many of us as want to go.” West stepped forward, let the author stand alone as he choked something smoky and snarling back down. “We need to end this now!”

The din was painful. Paul had never suspected such resistance to his plan, but—

“You cowards.” Jud’s knife-edged voice cut through Alina’s tongue. “You fucking cowards!” Her words could have enraged the crowd, but a silent truce sputtered to life across them. “What else do you have to live for? If we lose this, there won’t be much living at all, kids. If Maire breaks through entirely, you think you’ll be safe? She’s erasing both the Alpha and Omega lines. This isn't the Enemy rewriting history in their image—Maire's erasing the image."

"We'll begin loading the cache immediately." Reynald scratched his temple; another three lines appeared. "Best of luck to those who stay behind."

"I'm sorry," Paul managed as best he could. His hand went to the throb of his cardiac shield. "Please believe that."

They left the birth fields, the author limping along between Jean and Adam, Alina's hand on his shoulder.

"Gotcha," Maire said, and Michael Zero-Four's body streamered across the steel floor of the launch command center. The city's trunk shuddered below as Enemy forces quickly put an end to the pathetic civil war between tribes that had necessitated the launch of the zero-four probe.

She gutted him with a mechanical precision, popped his marble into her mouth and bit down. The sweet internals of the device pooled between her teeth and gums, and she knew. She knew.

Dozens of miles away, the probe erupted in its Gauss tube. Maire's Enemy companions flickered for an instant as their physics attempted to make sense of never having existed. Timesweep. She buffered them. She held them in place.

Which gave her an idea.

She walked quickly, eagerly to a console on one wall of the command, reached into the display and activated the upload link. Somewhere in the bowels of the room, a churning began. The display confirmed: there was a full pattern trapped in the buffer. Someone's soul hadn't made it to the probe.

She cooked him.

Hours passed, and she threw the download tank's hatch open. A tall, gray-eyed man crumpled to the floor with a splash and a thud.

"James Richter." Her grin was fangs and dimples. "Welcome to my future."

Richter wretched phased silica onto the floor. He tried to crawl to his hands and knees, but squeaked back down in a weak, naked pile.

He looked up at her. "Hope?"

༄

"Walk with me?"

"Paul..."

"Please?"

Judith Command was being systematically dismantled around them, the billions, trillions of soldats perdus uploaded into a pattern cache that Paul would carry. The bubble around the non-place had developed great cracks on its periphery, and in places, the blackness of the unknown beyond shined down through.

They walked to the edge, the place where they could look down into the Timestream. The Alpha Point sparked an eternity below them. As they walked, his hand was close enough to Alina's so that she could hold it, if she wanted. We know the distances between us; we test the lines and hope someone crosses.

Theirs was a heartbroken silence built of everything that had gone wrong, all the fights over nothing, the context of them, the place and time out of time in which they lived. They were both machines built from life's flickers.

They sat on the edge and still said nothing. Their hands were still close enough to hold.

Their feet dangled down over the universe.

He said, "It was good."

She said, "I know."

A thousand other lives tried to crawl into that moment, a thousand other faces, but as he sat there dying, Paul looked only at Alina. The angle of her jaw, the patterns of her freckles, the flare of her nose, eyes that smiled, upturned, even when she was crying. A thousand other faces tried but failed to replace her.

We can count down our final moments in the stillness between another's heartbeats.

We can search for a perfect moment and realize that we've already lived it.

We can ravel a ball of silver, wear a filament of it on our wrists. We can hear the music across the water, the stars falling above, and we can dance, reach out for a hand. The world falling apart around us, and none of it matters. Life is a series of moments, of splendor, of misery, the finest line woven between. We can sit on the edge with the love of our lives and not say anything at all.

He reached out, withdrew. They looked down at existence. He coughed.

She turned back to the bubble's center. "I think they're ready."

He looked. Judith Command was empty, except for them. There was wind, and it was cold.

"Are you?"

"No."

They looked into each other's eyes for the first time in months. Years. Time had no meaning at the edges.

He held out his hand.

She smiled. Her eyes were wet. He was bleeding metal.

There were echoes.

She took his hand and jumped off the edge.

They fell, but in that scale, they were motionless. Judith Command raced away above them, the bubble's edges cracking and releasing, great plates of metallish shattering down toward them, the whole of the last fort erupting and falling. And they flew, hands held, eyes open, as shards of Command danced around them. They wove, hands held, between the pieces.

They pulled toward each other, arms frantic, grasping, bodies shuddering to relearn their symmetries, to reseat the way they fit together perfectly. They tumbled, hands held, down into the past, into the deepest night, the places hidden away for lifetimes.

Paul wrapped his arms around Alina, couldn't hold her close enough. He pulled back, looked into her colorless blue eyes, remembered the taste of her, gone so long now, tumbling, hands held, end over end, a dizzying, frightening descent, picking up speed, whirling, faster, faster, and Command was nothing above them, a cascade of countless fragments running alongside.

He never looked away. Reached out, one hand shimmering, one hand clasping hers, so small and perfect. It was a beautiful hand that he couldn't see, enveloped in his own, but he could feel it, contact, reached out, one hand shimmering, and called the silver to him, the detritus of Judith Command, and it came, an ocean of metal, swarming, singing around them, wrapping and protecting, enveloping, consuming. He would protect her. He would hold her close. And it formed around them, hands held, silver forming and reforming, merging with him, the finest silver web spidering through him. She didn't look away from the horror of him as he shifted, merged, became something else. She was caught in an expanse within him. She was encapsulated inside of him, a ship, a living ship of silver, the last of Command, the machine sea, and an ancient silent song. She looked up and saw the last of the light before he closed around her, the pattern cache falling into place above, sparking to almost-life, his hand changing, snaking, draping. His face a distended mess of metal, and then flat, and then nothing. It was dark inside of him. It was quiet. She was cold. He never looked away.

remember me
remember me on the wind
in the autumn
please remember me
the reflection

The interface webs dug into her.
and I loved you. Know that I loved you.
They fell.

OMEGA

OMEGA

"Are you leaving?"

She stood in the doorway, her back to him. Heard him roll over and crawl deeper into their bed, pulling sheets around him in the cool autumn morning. The window was open. He was asleep. He'd spoken in dream.

She walked the short hallway to the bathroom, business, and returned. Levered comforters from him and wrapped herself. Draped an arm around him. He took her hand. Squeezed. He was asleep and she wasn't.

He's writing me in.

She felt his heartbeat, traced the scar on his chest.

Something wormed within her, something without meaning, intangible and cold. She'd be leaving soon, but not yet. The layers of meaning in his sleep-mumbled question drew focus on lines in her heart. He expected her to leave—and she would, eventually. That something spoke through his dream, that something was aware of the future while his eyes were closed and his heart was slow, that was the break.

So she held him tighter. She would leave tiny notes in hidden places. She would wake him up by crawling on top of him. She would smile into the window light, and he would fall in love in that moment. He would push her hair back from her eyes. She wouldn't leave yet. The question echoed.

༄

Are you leaving?

He lay there with his eyes closed, rolled to the left, his arm coming to rest on a pillow, a space, reached farther, and remembered that he was alone.

Opened his eyes to find the cat staring at him from the banister bounding the landing. The cat resented him. He had been a cat person before he got one.

Swung his right leg, muscled straight so as not to aggravate the shattered knee and its cap of scar tissue, to the cold tile. Wiped sleep from his eyes and craved a cigarette. Looped chicken legs into gray boxers and sat on the edge of the bed. There had been a picture on his nightstand. There had been books. Itineraries folded between pages. A booth photo. There had been many things.

Stood and pulled cotton over his sex. Jeans.

The stairs were narrow and tall, and he wondered the shapes of the people who had built them. The stairs were built to trip him. He'd bought replacement treads and two tubes of adhesive, but he'd forgotten to improve, and now there was no time.

Down right angles into the kitchen, and he was still alone. There were birds outside. The cat made angry barking sounds and tried to trip him for food.

Through empty rooms filled with many things into a cracked leather chair on wheels. The floor was tilted, and he could roll the length of the office with no effort. It was difficult to remain in place before the monitor.

Hooked glasses around his ears and there was an empty inbox. Grabbed yesterday's used coffee cup, three grounds, not much of a reading, at its bottom. There was a spoon. It circled as he walked, its bottom edge gummed to the cup with the residue of hardened hazelnut creamer. She had been allergic. He could drink that now.

His body woke him most days at 8:57, and he couldn't remember what significance that time had or why it had been imprinted on his body.

The paper was late again. He could tell because he looked out the patio door and couldn't see it sopping mud water in the puddled divot that was the end of his driveway. Sometimes it was in the ditch. He felt like an adult, reading newspapers that were delivered to him three hundred sixty days each year. He kept them stacked in a milk crate in his kitchen, out of the reach of the cat, which had once mistaken that archive for its litter box. The highlight of most days was the bra advertisements in the sale papers.

To the bathroom, still looking for tiny notes pressed into the edge of the mirror.

Four Kinney Brand acetaminophen tablets. Water. Two more to be safe.

He looked at pill bottles and ignored them.

Watered the cat. Stared for too long at a small ceramic vase, two dried yellow shoots of bamboo. He'd soaked them in his dishpan. Spent hours pondering their revival. Had decided to let them die.

Measured fifteen scoops of generic coffee into the twelve-cup maker, added water, waited, withdrew three. To the kitchen table. The first sip. The first smoke. He looked out the window and watched blue jays toss seed to the new concrete of the veranda. The cat wagged its tail and chattered. The coffee was hot and bitter. Considered the distance to the refrigerator to retrieve the creamer. Scratch flicker click. He breathed deeply of the smoke. It calmed him.

There had been other mornings, other coffee, places without cats. Eggs. The Tony Danza show. No underpants and yes plaid shirts. Messy morning hair and breath. The way people intersect.

There had been other mornings in other cities, or in cities at all. He looked out the window and saw fifty beef cattle across the road. He heard geese. The grass was too long; it was his responsibility.

Stirred the coffee and wondered if he'd painted himself into a corner. Two gallons of paint had been enough for eight corners, but there was still so much to do.

The kitchen had an island. He'd bought two stools for it in the hope of someday sitting with her. He'd have coffee; she could have tea. He could boil water. Quiet mornings sitting together. That's all he wanted. Counted the chairs in his house, the seating surfaces: twenty-four. There was one of him.

Swished the coffee in his mouth and swallowed. Chained a smoke to it.

Went to the bathroom and ate an antacid tablet, because when all you consume is nicotine and caffeine, the stomach attempts to burn itself apart. Two more painkillers to be unsafe.

Sat back down, his back to the window. He could hear the birds. The cat glared at him. There was room for three other people at his table. She could choose any of them. He'd give her his chair. She could use his lap. He could feel her weight against him. She had been so small. He had felt so much smaller.

Such thought shunts the mind down recollections that break. Remembered the feel of her legs around him, in a chair, on a couch. In bed. His name, whispered. *Oh, Paul Hughes. I love you, Paul Hughes.*

Reached for the cup, and his hand shook enough to spill the bottom two thirds. Brown plastic clattered to brown china. Coffee rivuleted out to the place the newspaper should have been.

His hand shook more than usual. He held it in front of his face, looked, knew. Wondered if his hand could still bend to the curves of her by sense memory alone. Wondered if he could remember her textures and tastes and scents. The architecture of her laugh. A face framed by sculptures of plastic and metal. The way, as she looked down at him, her tears had skated across her glasses, and how once, in the dark, one of those tears had fallen to his face and broken his heart as he held her tiny, shaking form closer.

He slumped out of the chair and fell to the kitchen floor. His head bounced from linoleum he'd glued down. The cat looked on, mildly amused.

A line of silver snaked lazily from the holes in his face.

"Midsagittal plane breached."

"It's spread into—"

"Ready lesioning probe on my—"

"Physiologic confirmation of the target location."

"Initial pass in three... two..."

Alina ran after him, just barely getting through the door into the construct before it slammed shut.

He spun, made to say something, didn't know what to say.

"It wasn't her, Paul." Alina walked closer, remembered holding a hand and what had seemed something deeper. "Just Maire. Hope's—"

"Merged. Maire took her." He slumped into a chair that flashed to existence just before his behind made contact. "And now—If Maire's merged with Hope, she knows everything that Hope knew."

Alina stood a distance.

"If Maire has Hope's code..."

"It's bad."

“More than bad. Hope had calculated the A/O line to almost perfect half. Now Maire has the modular calculus. The bleed—It’s going to get a shitload more than bad.”

Alina didn’t know what to say. She thought about the rough plain of his hand.

“And you—Jud, you there?”

“She’s here.”

Paul nodded. Something flickered behind his eyes. “I take it she needed mobility.”

“Something like that.”

“And you’re okay with that?”

“If it helps.”

He scoffed, tugged at his whiter hair. “I need to get back to the pool. I can find an answer in there, I know it. If Maire has Hope’s code...” He studied his hands on the table’s top. “I need to get back into the silver.”

He stood to walk past her, and she shoved him to the wall. His look was disbelief and confusion. His eyes were a foot above hers, and looking down was like falling. She bridged the gap and kissed him, standing on toes to do so. He bent to make it easier.

Frantic, grasping, they went to the floor, knees and elbows, rolling, combat for position.

He pushed her away and from the distance tried to see behind her eyes. “We can’t. I’ve been in the silver. You’re not—”

“Shut up.” She pulled him back down and cut off the possibility of further uncertainty with her tongue and lips.

They collided.

She felt him smile against her thighs. Enveloping, bounding, penetrating her sex. She shuddered and gasped

❧

“Don’t let go,” hitched out through sobs. Adam held her tighter, the stubs of once fingers smearing against his chest.

"It's spreading." Reynald fingertipped the glass, dragged a new plan into place. "Hank, reverse the phase."

He shifted. Nodded once. "Target locked."

Reynald's claw hesitated. Sweat blossomed across his brow. "Probe ready. Pass in three... Two..."

To fail to hit, reach, catch, meet, or otherwise make contact with.

To fail to perceive, understand, or experience.

To fail to accomplish, achieve, or attain (a goal).

To fail to attend or perform.

To leave out.

To omit.

To let go by

To let slip.

To escape or avoid.

To discover the absence or loss of.

To feel the lack or loss of.

To be unsuccessful.

To misfire.

To fail.

A young woman.

Miss.

Something's wrong.

"Jim?"

shut up.

"Jimbo?"

shut UP.

"Come on, pardner. You gotta talk to me sometime."

no i don't.

"You just did." Hank grinned from his command chamber. "Anyhow, what's it look like out there?"

whiter than jo's inner thigh.

"That white, huh? That must be pretty white. You know, one time I was at a saloon in—"

for the love of all things holy, shut UP.

Crawl, crackle.

"You feel that?"

certainly did. initiating full sensor sweep.

"Looks like we ain't alone out here, buddy."

indeed.

"Think it's Hunter and Lily?"

...

"Jim?"

secure your tether to the ME.

"What in—"

do it, hank. now.

The cowboy was disconcerted by Whistler's tone, urgent, honest. Afraid. "Show me."

The command display sparked to life as Whistler fed the exterior view of the Timestream to Hank.

His gasp was audible. "That ain't... Hunter. Or Lily."

secure your tether, hank.

His knobby hands skittered over the controls on his cardiac shield. He felt the tug of his constituent particles locking back into place on the Judith line. In an instant, he could be downloaded back into the thought ocean made possible by the author and shaped by the wounded god.

Following them through the Timeline was a nightmare armada.

"What is—"

enemy.

"Jesus fuck." Hank instinctively stroked his handlebars. "You runnin'?"

varying phase to lose them.

"S'it workin'?"

no.

"Shit."

There were hundreds, thousands, an incomprehensible number of vessels reaching toward them, an undulating mass of black edges flashing with silver, a school of embodied hate and desire. At its center, something horrific and laughing. They could feel the reach of fury.

Whistler dug deeper into Hank, tapping the pattern for something, anything that would throw the Enemy off their trail. His nacelles glowed with the effort, leaving a veil of desiccated lifetimes in his wake. The howling fleet lurched closer, smashing the fragile fabrics of reality, clawing toward the soul cache hidden away in Hank's marble.

"Uh, Jim?"

quiet, hank.

"We ain't getting out of this, are we?"

The vessel dived and shattered as an Enemy gained hold. Hank fell to the floor of the command chamber, his cardiac shield sputtering an alarm.

you are, old friend.

"Jim, don't—"

Hank flashed from the Timeline in a burst of static and dust.

come now, maire. show yourself.

The Black tendriled over his surface, piercing and stroking, merging and solidifying. Absorbing. Whistler felt a scrape across his pattern, dislodge, reformation. He found himself shifted back into human form, alone in an echoing cavern of burnt mercury, a blinding light lasering down to scan his image.

"Bravo, Whistler. Bra*vo*." The ruined child walked from the shadows.

He smoothed his cloak and stood defiant.

"You," she poked his thigh with one taloned, tiny finger, "were supposed to be on my side. Our side."

"He made a better offer."

She snarled. “I could have given you everything, James. The universe. History.”

He scoffed. “What possible use could I have for all that, poppet?”

“I trusted you.”

“You’ve a lot to learn, child.” He adjusted the tips of his gloves.

“Why’d you do it?”

“I’m tired.” He bent to her level, put his hands on her shoulders. “I was meant to be gone a thousand years ago. To be with Jo again, wherever that might be. When you tore me from that slumber, you ruined my heaven. Paul offered me a chance to sleep again.”

“Tired of bouncing around in his head, huh?”

“Your head, too.”

She nodded a smile. “You were good to me, bringing Lilith in. I can forgive this transgression. I’ll let you rest.”

“Dear child,” his eyes glinted, “thank you.”

“Just one more thing.” She took his hand, gently, tenderly. “Who does his maths?”

“Hmm?” Whistler frowned.

“You can tell me, or I’ll just take it from you. Who’s calculating the bleed? Who’s zeroing in on me? He’s no good with numbers. Can’t be his brawn, West. Is it Benton?”

Whistler’s lips opened over clenched teeth.

Maire’s tiny fist punched through his chest and closed over his silver projector. He gurgled with blood and shattered bone as silver laced through the mash of his heart and lungs. She yanked her arm out, leaving his dusted form to fall in a flop of grit and glitter to the floor.

Her fist shuddered over the marble, absorbing everything that Whistler had been. One more crack in the author; one more influence torn away and consumed. She looked through the folds of memory and saw that everything hidden from her echoed through the heart of one Hope Benton. The modular calculus that equaled her undoing, the intricate lattice of defense around the author's fading mind—it would be hers.

Her dimples deepened.

❧

Said while walking through a door: "Paul, Hank's—"

West cut himself off.

Paul sat on the edge of the silver pool, his legs dipping in. He turned around slowly, and West saw something horrible flash behind his eyes.

"They're back?"

West just shook his head, trying unsuccessfully to bury a wash of confused emotion. The author hadn't been the same since Hope's murder. He'd been spending more and more time in the silver containment chamber, that cache of machines gathered during their various engagements of Maire's forces. "Hank's back."

"Just Hank?"

West nodded.

"And Whistler?"

West inhaled. "Get out of there, and we'll talk about it." He turned and left.

❧

"Shit." Paul's hand went to his temple, kneaded.

Hank scooped another nervous pinch of chew into his already-dribbling mouth. The old cowboy's face was more wrinkled, stubblier. The downward slopes of the distinct halves of his moustache only reinforced the image of his broken heart. "I didn't—I would have stayed. We could have fought, but—There were so many of them. I would have stayed." He blinked over glistened eyes.

The newly acquired Jean Reynald baritoned the chamber. "No. That would have solved nothing."

"It's for the best that Whistler sent you back, Hank." West leaned toward the shaking man. "If she'd gotten your pattern—"

"Hope could have changed the math."

Nobody knew how to tell him.

"She's dead." Judith.

He chewed faster, brow furrowing, squeezing out two distinct lines of wet. "But—What the fuck next? Hope's...?" He let the question fade away.

"Maire's getting better at this." Jud curled deeper into her chaise. "With Whistler's pattern—"

"I'm going back in." Paul stood and walked toward the door.

"Where?" Jud frowned.

He hesitated. "Back into the silver."

"Paul, please." West couldn't look him in the eyes.

"I have to. Maire's—I have to."

"Paul—"

He whirled, fangs bared, his eyes swirls of black and metal. "Don't."

As the door cycled shut behind the author, the assembled remnants of Judith Command sat through a heavy silence.

Hank spit tobacco juice to the floor. Whistler's chair was empty next to him. "What next?"

Nobody answered.

"Jean?" Judith rose and walked to the window. "I want you to take over operations for the time being. Paul's... You know."

Reynald nodded.

The air hurt.

"Listen..." Judith said, her voice bouncing from the window. "I know it hurts. Whistler. And Hope. But we'll get by. We'll do this."

They all tried to believe her.

∽

His eyes raced behind fluttering lids. The cat, curious, approached slowly, stuck out a paw, carefully padded his cheek until another seizure wracked his body. The cat reared back, came to rest sitting up. It sniffed the linoleum, reached out, withdrew. It bent down and licked at the growing slick of blood. At the taste, the cat bristled and ran to hide under the couch, leaving a trail of red prints across the gray carpet of the living room.

Somewhere behind bone, pressure built, soft gray curves flooded. The newspaper arrived. The cat hissed at its still owner silvering out in the kitchen. Somewhere, a clock ticked. Somewhere, nobody thought of him.

"Are you leaving?" she asked, half asleep. His impression marked the sheet behind her, a curved kidney bean spooned into position over half a dozen hours and thirty thousand heartbeats. He pulled the blankets back over her shoulders, concealing any evidence that he had ever been there at all.

"Need to get back into the silver."

She woke in earnest, sat up. She wiped sleep from her eyes and tried to focus. "Don't go."

"Al—"

"Please."

"I have to."

A sad shake of the head. "Don't go."

He bent to kiss her cheek. She pulled back and forced a locked gaze. "Please."

His lips hovered inches from her. He frowned and

Maire smiled, bent to help Richter to his feet. He coughed another glut of phase to the floor. Tendrils and thick loops of the sludge slicked his chin and chest. He rocked against her, still solidifying, and she altered her form to match his memories of Benton. He was blinking away the birth blindness; she couldn't rely on a stolen voice alone. She cut into the remnants of Benton's pattern and searched for convincing.

"Hope?" he repeated, his hands now surveying Maire's face, which molded to the memories she pulled from him, the histories stored within herself. His hands traced down her sides, came to rest on hips that hadn't been hers for long. "Where are we? I thought—That light—"

"Shh, baby." Maire smiled with Hope's face. "It's going to be okay now. You were right. About everything. I knew you'd come for me."

"Baby—" He looked at the metallish expanse, the uplink chamber swaying at the top of a tower city jutting from a dead future. "Where are we?"

She stood on tip-toes, wrapping her arms securely around him. Richter tabled the question and responded, burying his face in her hair, dragging lips along her cheek, coming to rest in the angle of her neck. "I thought you were gone."

"I'm right here."

"I needed to see what was in the light."

"It's heaven, James."

"I thought—I needed to see. To find you."

"You did." Maire tugged with Hope's colorless eyes, and for an instant, a deeper blackness existed.

Richter's grasp on her weakened.

Maire lashed out with her claws, Hope's shape and form dissolving into nothing. Richter's neck hung in tatters; his look of surprise was endearing. Maire sneered with delight as she grabbed his head and bit the rest of his neck through. The assembly of blood and meat flopped to the floor. She took her time excising his projector.

"Too easy." She licked her lips and sucked wads of his viscera from the marble.

One step closer to Jud. Another piece of Paul fell into

the place was empty, just a scatter of overturned tables and splintered chairs. Napkins dispensing lazily from dented stainless bricks. The door shut the city out behind him, squeezing down and crimping off the sound of wind and the staccato vibrations of war.

A sign sat on the neglected counter: UNDER NEW MANAGEMENT.

Richter walked to the counter, was drawn to the sign. His hand, finding purchase, marred clean paths into the veil of dust. There was an empty cigarette pack on the floor. There was the flapping cellophane skin of a Zinger, the bottom residue of cream and unnaturally red coconut slowly yellowing across one plane of it. The tip jar was empty except for a small blue marble, clouded.

His hand went to his throat, found it intact. Confusions blossomed.

He heard movement from the back room. Something falling, something dragged. A female grunt of a nameless emotion.

The windows shivered with the sudden onset of rain.

An overturned cylinder of red plastic stir sticks. An eared copy of *Demian*, the pages crisp and cracking. A single black leather glove, glittering with something beautiful and heartbreaking.

Richter walked slowly to the back of the shop, wondered at his boots, the clothing from so far ago. He remembered a desert and the Styx. A spire. New memories dislodge. Timesweep. His jaw worked over new bends in history. He felt his neck again; it was whole. He walked through coffee grounds and crumbled ceramic, the green, furry remnants of pastry. He reached the door to the back room and jumped at a crash of something heavy and fragile.

The doorknob was cold. Its turn was rusted and audible. Hinges cracked ancient resistance, and the door pushed away from him.

Benton kneeled on the floor, flopping thick manila file folders from a cardboard box.

She looked up at his gasp and the quick backward retreat of his boots. "James?" A folder fell from her grasp, spilling an inch of photographs, postcards, love letters to the linoleum.

"Stay away from me." His hands shifted to silver.

She stood. "James? How did you—"

"Stay back!" His eyes flared white.

Benton halted her advance.

"You touch me again, I'll fucking kill you." The silver crawled up Richter's arms, consumed his form, leaving him a shadow, an implication.

Realizations slammed into place deep in the works of Benton's mind. "James—It wasn't me." She tested a step toward him. "I wouldn't—"

He lunged forward and lashed out with both hands, which passed ineffectually through the image of her. She bent toward his shimmer where he touched her, but her projection swam back into a solid, sparkling with her own shift. His fingertips dragged a merge out with that contact. New truths metastasized across lines of resistance.

"It wasn't me, baby. Please... Believe me."

The wind screamed through the collapsing city.

Her slurp was a cute annoyance. She was a loud eater. She smacked her lips. He couldn't remember ever having heard her chew gum, but he could forgive the cracking he suspected she would have allowed herself to ignore. Every brilliant mind controls an eccentric body, a collection of actions that set it apart.

She wiped aside a windrow of dust and put the teacup down on a laminated menu used as a coaster. "You were right."

His eyes asked.

"The signals were getting through, not bouncing back. Someone was listening, out there. They talked back."

He remembered an expensive restaurant lifetimes ago, a conversation broken off because of an unexpected flight to Wyoming.

"Who?"

"Maire. The Alpha Centauri system. Just one of infinite possibilities. The first to respond, because of the relative proximity."

"I don't—"

"We traded signals for thousands of years, neither civilization understanding that someone was listening. Someone was out there. And when the Sol system finally died, when Michael Balfour's probe finally reached Proxima Centauri, the aliens there—people with two hearts, black blood, but *people*—they considered it an act of war. Things bend out there in the empty spaces between galaxies. Things splinter into spectrums of possibility. Time thins out and doesn't mean much."

Richter broadcast his lack of understanding with a long draw of coffee.

"Life isn't a straight line. This time, Maire was there to catch you. Another time, Michael pulled you out, and you led the resistance against the Enemy. Another, Maire's forces got to Earth before Michael ever had a chance to build the probe. Sometimes life curves out and back again, intersecting places it's already been. This place—this ridiculous coffee shop dream—it's the place where everything collapses. It's the Delta merge, the place where the two most probable timelines collide. It's the place where a war between two solar systems begins and ends."

"What does that make Maire?" Richter couldn't look at Benton's eyes. "Or us?"

"She's the eraser at the other end of the pencil. The backspace key. The counterpoint to everything the author's written into existence. She's the unraveling. Revenge. And us? We're a part of her, now. She's torn us from him, and she'll use everything we know to win her war against Paul."

He opened one of the folders on the table. There was a photograph of the author in London. A postcard shaped like a sea monster. A tiny slip of paper on which a left hand had written a three-word note.

"There's boxes of this stuff stored here. Maire's built quite a collection. She's pulling things from him, storing them away in this construct, using each innocent little memory to destroy him. The whole back room, shelves and stacks. She's breaking him down."

"And you're going through it all, trying to find something to help him?"

"Trying. Not much luck. It's a mess."

"Why help him?"

She frowned at the question.

Richter shook his head. "If he's written these horrible futures into existence, if he's the cause of these wars, why help him fight Maire?"

Her fingertips traced over fading photographs, crumbling paper. She pulled a line of poetry from a notebook page, drew a memory of a skin's texture and taste from a passport photo. "He made this. All of this. Even Maire. Us. Without him, we never would have existed. Maybe I feel an obligation to help the person who gave me life."

"You really want to help him?"

Hope nodded her resolve.

Richter reached into his pocket and placed something on the tabletop. She saw small paper edges through the cage of his fingers.

"If this is the place where it all comes together, if the coffee shop is the place Maire hides the pieces of him," Richter lifted his hand, revealing a colorful book of matches, "then maybe it's time we end this."

She took the matches, popped the cover open. There was a number, a cartoon face. Pigtails. She wondered where James had gotten the matches, but it didn't matter. The Cafe Bellona was a focal point. Nothing had a satisfactory explanation. Nothing needed one. Sometimes life collapses into distinct moments of chance. Sometimes life, or the digital approximation thereof, is a spectrum of gray.

She picked up a photograph, let her thumb trace the eroding surface. He looked happy. Whole. A depiction of a time and place he'd never live now.

She took Richter's hand. Her face bent into a quiet attempt at a smile, but it only squeezed wetness across the colorless hemispheres of her eyes.

She'd been trapped so long here, searching for an answer to the calculus, the silver concretion savaging the author. She'd tried to prevent Maire from using her against Paul, but exiled to the construct, she'd been powerless, deconstructed. A silver marble held in a child's hand.

Hope tore a match from the book. Her third strike resulted in flame. She slowly, gently singed the edge of the manila folder on the table. Outside, the wind grew louder. A building collapsed. The sky tasted like ash.

She fed a postcard into the fire. The ground shook below them.

Richter pushed a note into the curls of flame. One of the front windows splintered.

"The whole back room?"

"And the basement. Stacks of boxes." She held the burning edge of a photograph. The author's face blistered and fell away.

Richter counted twenty-seven matches.

❧

"Are you okay?" Alina's voice echoed out into the command chamber. She adjusted the drape of the interface web, reached out to see for herself how he was doing, but felt nothing. There was none of the consciousness lockstep that interfacing with Sam had provided. Paul was wrapped in layers of silver.

The vessel shifted, walls realigning, nacelles stretching out, clawing. They fell.

Concern itched to life behind her eyes. "Paul? Talk to me."

Somewhere below them, rapidly approaching, was a small blue planet and the exile city and Maire.

i'm

"Paul?"

so many

She could feel him trying to contain the silver, the trillions of souls inserted not gently into his core.

too many

"Hold on, Paul Hughes. Almost

❧

there it is." Reynald fingered sweat from his forehead. The targeting laser arced over the author's skull. Reynald hesitated, looked up at Hank.

"Go for it."

He triggered. A stark lance of white light

❧

rocked the superstructure as a shard of silver tore from his caudal fin. Alina swung in the interface web, burying panic, unable to keep her hearts from racing. "Hold on, baby. Just

❧

come and get me." Maire grinned, leapt into the air as the city shattered beneath her, the planet imploding, great plates of continent glowing with ancient silver light. She could feel him, the line collapsing above her, countless futures dying in his wake. Every particle of her glinted with the shift, with the ocean of machines that defined her.

She could see him, the terrifying shiver of his form, as it tore through the fabric of that time and plummeted into the merge. Her claws cut into her fists in anticipation, spilling torrents of black blood and mercury into the sky. She could feel the god buried somewhere in

Alina saw through his blurred, dying eyes, the nightmare below them, the monster that was Maire, looking up and through, a smile on her face, her Enemy army surging below, an armada of them careening around the planet toward Paul. He shook, and she didn't know how to stop him. Didn't know the plan. He was silent. Alina sobbed, helpless.

Richter lit every match in the book, let the flame grow. Hope wrapped her arms around him. He kissed her forehead, finally home.

Was that an orgasm? I'll be the old man with cats. With loves.

This is where the fish lives. We did the 69. How do you catch a unique rabbit?

Kentucky City. Cover my feet. Horses don't get flu shots.

Paul Hughes, come here?

He dropped the fire into the tinder and

"Paul!" Alina surged in the silver umbilicals. "Tell me what to do!" She struggled in the unresponsive interface gauntlets.

The planetship that he was fell, uncontrolled, into the atmosphere. Maire's army rose to meet the threat, to cut into that silver flesh, to extract the guts of it, the pattern cache of the remnants of a species.

alina? His voice was forever away.

Head shaking, hearts breaking, two tiny hands pulling against silent systems, the witch below. "What?"

i love you.

And his presence cut a deeper distance as the umbilicals withdrew, the uplink severed, and he jettisoned his lifeboat into the sky, Alina and the pattern cache at its center, thrown savagely away from him. Where the hidden ship had rested, broken silver fingers snapped and fell away. He fell without control or direction into Maire and her horde.

Alina screamed as she felt him fall away.

I'm losing

౿

her, he thought as he put the truck into reverse, her image burned into his arc of vision as he checked his mirrors and pulled out onto the street. He smiled and waved, his right hand hesitating in that wave a little too long before retreating to the shift forward.

Are you leaving?

He felt his smile breaking as he pulled away, blinked through something overwhelming as he looked into his rearview. She was wearing his shirt and his pajama pants. She was wearing a smile all her own, and as he accelerated into the curves and down the hills, he catalogued the memory of her, everything, holding tightly to everything, because somewhere he knew that he'd never get that shirt back. She'd had the pants since that first night, making them more hers now than his. So ridiculously big on her, lost in fabric, accelerating into her curves and he remembered the landscape of her, the scent of her hair, that morning frizz and the sleep in her upturned eyes. He let the radio sleep. Drove past the field of tiny horses. *Horses don't get flu shots.* All the stupid fights they'd fought over nothing, all the disagreements over things that didn't matter; these are the edges that define loss. These are the frantic thoughts before the fall: please stay, please forgive me, please let me hold on to you, because you've become integral.

Left hollow and without purpose, these are the edges that define broken tomorrows, all the futures we'll never live, all the mornings we'll wake alone, hoping the pillow isn't a pillow, that the weight of her will be the incentive for waking, the dim angles of sunshine through a rusted ghetto window, the sound of the morning world outside, chill air stippling gooseflesh across arms and chest, we will remember those senses only so long, we will replace and forget, and each loss will take a little more of us with it.

He was leaving, and she slept on his shoulder. Speeding across the nighttime country on the wrong side of the road, running through concourses weighed down by a lifetime's collection of things; I need this to remember, I need evidence that I was ever here at all. She shifted against his arm, dug deeper into the overhang of his chin, spiraled hairs popping up to tickle his nose, and he inhaled, because this is life, such contact, and without it, he is lost. A coffee break in a Starbucks; he's never been in a Starbucks except for with her. The coffee burned his tongue, but not badly enough so he can't remember her taste hours later on the plane over plains of snow, a nearly empty plane, enough leg room in his own aisle to take off his cowboy boots, to pull out his wallet, the photograph from it, and the inscription that breaks his heart, he is so happy.

And sitting by the water in another's territory, the attacks of the morning forgotten or at least unspoken, cutting cheese with a key, he'd seen her upset and needing to run, and he'd driven her to the land's edge, because they both needed it, the sun burning their skins. He'd rolled up his sleeves, and the slough of that exposure had outlasted them. Looking out across the water, he wondered which of his lives was the dream. The wind brought her scent to him, the sand between his toes and the square cleave of the rocks grounding him to that place. Spider webs between the rocks, Zinger wrappers he collected and took home. Maybe the sandwiches got too warm.

And walking down the streets of her, that tiny hand lost in his. The streets that defined her, the cobbles of places far from him, the avenues she'd walked a lifetime and he'd followed a year. Sitting on a rock, hiding a cigarette from spying armies, he hated the way she grabbed his ass and loved it. Public. Displays. Her hand held him to that place and time, and he remembered her whispers. Wondered if it was real. Hoped he'd finally paid off the wages of a lifetime, and that finally he'd found her. He'd seen her eyes a thousand times before, felt her heartbeat in other cities and beneath other cages of bone, slowly edged toward that soul we search for all our lives, the one that so reflects us that we can't help but die a little each day after it leaves. Something fuses. Something breaks. We're left with pieces missing.

And the lifetimes we assemble into madness, the fragments of the departed we write into the days. He thought of Alina and knew that wasn't her name at all, that the scrawl of their love couldn't begin to emulate reality, that not even the Jud god inside of her or the Maire witch outside could approximate the feeling generated by staring across an antiques store in Lewes, making sure she's not watching, stealthily jogging to the cashier to purchase a teacup with feet, wrapped into the football pages, secreted away in a drab green ruck, returning to the rows before she noticed, hands tracing over the dust of centuries, settling on misshapen birds that have vented the steam from a thousand meat pies, over photographs of people dead now, crumbling, the photographs and the people, from times before we were born. That we run to train stations and weave through the schoolchildren, our hands held, collapsing finally into seats jangling with our change and the day's treasure, tiny old women sitting opposite, their accents thick and their skin thin like paper, speaking to each other but watching the two American kids pull out a bottle of water, a Yorkie bar, splitting it to share before dinner, curling together on the plastic bench, a head of curly hair, glasses, smiling eyes closed coming gently to rest under a stubbled chin, which lowers to rest, a tickled nose, a heart beating fast, knowing that this is heaven; this is all he needs.

Are you leaving?

Alina wretched as she felt herself break apart, the tangle of interface web sparking. Her vision doubled, trebled as she fell to the floor of the chamber, her form cleaving, new limbs flailing from the split of her form. Static and agony. Jud crackled to solidity and slumped from Alina, a glistening mess of wet silver and dried blood, chest grating over bitter air, hair dripping with something black and ancient.

"Get up," she growled over loose vocal cords, her tongues reaching for better words. She rocked with the exhaustion of being whole again.

Alina's hands splayed over a shattered cardiac shield. There were lifetimes of her missing. Two lines of tear fought through the slick of nervous sweat to bead out onto the floor.

"Get *up*." Judith grasped her hands and seesawed her to standing. The severed souls supported each other's stance. "Where's the cache?"

Alina was looking past Jud, who turned to meet the direction of her desperate gaze. The glass, cracked and fading, showed

Maire's army a whirlwind around her, the nightmare cacophony of the damned, the merged silver purpose. Paul could hear them, the collection of an eternity of broken tomorrows, the aggregate fury of the lost.

Maire paused in her flight, her claws a brilliant silver, garish strands of the machine ocean pouring from her eyes in a disconcerting ruin of a mask. Paul could hear her war cry spilling from between those horrible shimmering fangs. She was older than he'd ever written her, thick strands of white contrasting the black, dancing in the winds.

He ratcheted his wingtips, his nacelles forward, struggling against the gravity and drag of his descent.

And they collided.

༄

West flickered to life and snapped to grid, a stumbling, confused landing. He was even more confused by the fact that Reynald and Hank were standing next to him, before a lifeboat's glass, and Alina, and—

"Jud?"

Reynald's hand went to West's shoulder. His head shook an uncertain negative. His eyes directed a heartbroken look to the glass, and West followed just in time to see

༄

Maire smashed through Paul's central hub, a brilliant spray of fragmented armor and hemorrhaging silver racing after her exit wound. The vast planetship dived, Maire and Enemy vessels caught in its wake. As the imprisoned singularity at his center went critical, Maire and her horde tore at the air, attempting to escape the pull of his horizon. One by ten by thousands, the scrabbling silver forms collapsed into Paul, his edges red, melting away, great chapters of him rending away and bursting from existence.

He fell, the expanse of wailing souls spiraling after him.

❧

The lifeboat was far enough away to pull stubbornly from the collapse, but the vessel veered a spinning retreat, its contents shifting savagely.

"We need a lock on his pattern," Reynald barked.

"I'm on it." Jud stood before the glass, her voice a whisper.

Alina touched the display, shaking. "Please, Paul. Don't—"

❧

All of Puget Sound was erased from existence as Paul impacted, the field of vision instantly blinded, a stark assault of silver light boiling across the planet's surface. The cataclysmic deluge of liquid metal erupted from his savaged superstructure, dusting the sky, then drifting lazily down to blanket the world with argent. The Enemy forces not caught in his wake, neatly clipped from Maire's mind essence, stippled the new surface in craters of shattered phase. All across the barren scar, new oceans of silver coalesced.

Paul's chassis shuddered, grappled with its new foundation. Then stillness.

❧

Alina screamed. She sobbed, throwing herself against the display until her tiny hands wilted. West heard flesh split, fingers crack. She kept beating against the glass, kept beating, kept screaming, even as he pulled her away, the stubs of fingers smearing that image with bloody letters; hers was a language written in despair.

West held her tightly, but she still struggled, her crumpled hands pressing against him only jarring loose more of that loss; she seeped through his shirt, and he felt warm copper run down through the hair on his chest, pause to circumvent his navel. She eventually relented, slumped into him, allowed herself to bury her eyes under his jawbone, anything to force away the screen, to erase that image.

West watched it all, even as he held Alina so she couldn't.

❧

Inhale: no lung, no mouth, but why the sensation of drowning, of choking, the scent of burning flesh when there was no nose, no body?

All around him, silver. Waves still came back to slap at his shallow corpse, near-corpse. It burned; it froze.

He struggled to sit up and remembered that things were no longer attached to him in the way he remembered. His starboard nacelle lazily rose, slammed back into the silver ocean, stirring the metal again, angering what sensors he had left operational.

The nacelle crawled through half-crystallized mercury slurry until it met his main chassis. He was disturbed but not surprised to find that his pelvic fin had been shattered on the impact, and his caudal fin was twisted into an array of broken metallish.

s
paul hughes((?))
come here ((?))
cover my feet ((?))
rupture rend rive split cleave

Maire had pierced through his chest, heavy silver armor cracking and splintering before it. Reflex forced his head back; agony kept it there as spasms wracked his entire form. The hole in his hub was slick with his blood, mechanicals, the shimmer of venting containment chamber exhaust. He finally settled in the shallow silver, nacelles digging into the flooding ground.

Too tired to move his port nacelle. Too broken.

Starboard nacelle feels around the hole. The wingtip snaps off, falls to his belly, slides into the silver.

Focus, but

It's flooding, that alien, that lifeblood. Choking, gasping. Somewhere, a line of code reminds him that there's a human buried inside that ruined sculpture of metal.

i'm sorry

i'm

His nacelle falls back into the ocean, the wingblades now useless.

i'm

~

Paul finds her in the exile city. He finds her sitting in the street, a young woman again, covering her face with clawless hands. A few tears have spilled between her fingers. She snuffles a few more to the back of her throat.

He sits down next to her.

The Cafe Bellona is a ruin, the detritus of the fire still smoldering. He can see bones under blackened beams. Maybe the bones are broken coffee cups. Tarnished metal stems poke up, twisted stools crushed under the collapsed roof. There is no wind. The city is silent except for popping knots and the slow burning deep down.

He thinks of cigarettes and inhales the smoke from one, passes it to Maire. She takes it. Her arms rest on her knees. Her body stretches toward the Bellona waste as her hair flops down, obscuring her face from him. Her eyes are blue now, and he looks away.

"Why didn't you kill me?" Her brow works over the question, her face torn between thin probabilities of rage and despair. She shakes with it, a fading question, a veiled surrender.

"Tu crois être le doute et tu n'es que raison. Tu es le grand soleil qui me monte à la tête quand je suis sûr de moi," he says.

"Comme on oublie," she says.

"Je t'aime contre tout ce qui n'est qu'illusion."

"I know." She exhales smoke. She extends her hand. She offers him the three silver marbles rolling the folds of her palm.

He closes her fingers around them.

We are machines of a horrible beauty, and life is a collection of moments. Fundamental redefinitions of trust. The suffocating intersections of coincidence. Rejection mechanisms. We are forgotten as easily as the quiet desperations of our madness.

And it's okay.

༄

In the lifeboat's command chamber, Reynald swiveled the targeting laser of the lesioning probe to a new position over Paul's skull. They'd successfully downloaded his pattern from the dissolving devastation of his superstructure, but the final tendrils of silver had entrenched themselves in his mind, lacing, consuming.

"I—I can't." Reynald stepped away, kneading his temple. The code burns were gone.

"Please," Alina sobbed. "Help him."

"There's too much of it. I can't separate the silver from his brain without damaging him."

West turned from the display. "There's no sign of Maire. And the Enemy... They aren't moving."

"That's good. Right?" Hank searched their faces.

"She's not gone." Jud said from the corner into which she'd hidden herself. Her eyes no longer glowed. "She's in there." She motioned at Paul, then tapped her head. "They're together, somewhere in there."

Alina held her arms tightly, shook her head.

"Better believe it, baby." Jud stood and walked to the motionless author. "They've merged."

"He wouldn't—"

"It's what he always fucking wanted." Jud said through gritted teeth. "Can't you see that?"

"But—He hated her."

"And he loved you?" One side of Jud's mouth upturned. "Life isn't that simple, kid."

Reynald cleared his throat. "If the silver spreads through his mind again—"

"That's not gonna happen." Jud swung the targeting laser into place above Paul's forehead, the barrel's glow intensifying.

A veil of surrender obscured the room.

"Do it, then," West choked out, his growl stumbling over resignation. "If we're going to ruin this, let's ruin it forever."

Reynald's hand joined Jud's on the barrel. "It's been an honor."

Hank crumpled his hat in his callused hands, spit tobacco to the floor. "Yeah, a real fuckin' hoot."

Alina bent to the author, kissed his cheek. Took his hand. She tried to smile, her freckles shifting to new constellations.

Jud met each gaze. Histories and universes collapsed behind her eyes.

"Okay." She grinned through tears. "Let's go home."

She pulled the trigger.

Flatline.

∽

They walked, the streets shifting beneath their feet, sometimes cobble, sometimes pavement, sometimes the wooden planks of the pier. The buildings were different and all the same. People came and went around them, between them, through them. Sometimes she held his hand.

They took a left.

"You know where we're going?"

He laughed. "Does it matter?"

She shrugged.

They stopped in front of a coffee house.

A heavy wooden door to a nameless, dark place. He held the door for her.

He didn't recognize anyone. There were two stools empty at the counter. Ashtrays. The server was busy placing steaming cups in front of other customers, her hands balancing coins and receipts. They sat.

"What would you recommend?" She couldn't read the menu.

"What do you like?"

"I've never had coffee."

He felt an emotion for her, and it wasn't fear.

"I'll order," he said, bringing the server over with a motion. "Hi, I'll just have coffee, black, and she'll—" He turned to Maire.

And she was gone.

Paul slowly turned back to the counter, struggling against the sudden stillness of the place. Took a Marlboro from the hardpack in his pocket, lit it. Inhaled, and the smoke tore at his eyes.

"Will that be all, sir? Just the coffee?" The server's pencil hesitated over an order book she really didn't need. There was a flicker of recognition that could not be. There was a system of desire that was fundamentally flawed.

And Paul felt decades older, the empty stool next to him only deepening that sensation of age and loss. He surveyed the shop, the people sitting together, engaged in important conversations that meant nothing, sipping and slurping and spilling, laughing, falling in and out of love. The stool remained empty.

Something's wrong.

The server faded, the customers, the tang of bitter coffee and the jostle of cell phones, the tables and chairs, the street outside. He inhaled smoke. No more neon or important books, no more pastries or expensive soups, no more undercurrent of conversation. He was at the end of the pier. He was looking at the lightning over the gulf. His pockets were empty, the marble gone, the jigsaw Michigan. His wrist was bare, the silver bracelet lost. His hair danced in the wind and sand eroded the planes of his face. He couldn't remember. He was lost. He exhaled, closed his eyes to the midnight winds. He could still see the lightning out in the gulf, still feel her touch.

He opens his eyes and finds himself at his kitchen table, the cat stalking a fly around the linoleum. The coffeemaker sputters its completion. He stands on grating knee. Stacks of newspapers. Boxes of memory. Photographs hidden away upstairs. An empty inbox. And he can't remember what made him. Can't remember the faces of the lost, the tastes of the dead. Can't remember their songs or the textures of them, the warmth of skin or the secrets between them. Forever poised in the moment before a first kiss, the phantom scents of cheap beer and cigarettes and something rich and hidden, something fading from him no matter how he claws to hold it, something rending and beautiful hiding behind blue eyes.

He reaches into his chest and feels nothing at all. He's hidden the artifacts, or someone's stolen them. There are pictures on his walls of people he doesn't know.

He has coffee. Another cigarette.

January cuts a deeper distance.

He stands at the window and watches the snow fill in the morning's tracks. He loses something in that.

Love is the farthest unsteady light.

He knows they'll all go eventually, leaving behind an unfinished equation, an unwritten song, a fragile calculus in which nothing is integral. Forevers are redefined in departures. He doesn't have to do anything at all to deserve nothing. He can travel around the world to end up where he began. He can search a lifetime to find the one who will ruin him. He can fall to the floor, stumbling through bent physics, hands searching for the ineffable past, sobbing for the war dead, the faces he can't remember, the whispers, the gasps: *Paul Hughes, come here? Paul Hughes, I love you.*

Because suddenly he's looking back and a week is gone, a month or a year, five, a decade, a lifetime, and it feels like a lifetime, a decade, five, a year or a month, a week, a day, hours, minutes, she's there, seconds, she's there and they're together, instants, she's there, moments, there, now, she's there, now, there forever, there, walking together down thin paths into broken futures and todays, and they contain multitudes, lifetimes of stillness hovering in the air between them.

And they're running down those ancient streets, hands held, eyes open, laughing and whispering and knowing.

Staring, but not seeing.

Thinking of the thought [itself].

Breathing, but not living.

In the struggling light, the snow looks silver.

He inhales.

I don't know who I am anymore.

He exhales.

Bracketing those dead to us, delineating the forms and histories of our desires, in a breath, in tears, in the pattern two opposing collections of striation compose in the catalytic reaction of palm to palm, all physics are bent, and all probabilities, all convenient presuppositions and extrapolations of futures not yet lived are erased: all we have is now, this moment, this beautiful, fragile moment, and

Ω

www.ingramcontent.com/pod-product-compliance
Lightning Source LLC
Chambersburg PA
CBHW020256030826
48979CB00026B/1287/J

* 9 7 8 0 9 7 7 4 1 1 0 1 6 *